Fatemaker

Book 3: Fatecarver Series

Robinne Weiss

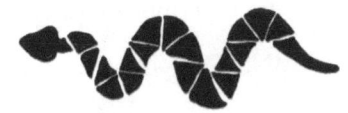

Published by Sandfly Books

ISBN: 978-0-473-68990-2

Cover design by Jenn Rackham.

This book also available in electronic formats.

Discover my other books and stories at robinneweiss.com.

CAST OF CHARACTERS

Fatecarvers

Formerly of Flintcrag Clan, now Fatekeepers

> ### Prime Terrace
> Kalish—Fatewalker
> Dayo—Kalish's partner
> Wathi—Dayo's mother
> Jenti—Dayo's father
> Grandmother Ma—Kalish's paternal grandmother, dead
> Benut—young woman, friend of Kalish

Formerly of Point Clan, now Fatekeepers

> ### Prime Terrace
> Lela—Fatecarver
> ### Lone Tree Terrace
> Kofri—Elder
> Jalen—Kofri's daughter
> Wend—Jalen's husband
> Tili—Jalen's daughter
> Ino—Jalen's son
> Arnid—Jalen's son
> Leithe—young woman
> Pentel—Leithe's husband
> ### Dry Terrace
> Umbel—Elder, Kofri's sister
> Fino—young man
> Yinlan—young man
> Linc—young woman

Formerly of Surefoot Clan, Now Fatekeepers

> ### Western Terrace
> Lofi—middle-aged woman
> Boled—Lofi's husband
> Zev—young man
> Nenu—Zev's brother

Surefoot Clan

Norili—Kalish's mother; originally of Flintcrag clan, now fatecarver of Surefoot Clan

Riven—young man

Tana—young man

Caverna Clan

Farlin—clan's fatecarver

Wex—young man

Southcrag Clan

Margali—clan's fatecarver

Garen—young man, guard

Tensa—Fatewalker from folk tales

Treekeepers who have joined the Fatekeepers

Upper Falls

Hana—middle-aged woman, Boluso's wife, formerly of Weaver's Retreat

Boluso—middle-aged man, Hana's husband, formerly of Weaver's Retreat

Rista—young woman, Qin's wife

Qin—young man, Rista's husband

Sendalee—young woman

Jando—young man

Londra—young woman

High Reaches

Benha—Speaker

Flatwater

Sarafee—Speaker

Lower Falls

Onola—Speaker

Treekeepers loyal to Norili

Sintala—Speaker of Weaver's Retreat

Zel—Speaker of Upper Falls

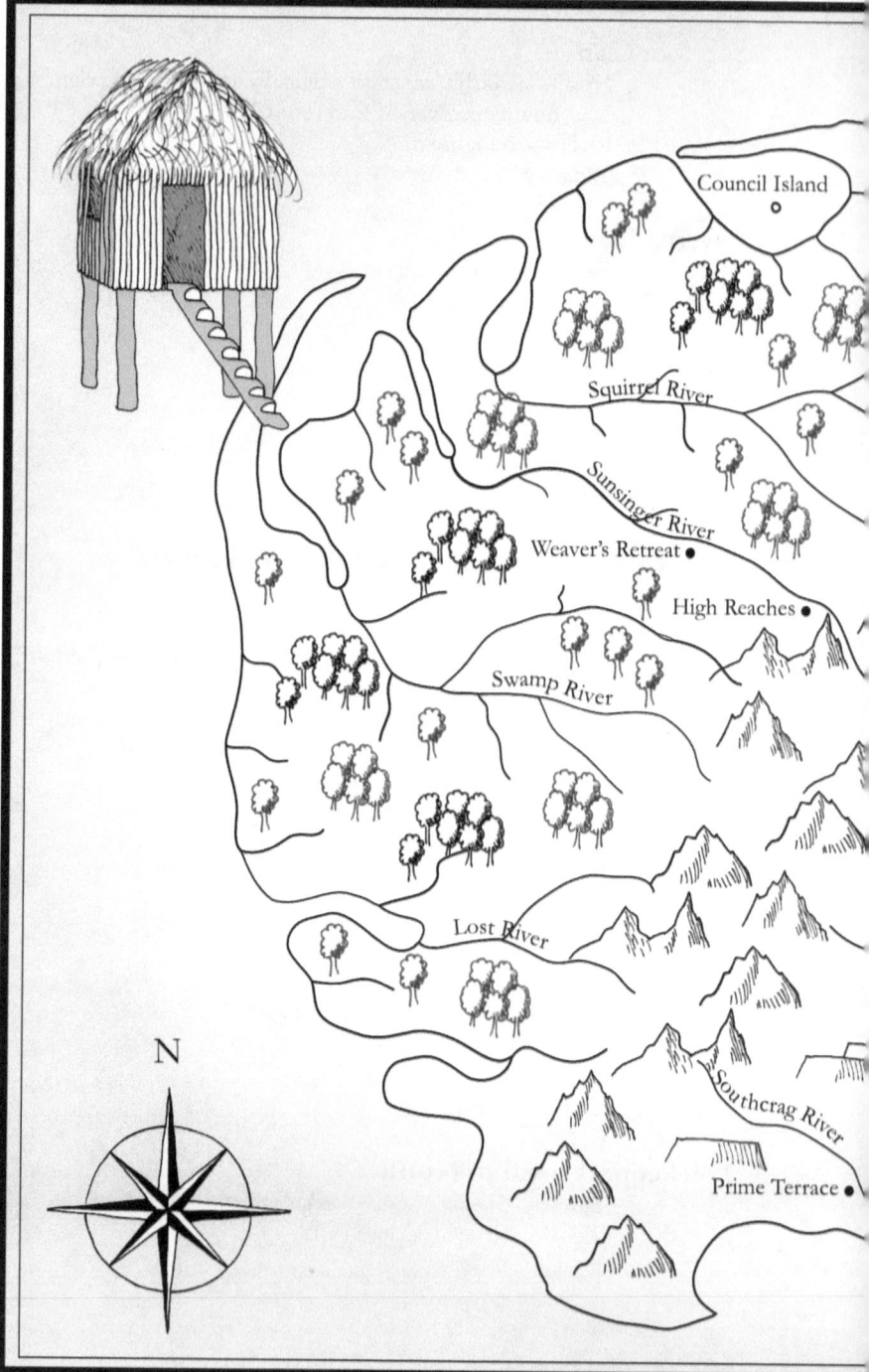

Council Island

Squirrel River

Sunsinger River

Weaver's Retreat ●

High Reaches ●

Swamp River

Lost River

Southcrag River

Prime Terrace ●

N

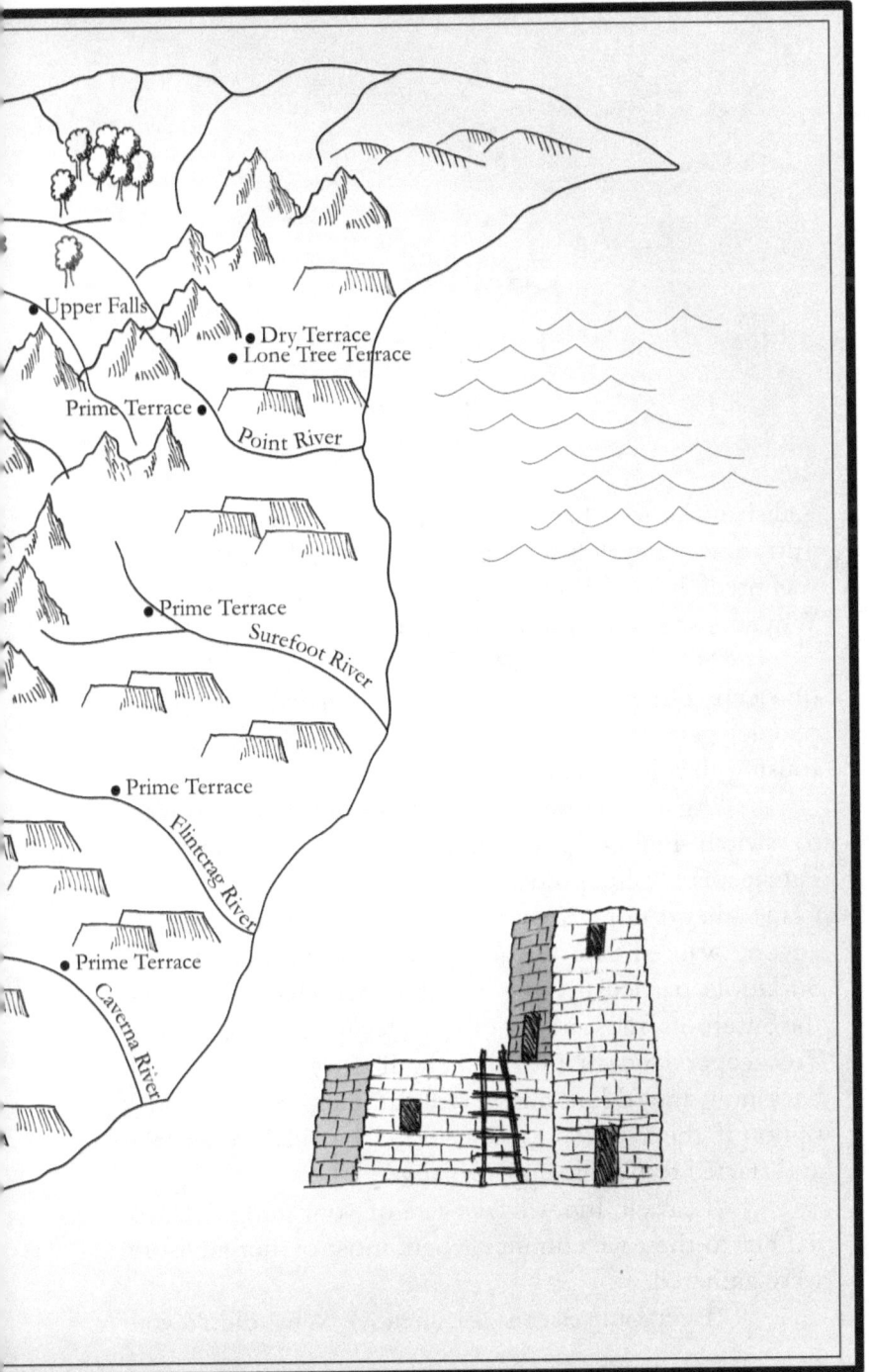

CHAPTER 1

Kalish woke to a hand on her shoulder. Her eyes were gritty and her eyelids felt weighted with rocks. Spines, she was tired! Stars glittered in the dark sky outside the cave. Why was she being roused at this hour?

"They've found us." Dayo's words jolted her out of sleep. The cave echoed with the hurried rustling of people gathering supplies, rolling up blankets, and rousing sleeping children.

"Again?" How many times would they be forced to switch hiding spots? Kalish stifled a groan. The Fatekeepers were prepared to flee from the Surefoot Clan—they'd done it twice already—but it wasn't what anyone wanted to do. Kalish *wanted* to stand up to the Surefoots, particularly to her mother, who had taken over the Surefoots, most of the other Fatecarver clans, and the Treekeeper lands. Unfortunately, if they tried to fight back now, they'd be slaughtered. Running was their only option if they wanted to stay alive. She rolled to her feet and started to bundle up her blanket.

"Leave it. Ino will take care of your things." Dayo led her to the cave entrance where most of her advisors were gathered.

"Everyone else is up already? Why didn't you

wake me earlier?"

Dayo squeezed her arm. "You spent half the night in the Fatewalker Realm. You were exhausted."

Kalish didn't tire as quickly when she was in the Fatewalker Realm—the spiritual realm in which her power of shape-shifting felt as natural as breathing, where she could speak to the god Iskra—but it wasn't restful like sleep, even though her physical body appeared asleep while she was in the Fatewalker Realm.

Umbel, Elder of Dry Terrace before it had been taken over by the Surefoots, nodded. "We've got it under control. Everyone knows the plan. When the scouts returned with news of the Surefoot force, I sent three hunting parties out to try to slow them down."

"And they know they're not to kill?" Last time, the hunting parties got carried away and went on full-out attack, killing several Surefoot scouts before they remembered their Fatekeeper pledge of non-violence.

Umbel raised a hand. "I made sure to remind them. Not that I can guarantee it's not going to happen in the dark—mistakes can be made—but their orders are to harass and engage, not kill."

"The injured, sick and elderly are already on their way out," Jalen reported. "Wend and a handful of warriors went with them."

"Everyone else will be out of here soon. They all know what to do," Leithe added.

"And the gliders?" The gliders were their main tactical strength—they'd spent months doing little but construct them, and their fleet was larger than even the Surefoot fleet. Best of all, the Surefoots had no idea just how many gliders the Fatekeepers had. They were in for a surprise.

"Ready to go."

Kalish nodded. "Let's get to it, then."

Most of the glider pilots were already on top of the ridge—the encampment there protected the gliders and also gave the Fatekeepers a good vantage point from which to see approaching enemies. Fabric rippled in the breeze, and the ghostly wings stood out in the dark.

The sky was just beginning to lighten in the east. Good. The idea of flying at night had Kalish's stomach flipping over.

Besides, the point was to be seen. It was a tactic they hadn't tried before—it seemed counterintuitive if they were trying to flee. But Kalish had been sneaking around, trying to gain supporters surreptitiously for months, and it wasn't working fast enough. Maybe a show of strength would help.

"What do we know?" she asked as she drew alongside Yinlan, who was organising the glider contingent.

"They're a force of about a hundred and fifty. All men."

So they were definitely here to fight, not chat. Norili would never have sent men to negotiate. That could work to the Fatekeepers' advantage—men had more to gain by joining them. And they were used to taking orders from women, at least among the Surefoots.

"Do we know if they're Surefoot born?"

"Impossible to tell, but I'd guess they are. The Surefoots would be foolish to send out anyone from the conquered clans."

Dawn crept to the edge of the sky, tingeing it a deep azure which slowly gave way to magenta. The assembled pilots waited in tense silence, the only sound the occasional snap of fabric in the wind. Kalish kept her back straight, shoulders up, hoping the magnificence of her Fatewalker cloak hid her jittery hands and pounding heart.

"There." Yinlan pointed. The raiders were a smudge on the landscape below.

"Time to fly," Kalish said.

There were no rousing speeches for this launch as there had been the last time the entire glider fleet took to the air. They were all business today. Surprise and shock were the goal, and they needed a speedy, silent launch.

Dayo was already harnessed into his glider, and Kalish joined him, strapping in next to him and giving him a nod. With a running leap they lifted off from the ridge.

Her nerves fled the moment she was airborne. Flying next to Dayo banished every emotion besides joy.

They arced into the wind, using the lift to soar out over the plain below, heading for the raiding party. In her peripheral vision were others of their fleet, and she smiled. In moments, the sun would breach the horizon— their two hundred gliders would positively glow in the light, while the plain below remained in shadow.

They couldn't have timed it better if they had tried.

She and Dayo turned their glider into a wide spiral as they neared the raiding party, which afforded her a good view of the rest of the fleet. The gliders were magnificent—like a flock of great white birds.

"I'm going to shift," she warned. It had taken Dayo a while to learn how to manage a tandem glider during the sudden weight change that happened when Kalish shifted form. Surprising him with the shift wasn't a good idea.

Freaking him out with the shift, however, was too much fun to pass up. Kalish slipped out of her harness, shot Dayo a mischievous grin and then dropped like a stone.

Who would have thought falling would be so

4

much fun? When there was no worry over the landing, the sensation was exhilarating. She closed her eyes against the rush of wind and imagined her falcon form.

Feather, beak, claw. Her transformation rippled over her and her eyes flew open again. Falcon eyes now—keen and far-seeing. The sun's first rays shot over the horizon and illuminated the fleet, and Kalish let out a wild war cry. The men below turned surprised faces upward. A few stumbled.

The gliders swirled above the raiding party like a kettle of hawks, keeping pace with them as they jogged over the dusty ground. Groups of gliders dropped out of formation to swoop close to the raiders, risking atlatl strikes, but demonstrating the fleet's manoeuvrability and speed. If their goal had been the destruction of the raiding party, the confrontation would already have been over.

The raiders stuttered to a halt, every face painted with fear and uncertainty. They milled about, brandishing spears and atlatls. A few darts flew toward the gliders, but none struck home.

It was time for Kalish to show herself.

She folded her wings and dove.

Wind screamed past her face and the ground rose to meet her. A shout, and someone below pointed at her.

Yes. Watch. See what I am.

One man raised his atlatl. It was beaten down by a fellow clansman. Angry faces and gestures.

When she was close enough to pick out individual pores on the men's faces, she opened her wings. She swooped out of her dive, buzzing the men's heads, even as they ducked away from her. She hovered for a moment, and then transformed back into her human self, dropping to her feet and giving her cloak a dramatic swirl.

Every eye was glued to her. The glider fleet

swirled overhead, but the raiders before her looked as if they were carved from stone.

"Greetings, men of Surefoot Clan," she began in a voice taught to her by her mother. A voice that demanded respect, expected obedience. "I am Kalish. Fatewalker. Chosen by the Fates to save our people. You have come to destroy me and my followers, the Fatekeepers. You have already failed."

Kalish recited a speech she'd polished over many repetitions. A speech encouraging the men to break with the Surefoot Clan and join her Fatekeepers. A speech that emphasised what they stood to gain by joining her—equality, respect, opportunity. All the while, her mind was playing a vision of her people—homeless, landless, currently scurrying away. Could she ever deliver what she promised her followers? Her voice faltered.

The snap of fabric overhead reminded her of the fleet of gliders at her back, reminded her of what the Fatekeepers had accomplished, in spite of their hunted status. If enough people believed in her vision for a more just world, they *could* make it happen. They could overthrow Kalish's mother, Norili, and break the Surefoot's hold on the other clans. *Keep telling yourself that. If you don't believe it, no one else will.* She straightened her shoulders and continued.

"I ask you to go home. Think about the world *you* want to live in. Do you want to remain second-class citizens, sent to do the raiding, ignored except when the elders want something from you? Or would you rather have a voice in society, choose what you do each day, and be respected for your ideas and your skills? If you choose our path, then we will welcome you on another day, when you come to us willingly, and not as a raiding party. Together we can embrace new ideas of equality. Together we can usher in a new age of innovation and prosperity for all people."

"How do we find you?" A faceless voice from the back.

Kalish raised her eyebrows. "Well, I won't tell you where my people have fled to, seeing as you're here to kill us. But if you choose to join us, the god Iskra will guide you. And if you choose to support us from within your clan, keep your eyes and ears open. A messenger will come to you. And I promise, you will see me again." In a swish of vanishing cape, she transformed, beating feathered wings to rise above the gaping men. No one raised a weapon this time. Kalish joined the fleet in their swirling kettle and led them streaming away into the hills.

CHAPTER 2

"Fatecarver Lela?" Kalish hated surprising people in the Fatewalker Realm, but it was the only way to communicate across long distances.

The young woman's head whipped around, eyes wide. Then she smiled. "Fatewalker!"

"Please. Call me Kalish."

"Only if you'll call me Lela." The fatecarver's eyes twinkled. "I'm so glad you're here. I didn't know where to find you."

"And I'm glad to see you here. I was worried you hadn't survived the Surefoot invasion."

Lela nodded. "We learned from the Flintcrag Clan's experience. We put up no fight—they left our terrace intact and most of our people alive." She pursed her lips as though she'd tasted something bitter. "Though they've not been shy about letting us know who's in charge now, and they've been confiscating food."

Kalish could easily imagine the repression the Surefoot Clan had imposed on Point Clan. It would feel especially harsh to Point Clanspeople, who were less strict about the traditional roles of men and women in society, and more open to new ideas than other clans.

"I'm so sorry." Kalish couldn't help apologising

for her mother's actions.

Lela waved a hand. "You have nothing to be sorry about."

"But you're suffering, and I'm here to seek your help."

"You are surely suffering more than I am." Lela glanced around, as though looking for eavesdroppers—unlikely, given they were in the Fatewalker Realm. But as more people learned how to enter, the realm was becoming increasingly busy. And Norili could show up at any time. "Let's walk."

Lela led Kalish down from Point Clan's prime terrace and through tangled brush along a narrow goat path that skirted the base of the butte. They wended their way between boulders that had tumbled from the cliffs above. When they were far from any of the heavily used trails in and out of the terrace, Lela pre-empted Kalish's questions. "You should know that Norili has asked me to look after Point Clan's fatecarving duties as her apprentice."

Kalish sucked in a breath. "And you've agreed?" Maybe talking to Lela was a bad idea. The young fatecarver had seemed supportive before, but if she was Norili's apprentice now …

"You know what they say—the best way to defeat the enemy is by crawling under the furs with them." Her grim expression morphed into a wicked smile.

Kalish laughed, the tension in her muscles easing. "I was going to ask you to help me keep tabs on Norili in the Fatewalker Realm. Being her apprentice is the perfect cover for doing so, if you're willing."

"Gives me an excuse to find out where she is and what she's doing. Meanwhile, I can maintain my influence with the Point Clanspeople. Eventually the Surefoots will show a moment of weakness, and I intend for us to be ready to exploit it."

Kalish could have cried with relief. She'd half expected to arrive at Point Clan's prime terrace to find it destroyed by the Surefoots like her own home terrace had been. She had feared Lela was dead. She was surprised her mother hadn't ordered her killed—a rival fatecarver could represent a problem for her.

They wound through the brush for some time, discussing how and when they would meet to share information, and how they might work together to topple Norili. Nearing the main path back to the terrace, Lela halted. "You should probably leave from here. Your mother tends to show up unexpectedly, usually in the afternoon. Keeping an eye on me, no doubt. It would be bad for both of us if she saw us together."

After Lela had returned to the terrace, Kalish transformed into her snake form, slithering silently to a vantage point in the sun near the path. She coiled up in full view, trusting the lantan's camouflage to hide her.

Her snake form was patient. She lay for a long time beside the path, tongue flicking out now and again in search of her mother's telltale tang.

There. A tiny whiff of piromanga smoke. A second flick of the tongue and the smell intensified. She was coming. Soon Kalish heard her mother's footsteps in the vibrations resonating through her jaw resting on the ground. She froze, not even a flick of the tongue to give her away.

Her mother strode purposefully down the path. A new cloak swirled in her wake, made of the finest sugarspike cloth and heavily embellished with both Fatecarver beads and bright feathers from Treekeeper lands.

Trying to outdo my cloak. She looks like a Fatewalker.

Irritation surged through Kalish and her tail

twitched. One bite could do it. Norili always carried alna leaves—the antidote to the bite of a lantan—but once the venom took effect, Kalish could overpower her and take her herb pouch. It would be easy. If Norili wasn't her mother. Spines! How was she supposed to defeat her mother without killing her? Norili would never quit seeking power.

Kalish's tail twitched in irritation, and her tongue flashed black in the sun.

Norili's eyes snapped to the side of the path, searching. *Would she know me if she saw me in this form?* Kalish uncoiled and slithered away into the tussocks. She would go see Iskra—they would have advice for her.

Kalish walked among the nalati trees on Council Island, breathing in the humid air and soaking up the stillness and peace the grove exuded. She was alone in the sacred grove. It felt abandoned. Did Norili ever walk here and speak to Iskra? She doubted it. In any case, she wasn't overly worried about meeting Norili right now—hopefully she'd be busy with Lela for a while.

Sunlight dappled the forest floor and a sunsinger bird called overhead. Kalish pressed her palms against the largest of the giant trees in the grove. *Iskra?*

The low hum that indicated the presence of the god swelled, and then the leaves overhead seemed to shiver and whisper directly into her mind.

Kalish. Falcon. Lantan. Pebble. You are distressed.

Kalish let out a sigh. "We were so close to freeing the Treekeepers, protecting your grove. Now I don't know what to do. I had a chance to kill her—to kill my mother. I couldn't do it."

Of course you couldn't, child. No one would expect you to, least of all me.

"But she's worse than the old Treekeeper Council! You killed one of them."

Because he was intent upon harming you. Kalish, I am life. I will never advocate for its destruction, no matter what form it presents itself in. Of course, one cannot have life without death, and I am fully prepared to mete out death when it is necessary. You, however, are not me.

Kalish laughed. "Thank the Fates."

The leaves overhead shivered in mirth. The Fates, Nalatassa—these were also Iskra, simply by different names.

"So how will I stop my mother without killing her? I used to think I could change her, but I know she will always hunger for power. If we dislodge her from the island, she'll simply find another way to dominate others and commandeer resources. She'll never stop."

Just as I will never stop trying to regain my power. I thirst for it as keenly as your mother does.

"But you're a god. You're supposed to be powerful. You use your power to ..." What did Iskra do?

Maintain the equilibrium among living things and manage the spiritual world—what you call the Fatewalker Realm. It is my energy that fuels the Fatewalker Realm.

A flicker of fear ran through Kalish. "Does that mean that if you ... die ... the Fatewalker Realm will vanish?"

Not immediately. It will slowly degrade over time. And with it, the physical realm will also degrade.

Kalish's fear spiked. "But you are strengthening, right? Now that more people are entering the Fatewalker Realm?" That's what Iskra had implied when her people ousted the Treekeeper Council.

Provided the nalati grove remains. It is the seat of my power. Without it I am nothing. It was, perhaps, a mistake in my youth to concentrate myself in one place.

Kalish couldn't imagine a god having a youth. Did that mean they had an old age? Weren't gods immortal?

Iskra continued. *My pebble. You have created one landslide. It is time to tumble again and bring down more of the mountain. Look after your people. Draw from their strength. And do not be afraid to reach for power—you have much unrealised potential still within you.*

Reach for power, like her mother? It was the last thing Kalish wanted.

"But what about Norili?" Surely Iskra had some ideas on how to get rid of her.

You will know what to do when the time comes.

What kind of answer was that? "But—"

Hush. Seek your power. It will guide you.

It was a relief to return to her body, to Dayo waiting patiently for her.

Well, maybe not patiently.

When she opened her eyes, he was pacing the ground beside her.

"What's happened?" It couldn't be immediately life-threatening, or he would have called to her in the Fatewalker Realm.

He whirled around and crouched beside her as she sat up, bending her head to avoid hitting the strut of the glider she was lying under. Their current camp was nestled deep in the foothills of the mountains. They were harder to find here, but there was little shelter among the low-growing tussocks. The wind was relentless, and they'd begun using their gliders as makeshift shelters against the cold gusts.

Dayo held out a pair of darts. Kalish opened her mouth to ask why he was presenting her with atlatl darts.

Then she saw the tips, glinting dully in the sun.

She drew one from his grasp. The tip was triangular and barbed, as all dart tips were. But instead of the characteristic knapped scallops of traditional dart tips, this tip tapered smoothly from the centre to the edge. She ran a finger over the edge, and it sliced effortlessly into her skin. The finger came away bloody.

"Bladestone. From a Surefoot scouting party?" she guessed.

Dayo nodded. "Didn't take long."

No. It hadn't taken long for Norili to recognise the potential of bladestone for fashioning superior weaponry. The stone was mined in the mountains by the Treekeepers. There was, no doubt, plenty of it to be found on the Fatecarver side of the mountains, but the arid scrub on the Fatecarver side didn't provide the large quantities of fuel needed to melt the stone in order to turn it into useful objects. Fatecarvers had never used it, didn't know what it was until Kalish had brought the two cultures together.

She sighed. "Well it was going to happen one way or another, with trade opening up between the two. Do we know this is Norili's work?"

"Who else's could it be?"

Only a Treekeeper who had encountered Fatecarver weapons and seen the potential for commerce. But it wasn't within Treekeeper culture to either innovate like this or to create weapons. No. It was her mother's doing. How many of these had she made, and how many were now circulating among the Surefoots? How many would be used against Kalish's people?

Kalish rubbed her temples. She and her people had been hiding out in the hills for months now. She'd sent dozens of small parties out to visit outlying terraces within Surefoot and the former Point Clan, trying to gather supporters and put spies in place. But the pace was slow. People were afraid of change. Even the men, whom she expected to flock to her because of the equality she offered, were reluctant. Now the Surefoots had superior weaponry, provided by Norili, who championed *traditional* values—women and men in their rightful places, girls with storyscars dictated by the Fates and tattooed on their faces by official fatecarvers, the moral and social superiority of the fatecarvers and all-female elder councils.

Kalish wasn't a fool. She knew many Fatecarvers would be swayed by shiny new weapons.

"Are you thinking what I'm thinking?" she asked Dayo.

"That we need to start giving out gliders?"

She nodded, hating the idea. The only thing that kept the Fatekeepers safe was their large fleet of fully steerable gliders. Gliders she and Dayo had designed. Other clans' gliders weren't steerable, and even landing safely was dicey. Flying one was risky, and even if you reached the ground in one piece, there was usually a long walk home afterwards. "It'll be the end of our ability to hide."

"Yes, but if we give them to Caverna and Southcrag, we could gain some important allies."

"Provided we get there before Mother does," Kalish agreed. "We should talk to the advisors about it." She stood and stretched, shivering in the keen wind that whipped through her clothes. "Spines! It's gotten chilly."

Dayo smiled as he rubbed warmth into her arms. "Put your cloak on. I'll find you some stew."

He picked his way between the tussocks dotting their camp, passing Kofri coming towards Kalish. The furrows between her eyebrows spoke of trouble.

Several paces away, Kofri raised her eyes to Kalish, and the furrows vanished in a smile. "I'm glad to see your young man is taking good care of you."

Kalish's gaze shifted to where Dayo stooped over a steaming pot of food, ladling some into a bowl for her. "It's a little embarrassing. Here I am espousing gender equality, and he insists on waiting on me hand and foot."

Kofri squeezed Kalish's arm. "He does it out of love, not duty."

"I know." A sigh escaped her lips. If only they could have a normal relationship—if they could proof like any other couple and eventually marry. She shook the thoughts away. It was foolish to hope for any normalcy while they were hunted nomads. It was a dream for the future. "You're not here to tell me how lucky I am to have Dayo. What's the problem?"

"We—Umbel, Wathi, Jenti and I—don't think we'll be able to support the Fatekeepers through the winter on what we can hunt and gather while we're on the move like this." She waved an arm around their makeshift camp. "Also, we can't keep sleeping out in the open under our gliders—winter will hit hard one of these days."

It wasn't news. They'd been managing, but their grain had long since run out, and everyone missed the pola they were accustomed to eating daily. And the camp bread, even before the wheat was gone, was a far cry from bread baked in a proper oven like it was in the terraces.

"What do you suggest we do?" Kofri wouldn't have come to her without a plan.

"Wathi and Jenti think we should reclaim Flintcrag's prime terrace. It is large enough to shelter us all, and there may be grain the Surefoots didn't destroy, either in the fields or stored in the terrace."

A jolt of hope and longing at the mention of Kalish's home was quickly replaced by despair. She shook her head. "It was badly damaged when Surefoot attacked. They used incendiaries." She remembered the blackened, crumbling walls and shuddered. "Besides, I'm sure they're guarding it to prevent Flintcrags returning."

"When you saw the terrace, you were devastated. Did you really look closely enough to tell if it could be inhabited?"

She had a point. By the time Kalish was close enough to make out the terrace's details, her eyes had been blurry with tears, and she wasn't exactly thinking coherently.

"And as for guarding it? The Surefoots know by now that the Flintcrags have joined you. Their eyes are not turned toward Flintcrag territory."

"Until we go there. They may not have pinpointed exactly where we are yet, but they manage to get close every time we move camp. They'll follow us there."

Dayo had arrived with a steaming bowl, and he chimed in. "What if we convinced them we'd gone the other way?"

An interesting idea, but it could get complicated. Kalish accepted the bowl of stew Dayo held out. "Let's talk about it at tomorrow's advisor meeting."

They were making too little progress on gaining support, and if they had to spend the next month laying false trails, they wouldn't be able to focus on their real goal. Kalish felt like tearing her hair out in frustration. They needed to move more quickly to undermine Norili. Once she was fully established, once she'd taken over all the clans, it would be almost impossible to unseat her.

CHAPTER 3

Hana crouched in silence at the edge of the clearing at the centre of what had once been the village of Upper Falls. Norili and Speaker Zel faced off a few dozen paces from where she hid. Norili had just dismissed Zel as Speaker, and Zel was growing more and more desperate as he argued with her.

Norili gestured at the heaps of ash that had once been homes, destroyed by the previous council. "Even if men *were* capable of spiritual leadership, there is no one left here to lead."

"The villagers are nearby, I know it. They'll return now that the council's—your—fighters are gone. Please, you must allow me to remain here. They trust me. They look to me for guidance."

Hana nearly snorted out loud at the blatant lie. No one in the village trusted Zel. He'd lived high off of council bribes, and the meagre goods the council sent to the village he withheld for his own use.

Zel continued to beg. "I will tell them of your benevolence, your greatness, how you glow with the power of Nalatassa. You must let me remain their

Speaker."

Norili barked a laugh. "You speak sweetly. Let's hope your cooking tastes as good on the tongue."

"My—you expect me to cook? For myself?"

Norili laughed again. "No, you idiotic man. For my warriors. You may eat what's left when they are through with their meal. I expect you on Council Island in three days. You will leave the Fatewalker Realm and not return here. If you do not appear for duty within three days, I will have you hunted down and given to the trees. They've been extraordinarily hungry lately."

Zel blanched. Most Treekeepers believed the trees awoke at dusk to prey upon anyone foolish enough to be outdoors at night. Criminals were given to the trees—tied up and left in the forest at nightfall. Few survived, but the trees weren't the cause. Hana had long known that the real danger at night was the large black cats that prowled the forest, and they were avoidable with the right precautions. The entire village of Upper Falls had become largely nocturnal to escape the previous council's fighters. They'd built a fleet of boats to attack Council Island right under the noses of the fighters and Speaker Zel, all of whom were too frightened of the trees to investigate the noises drifting through the night-time forest.

Well, at least one good thing had come of Norili's takeover. With Zel and the fighters gone, the villagers could resume a diurnal lifestyle. Maybe they could even begin rebuilding the village.

Unfortunately, they were going to have to attack Council Island again, to take it back from Norili, and this time they'd have to do it without Fatecarver help.

The thought burned in Hana's chest. She'd trusted Kalish and the other Fatecarvers. The village of Upper Falls had welcomed them with open arms. They'd all been deeply affected by the discovery of the mural in the cave to which they'd escaped—a mural depicting friendly trade between Fatecarvers and Treekeepers, drawn in charcoal generations ago. Hana dreamed of reviving trade between their two people.

But since Norili's takeover, the fledgling trade they'd begun had ceased. Hana refused to attend the regular meetings of Kalish's advisory group, although Sendalee and Qin continued to go.

Kalish claimed she had been as blindsided by her mother's actions as anyone, but Hana wasn't a fool. Norili's actions were a blatant attack by the Fatecarvers, and Kalish was a Fatecarver. She'd betrayed the Treekeepers' trust. Worse, she'd betrayed Hana's trust. After years as an outcast, relying on herself, trusting no one, Hana had allowed herself to trust Kalish. Clearly it had been a mistake, and now all the Treekeepers were paying for it. The weight of responsibility pressed on Hana's chest. She wasn't sure who she was more angry with—Kalish or herself.

Lost in thought, Hana hadn't noticed Zel and Norili leave the clearing. She focused for a moment, listening for footsteps, but heard nothing. She was alone. Time to return to her body.

"We'll need to strike as soon as we can," Hana urged.

"Do we have enough boats? We lost quite a few last time," Rista said as she nursed her new baby.

Jando frowned. "Forget boats, do we have enough fighters? Hana, you talk like we've done this before, but all *we* did was transport two hundred Fatecarver warriors to Council Island."

"We've fought the council's men for months. We can do this." Hana was determined that her people—the

Treekeepers alone—would oust Norili. They couldn't rely on the Fatecarvers again. "The people of High Reaches, Lost River, Rocky Glen and Pinnacles are all with us."

Qin leaned forward. "That gives us, what, a hundred people willing and able to fight? Hana, it's not enough. Not when we're up against a Fatecarver. Benha says Norili has brought in Fatecarver warriors. How will we fight against them? If they're even half as good as the Fatecarvers who helped us last time, we'll be destroyed."

Jando nodded. "He's right. We can't simply attack like we did last time. We need a different strategy."

"But what?" Hana clenched her fists. Treekeepers weren't good at this. They didn't fight. They didn't know anything about strategy, weapons, or planning an assault. Her husband Boluso laid a hand on her shoulder. "We'll come up with something."

Sendalee, who had been quiet so far during the meeting, spoke up. "Kalish would know what to do."

Hana rounded on the girl. "Kalish's *mother* is sitting there on Council Island. Do you think she's going to help us?"

Sendalee's voice was as hard as Hana's. "Yes. I do." Her shoulders slumped and her voice gentled. "Hana, Kalish had nothing to do with Norili's takeover. She hates her mother and is doing everything she can to remove her from power. She's heartbroken about everything that's happened. Every time we meet, she asks about you."

It wasn't the first time Sendalee had told her this, begged her to give Kalish a chance, reminded her of all that Kalish had done for them. Part of her wanted desperately to believe in Kalish, to believe in the vision she thought they both shared of a people united in peace and mutual respect. But the part of her that tallied their failures and losses clung to anger. It was easier to be angry than to admit they had all been naive. It was easier to blame Kalish of deceit than to recognise that anyone with a lust for power could have taken control at the moment they toppled the council, because they hadn't planned for what would happen *after* the battle. They'd created the perfect opportunity for Norili, and no one had realised it until it was too late.

Hurrying feet sounded on the path to the clearing, giving Hana a reprieve. She forced a smile as Benha, Speaker of High Reaches jogged into view, along with several High Reaches villagers.

"Sorry we're late." Benha was breathless. "The river was up—it was brutal paddling."

"You needn't have hurried. I could have filled you in later," Hana assured her.

"No. What I have to say can't wait, and you all need to hear it." As a female Speaker, Benha had been treated well by Norili—the Fatecarver understood how to buy loyalty, and she wanted all the Speakers to be her own personal spies among the people. Speakers were showered with gifts.

Benha, however, couldn't be bought. She fawned over Norili while in her presence, but everything she saw and heard was communicated to Hana and the others who intended to bring Norili down.

"Norili ordered the entire nalati grove on Council Island chopped down for use in building a huge shrine to what she calls the Fates. She says it's called a fatechamber and in it she will perform the ceremonies to invoke the gods the Fatecarvers worship."

Hana's stomach flipped. "She's going to cut down the nalati grove?" She knew from Kalish's experiences that the god Iskra's power was centred in the nalati grove on Council Island. "But cutting down the trees will destroy Iskra. Destroy the very Fates she intends to worship."

Kalish would never do that, would never allow it to happen if she knew about it. She walked regularly among the nalati trees to speak with Iskra. Iskra was her guide, her touchstone. Hana squeezed her eyes shut, a heavy weight lodging in her stomach. Sendalee was right—Kalish had nothing to do with her mother's takeover.

"We need to warn Kalish."

The Fatekeeper advisory group met every five-day in the Fatewalker Realm. Hana had refused to attend since Norili took over Council Island. Now she paced, stomach churning, while she, Boluso, Qin and Sendalee waited for the Fatecarver delegation to arrive.

Boluso caught her arm as she passed him for the sixth time. "Relax, Hana." He pulled her into a hug.

"What if she doesn't forgive me?" Hana whispered into his shoulder.

"She will forgive you."

"And if I can't forgive myself? I was horrible for not believing her."

"Oh, Hana." Boluso squeezed her tighter.

Footsteps announced the approaching Fatecarvers, and Hana loosed herself from Boluso to face them. The elders Kofri and Umbel—sisters whose intense energy had not diminished with age—set the pace. Behind them came Wathi and Jenti, Dayo's parents, chatting with Kofri's son-in-law Wend. The young adults Tili, Fino and Yinlan were next, followed by Dayo and Kalish, who walked hand in hand, deep in conversation.

As if she sensed Hana's presence, Kalish looked up, zeroing in on her. "Hana?" Emotions warred on her face—surprise, then hope, settling into uncertainty.

Breaking away from Dayo, she strode to Hana, but her steps faltered as she approached.

Stomach tied in knots, Hana held out a hand to Kalish. "I'm so sorry."

In an instant, Kalish closed the gap between them to embrace her. "No. *I'm* sorry. I should have known my mother would do something horrible."

"We were foolish not to think ahead—it's as much my fault as yours. I'm sorry I blamed you." Tears pricked Hana's eyes. She blinked them back, forced herself to pull away from Kalish. "It was your mother who convinced me you weren't involved. She's ordered the destruction of the nalati grove on Council Island."

Kalish gasped. "No!"

Chapter 4

Kalish was desperate to do something to stop the destruction of the nalati grove. Maybe this was the time Iskra had spoken of—the right time to overthrow Norili. While her advisors waited, she sped to Council Island to warn Iskra.

I have heard of her plan. Iskra's whispery voice gave no indication of how the god felt about the news. *If the nalati grove falls, this will be the last time we speak. If I am destroyed, it will be up to you, Fatewalker, to preserve the spiritual realm.*

"How?" Kalish asked.

The leaves overhead rustled in a long sigh. *I don't remember. What came before me is hazy in my memory. I remember only that I was created by myself, and in my creation, the Fatewalker Realm flourished.*

"I have to … create a god?" How was that possible?

There must be a Spark. Without one, no life can survive for long. You must restore the Spark if I should fall.

"And you don't know how to … restore the Spark?" How could a god not know?

It is beyond my remembering.

Spines! Better to focus on preserving the grove,

keeping Iskra alive. She at least had some ideas on how to do that much.

When she returned to her advisors, she presented her idea. "I could lead a small force over the mountains. We could go by glider, and meet up with the Treekeepers, if there are some willing to fight." Kalish looked to Hana.

"There are several villages willing to send fighters," Hana replied.

Qin shook his head. "We have about a hundred people who have been taught how to use a spear. They'll be no match for the Fatecarver warriors on the island."

"Qin's right," Dayo said. "We'd have to send a large force of good fighters over, if we want to take the island by force."

Umbel looked thoughtful. "We don't actually need to take control of the island to save the nalati grove. We simply have to stop Norili's people from cutting the trees. That could potentially be done with a much smaller number of people, and with minimal fighting."

"If we knew where their tools were stored, we might be able to destroy them," Hana suggested. "It might not stop them forever, but it would slow them down if they had to make new ones."

"It would still mean getting onto Council Island," Kalish said.

"Maybe not," Boluso argued. "The nalati grove is the only stand of trees on Council Island. The wood for building on the island comes from the forests surrounding Council Bay. That's where we'll find the tree-felling saws."

"But we'll have to move quickly, before they take the saws to Council Island," Qin warned.

To delay the felling of the nalati grove was good enough, provided they managed to unseat Norili soon. It was the best they were likely to be able to do, with winter closing in on them. The truth was, sending a party over the mountains at this time of year was risky—there was little chance they'd even make it.

After discussing the options, they agreed that Kalish would seek out the location of the tools, using the Fatewalker Realm. Meanwhile, Hana would gather a group of twenty to forty Treekeepers who could sneak into wherever the tools were kept and steal them.

"What if Norili's fighters are nearby? What if you're caught?" Tili's worry showed in the lines between her eyebrows.

Hana smiled. "Norili's Fatecarvers won't catch us in the forest. We won't try to fight, we'll simply vanish into the trees."

While the others returned to the real world, Kalish remained in the Fatewalker Realm. She shifted into her falcon form and soared once again toward Council Island.

Something about Kalish's falcon form calmed her. As she soared over the forest, the panic over the imminent destruction of the nalati grove settled into determination to stop it. They would prevent Iskra's demise. Their plan would work, as long as she found the tools. What had Boluso called them? *Saws.* She should have asked what they looked like.

It felt like only moments before she was spiralling down toward Council Island. To her relief, the nalati grove was unchanged. Her mother's followers hadn't yet begun its destruction.

She longed to walk among the trees, to hear Iskra's voice. But she wasn't here for that.

Boluso had suggested there would be few tools on the island, but Kalish wanted to make certain of that.

Circling the island, she examined the buildings and kept her eyes open for anyone wandering the Fatewalker Realm. The place was deserted, as she'd expected—Norili wouldn't want anyone to be here. Good. At least Kalish wouldn't have to sneak around.

Where would they store tools for wood cutting? There was no point searching the rich former council members' houses—those people had never cut trees or fashioned houses. But on the outskirts of the settlement, near the great furnace used for melting bladestone, there were several small buildings that could contain tools needed to cut the wood used in the furnace. She swooped down between two likely buildings and shifted to her human form.

Unlike the houses in the villages, which were built on stilts, most of the buildings on Council Island were constructed at ground level. Council Island buildings were also different from village houses in that they were made with thin, sawn planks instead of sapling poles, and their roofs were tiled with wooden shingles instead of the thatching used in the villages. There must be hundreds of tools for cutting trees and shaping wood on the island. Would they have to find and destroy them all?

The wood of the nearest door was worn smooth by countless hands. Kalish pushed it open and peered into the dim room. Rows of tightly woven, lidded baskets lined the walls. She lifted a lid to find a basket filled to the brim with corn. The next basket was nearly empty, and as she peered into the depths, a mouse dashed up the side of the basket, leaping to her arm to make an escape. Kalish jumped in surprise, and then laughed at herself.

This was clearly a storeroom for grains, not tools. She moved on to the next building. Pushing open the door, she wrinkled her nose. It smelled of sweat and smoke. Sleeping platforms were stacked three high along the walls, with short ladders propped up against the upper ones for access. It reminded her a little of the children's rooms in her home terrace. But unlike the children's rooms, this barracks was sparse in comforts. There were no soft furs, no toys tucked underneath the platforms, no sense that this was a home.

She moved on. There was a pavilion for cooking, with a bread oven and several cooking fires. There was a storehouse for raw bladestone—nearly empty. Good. Norili wasn't able to replenish her supply without the cooperation of the mining villages.

At the end of the row of buildings was a tiny shack beside an enormous pile of cut logs. Aha! Inside was a range of tools, the likes of which she'd never seen before. All were made of bladestone. There were sharp knives with two handles, viciously serrated blades set in rectangular wooden frames, strange sharpened hoe-like tools whose function she couldn't fathom, heavy wedges, long-handled axes, and a double-handled serrated blade of such enormous proportions she scarcely believed it was real. It hung from pegs on the wall and stretched the entire length of the building—five long steps from end to end.

"Spines!" This must be a tree-felling saw. She shuddered at the thought of those jagged teeth ripping into Iskra's giant nalati trees.

She searched the other small storage buildings on the island, but found no more of the giant saws. How fast could you cut a tree down with one of those things? Was one saw enough to fell the entire grove? Surely they would need to bring more saws to the island. Those trees were enormous; it would take a long time to remove the grove with just one saw.

She transformed into her falcon form and lifted off, widening her search for the blades. Where were there freshly felled trees? That's where she'd find saws.

From the air, it wasn't hard to find the patch of forest ravaged by the felling blades. As someone who had grown up on the dry side of the mountains, where trees of the dimensions found here were unimaginable, the number of trees that had been felled was shocking. Stumps jutted up out of brambly new growth. From the tree-felling area, a wide muddy scar led to the edge of Council Bay, where a stack of logs awaited transport. Did they float them across to the island?

Once she identified the fresh cuts, she began to see places where the forest had been felled in the past. Places where vines and brambles dominated. Places thick with saplings. Massive trees standing alone among seedlings. The older clearings were smaller, and it was obvious that the pace of tree felling had increased in recent times. She knew it wasn't necessarily her mother's doing—the previous council had been hungry for bladestone and eager to build a great structure filled with luxury for themselves.

Now, where did they keep the tools?

The following day, Kalish met again with her advisors from both sides of the mountains.

"There's a spot near the coast." Kalish scratched a rough map of Council Island, Council Bay, and the surrounding land into the dirt with a stick, and then tapped the spot. "Right here. They're actively felling trees in this area."

"Where are the saws?" Dayo asked.

"In the forest near the felled trees there are ..." How would she describe them? "Houses made of barkcloth."

Tili snorted. "Houses of barkcloth?"

"Tents," Hana said. "They're light and easily moved, so when they cut all the trees in one area, they can quickly move on to another."

Umbel grunted. "That's a good idea. Better than sleeping under our gliders."

"And if you made them from furs, they'd be warm," Tili added.

It was exactly what Kalish had contemplated on the flight back, but they needed to focus on the task at hand. "Let's talk about that later. One of the cloth buildings is a storehouse for tools—there are probably thirty or more of the big blades there, along with a heap of axes and smaller tools." She'd been shocked by the massive pile of blades. "I think we should take the lot."

Hana nodded. "We'll need at least sixty people— it takes two people to carry each one of those tree-felling saws, especially if we're fleeing through the forest with them."

"Where will you take them?" Wathi asked.

"We should spread out," Sendalee suggested. "Once we have the saws, we should scatter. We can drop the saws in the forest somewhere, hide them. Norili's people are unlikely to find them, and even if they find one, they won't know where the others are."

Kofri chuckled. "Clever thinking."

"How many people are at this site?" Boluso asked.

Kalish shook her head. "I don't know for certain. In the Fatewalker Realm, I don't see the people. At a guess, there might be as many as a hundred."

"A hundred." Boled frowned. "Can you draw a picture of their encampment? I want to know where the storage tent is situated in relation to sleeping tents."

Kalish drew another diagram in the dirt, and the group discussed what tactics the Treekeepers might use to sneak in and out with the tools. When they were satisfied with the plan, Kalish asked the most important question.

"How soon can you go?"

Hana and Boluso shared a glance, and Boluso spoke up. "It will take at least two days to gather sixty people from the villages. We'll spend another three days travelling. So five days, minimum. And it may take another day or two to scope things out and find the right opening to strike."

A full five-day or more.

The thought twisted Kalish's stomach. What if Norili's people moved the saws to the island in that time? Once the cutting in the nalati grove was under way, there would be nothing they could do to stop it.

Dayo squeezed her hand. "We'll let you get to it then. Is there anything we can do from our side to help?"

Hana shook her head. "Just get rid of Norili."

CHAPTER 5

Light rain fell as darkness crept through the forest. The river rushed noisily, swollen by recent rains. It would be a swift journey to Council Bay. The sixty Treekeepers gathered with Hana by the river were jittery—many still feared the trees, despite Hana's repeated assurances that trees didn't eat people at night. Hana was jittery, too, but only because she was eager to get moving. They were finally doing something, rather than waiting around to be attacked by Norili's forces. Maybe they weren't taking back control of their lands from Norili yet, but they were preventing her from doing more damage.

Hana took a calming breath and slowly let it out. Find the wood cutters' encampment, steal the saws, and come home. If all went well, they wouldn't have to fight, and no one would know what they'd done until they were far away. They could do this.

"You'll meet me in the Fatewalker Realm tomorrow?" Boluso asked. He would stay behind—his missing toes slowed him down, and for this mission they needed everyone to be fleet of foot.

Hana squeezed Boluso's hand. "If it's safe to do

so. I've told Kalish the same."

The boats were drawn up to the bank, and Hana's people settled into them.

"We're all ready," Qin called.

"Be safe." Boluso kissed Hana.

She smiled. "You know this is what I'm best at—sneaking around not being seen." She and Boluso had been outcasts among their people for years, living on the fringes of society, unwelcome in their village.

Boluso chuckled. "Then keep everyone else safe."

Hana clambered into Qin's boat, and they shoved off into the current.

Their fleet of boats bobbed swiftly downstream through the silent forest. People spoke in murmurs and whispers, when they spoke at all, and Hana's nerves were lulled by the rush of water and motion of the boat.

The drizzle had turned to a steady, drenching rain by the time the sun came up and they stopped to hide and sleep through the day.

"Good thing we haven't got any Fatecarvers with us," Sendalee commented as she wrapped a damp blanket around her shoulders.

Hana laughed. "Because they'd be complaining about the rain?" Her mirth faded. "Let's hope we're not wishing for their fighting skills later."

Another night of paddling in the rain brought them to the mouth of the river. They slipped silently past the village at the mouth and skirted the shore of the bay until morning light threatened to reveal their fleet to any lookouts on the island.

"From this point, we're on foot," Hana warned her people. "Hide the boats well and leave behind as much as possible. We'll need to be light on our feet once we have the saws."

"Will we travel at night again?" Some people were

still terrified of the night-time forest.

"Yes. It's the only way we can move without being seen. But bear in mind that any Fatecarvers we encounter have no fear of the trees at night."

"And you think the Treekeepers here in the lowlands support Norili?" another villager asked.

"We don't know. I'd like to think they don't support her any more than we do, but many Speakers have been appointed by Norili, and they might easily convince the villagers Norili means well. And even those who don't like Norili might mention they saw us to the wrong person, so we need to remain unseen. So get some sleep now. We leave at dusk."

"I'm going to scout ahead in the Fatewalker Realm, so we know exactly where we're going tomorrow," Hana told Qin as they prepared to settle in for the day.

Qin nodded. "I'll watch over you while you're there. But eat something first. If you're going to miss sleep, you should at least have some food or you'll be running on nothing tonight."

Hana ate a hasty, cold meal and then lay down on her bedroll and shut her eyes. She relaxed her shoulders and uncurled her fists—she didn't enjoy the sensation of stepping out of her body into the Fatewalker Realm, but being tense made it worse. It took conscious effort to relax enough to make the transition. Breathe in, breathe out. Breathe in, breathe out. Visualise the threshold between the two worlds and step forward.

Hana grunted and rubbed her temples. Dappled sunlight on her eyelids, combined with the instant headache she got every time she entered the Fatewalker Realm told her she'd successfully made the transition. It took another five slow breaths for the headache to subside. A sunsinger bird called overhead. Hana smiled and opened her eyes.

She knew vaguely where they needed to go tonight, and she hoped she could quickly locate a path to take them there. Paths were potentially dangerous, but they were also the fastest and quietest routes through the forest.

Drops of water on the leaves above sparkled in the sun, as though it had recently rained. How did that work, here where it was always sunny? In the real world, the rain had stopped, but the sky was still overcast.

Hana picked her way through the forest perpendicular to the shore of the bay. There was likely to be a path that ran parallel to the shore, as there was along nearly every waterway in Treekeeper lands. That path should eventually intersect with the track along which Kalish said the logs were being dragged to the bay.

Dense brambles and vines made her progress slow and laborious, but eventually she made it to the expected path. Was there a better spot they could pull up to so they didn't have to crash through that mess? As she began striding down the path, she considered whether they should paddle further, maybe even as far as the stacked logs Kalish had seen.

But somehow, marching up the log track, with their boats docked at the end of it, seemed like a foolish idea. Better to have their boats hidden further away. Better to tiptoe through the forest and catch Norili's people by surprise.

Hana found the muddy log track while the sun was still high in the sky. Did the sun even move here in the Fatewalker Realm? She hadn't spent enough time here to consider it. In any case, it wasn't too far from where they were camped.

Expecting no company in this realm, she boldly walked up the track toward the wood cutters' encampment. It was slippery going—the slope had been thoroughly churned by the moving logs. Mud sucked at her feet, and loose rocks shifted when she stepped on them. This was definitely not the way to approach the encampment.

The camp was exactly as Kalish had described it, and Hana didn't waste time looking into all the tents. She went instead directly to the storage tent.

Wow! Kalish wasn't exaggerating. The tent was filled with tools. The ones of interest to Hana's thieves were piled along the far wall. She hoped they'd be able to carry them all.

As she left the tent, Hana paid attention to the details of the camp. The tents were arranged in a circle around a cooking fire. All the entrances faced inward, toward the fire. The tent cloths were stretched over frames and anchored to the ground with rocks and bladestone pegs. It would be easy to sidle up to the back of the storage tent, lift the edge of the fabric, and slide the saws out.

Now she just needed to mark a route through the forest to the back of the storage tent so they weren't flailing around in the dark trying to find the camp. But how was she going to make marks they could see in the dark?

Colourful feathers wouldn't work. Neither would breaking branches or scoring tree bark. What could she possibly see from a distance in the dark?

A rustle of leaves nearby startled her, and she tensed, ready to flee if necessary. Was someone else here? The rustle turned into the unmistakable scamper of a squirrel bounding across the ground.

That was it! Visual markers wouldn't work at night, but auditory ones would. Rain was often followed by several days of wind. All she had to do was find something that made a distinctive sound in the wind. She searched the area behind the storage tent, but found nothing useful. Nalati pods would be the best, but there were no nalati trees nearby, and the pods needed to dry in order to rattle, so she wasn't likely to be able to use them, even if she found some.

But then she had another thought—would the markers she created in the Fatewalker Realm be present in the real world? And if changes made in the Fatewalker Realm were echoed in the real world, could her people simply steal the saws in the Fatewalker Realm where no one would see them do it?

Think! What had she seen in the past? A trail of sunsinger feathers Kalish had left for her in the real world had been visible in the Fatewalker Realm. A message Kalish had formed of feathers while in the Fatewalker Realm had been visible days later in the Fatewalker Realm. But when a small group of delegates had rowed to Council Island in the Fatewalker Realm, their canoe had remained firmly rafted up with the others in their fleet in the real world.

Well, that was inconvenient—no markers and no stealing the saws with impunity.

On her way back to her group's camp, Hana carefully noted every large tree, every dip and rise in the land, every rivulet. It would have to be enough to guide them in the dark.

As dusk fell that evening, Hana and her thieves crept away from their hidden boats, heading toward the tree-felling camp. Hana's hands were jittery, and she gripped her spear tightly. The last time she had participated in a bold attack, she'd mostly been following Kalish's direction. Now she was in charge, and she was quickly gaining new respect for Kalish's ability to hide her insecurities behind her Fatewalker persona. Every one of the people with Hana was depending on her planning and leadership to keep them safe. If she failed, the cost could be in the lives of her people, her friends.

The air was still and the sky had cleared. Hana caught glimpses of glittering stars through the treetops. As she listened to her people's footsteps rustling through the leaves around her, she wished for a little wind, or even rain, to mask their sounds.

Once they reached the path, they were able to move more silently, easing some of Hana's tension. Unfortunately, they would have to enter the forest again to approach the camp.

"How much further?" Sendalee asked after they'd been walking for some time.

"Not too far until we leave the path. Look for a large tree leaning against its neighbour on our left," Hana answered.

When they reached the tree, Hana halted them all. They were strung along the path, so she walked back the line, quietly briefing everyone as she went.

"Qin's group will remain on the path. They'll approach the camp from the front, hopefully drawing the attention of any guards they have posted. They won't draw close to the camp, however, until we're all in place near the storage tent."

"And you'll signal us with the call of a grigi?" Qin asked.

Hana nodded. The grigi was a nocturnal bird with a piercing screech for a call. Most Treekeepers believed its call was the sound of the trees making a kill, but Hana's experience had taught her that the tiny, big-eyed grigi was a danger only to the moths it liked to eat.

While Qin and five others continued down the path, Hana led the rest uphill through the undergrowth.

Their progress was slow—Hana struggled to find her way in the dark, and they needed to move as silently as possible.

"Do you think the wood cutters are Treekeepers?" Sendalee asked as they picked their way through a tangle of vines.

"I hope so. If they are, they'll be too frightened to come outside, even if they hear us."

"I wish we knew more about what was happening in the lowland villages."

"You mean so we'd know whether they hate Norili as much as we do?"

"Yeah. And so we had a better feel for how many of her own people she's got here. I'd like to know exactly what we're up against."

They cleared the tangle of vines and Hana stopped, peering ahead for her next landmark, which should be a tiny stream running through a narrow channel. In the darkness, the contours of the forest floor were invisible.

"Hana?" Sendalee said.

"I'm not sure where to go from here," Hana whispered, her hands sweaty against her spear.

"We've been heading uphill and to the left across the slope. Maybe if we continue the same way, we'll see your next landmark." Sendalee's confidence in Hana's way finding skills may have been misplaced, but Hana grasped at that confidence and tried to make it her own.

"You're right. Let's go." She forged ahead.

As they travelled further without encountering the stream, Hana began to question her ability to find the camp. Maybe they were above the spring where the stream began. Could they be that far off course? Was the tangle of vines they recently traversed the wrong one? Her grip on her spear grew tighter and her hand began to ache.

Just as she was considering turning back to find the path again, her foot met air instead of soil. She pitched forward, landing on her hands and knees in a cold trickle of water. She'd never been more happy to take a fall.

"We're almost there," she said as she stood. "Here's where we split up."

Once everyone had caught up to her, she explained the next step of the plan. "The camp is about two hundred paces from the stream. We will come out into the clearing about fifty paces before we reach the tents. The storage tent is the small one set slightly apart from the others. Do not enter the clearing until after you hear the second grigi call. That will tell us that Qin's group has either caught the attention of the guards, or that there are no guards present."

Once the signal was given, everyone would creep to the storage tent with their partner, grab a saw, and carry it into the forest. If they weren't pursued, they'd take the saws with them back to their villages, where the tools would come in handy. If they were pursued, they'd scatter and hide the saws in the forest.

Hana and Sendalee formed one of the pairs, and they picked their way toward the edge of the clearing. Hana was glad to note that she couldn't hear any of the others—maybe they'd be able to pull this off.

A rustle on the forest floor ahead froze both of them in their tracks. Hana held her breath and listened. Another rustle and a low moan—a person? Straining her eyes in the direction of the sound, Hana made out an indistinct dark blotch on the ground.

Sendalee sucked in a sharp breath, and then whispered. "Someone's been left out for the trees."

Another sound caught Hana's attention, and she

scanned the nearby forest. "More than one person." She made out at least five bound forms on the ground. "Come on." Hana despised the practice of leaving people out to be eaten by the trees—it was a culmination of the worst of her people's beliefs and misconceptions. She didn't care who these people were or who they were loyal to—she was going to release them.

The first person they approached thrashed in a panic. He grunted through the gag stuffed in his mouth. "Shh," Hana said as she crouched. "We're going to cut you all loose, but you need to be quiet." She reached behind the man's head and began working on the knot of the gag first. "We're with a large force of Treekeepers. If you are loyal to Norili, we will tie you right back up." She wouldn't, but she hoped the threat would keep the man in line if he was hostile.

When the gag was free, the man gasped his thanks. "I'm here, along with eight others, because we defied one of Norili's orders," he growled. "She's cutting the sacred nalati grove on Council Island."

"We know. We're here to stop it." Hana pulled out her knife and sliced through the vines binding the man tightly to a long pole which was meant to prevent him from crawling away.

"Well you're too late then."

Hana froze. "What do you mean?"

"A group of Norili's Fatecarvers showed up in camp today to take half of us to Council Island to cut the grove. Some of us refused. Some of us tried to fight back. The Fatecarvers killed two dozen people and tied the rest of the rebels up for the trees to eat." The man rubbed his newly freed limbs, and Hana turned to whisper to Sendalee. "Start releasing the others."

"So your rebellion was unsuccessful?"

The man grunted. "The Fatecarvers took forty of

us along with half our saws. Nalatassa help those poor people, forced to cut down the grove. I'd rather be eaten by the trees than destroy that sacred place."

"Well, you're not going to do either tonight." Hana's heart was heavy. They'd failed. If they'd only been one day earlier, they could have spirited away all the saws and saved not only the grove, but also the lives of twelve Treekeepers, who wouldn't have had to resist Norili's fighters. She stood and held out a hand to help the man to his feet before she released the others who were bound.

When they'd freed all nine, Hana questioned them. "Are any of Norili's people still in camp?"

"A force of fifteen remains. It wouldn't surprise me if they're waiting for orders to kill or capture the rest of us, after our rebellion yesterday."

"And how many Treekeepers are left here?"

"About thirty-five."

Making thirty-five people vanish under the nose of Norili's guards would be a challenge, but Hana wasn't about to leave them here to face the tyrant's wrath.

"Okay. Slight change of plans."

Hana hoped Qin's group was ready to run, because they were going to have to. She gave the call, signalling Qin's group to approach the camp.

She addressed the freed wood cutters. "As soon as we get the signal from Qin that they've drawn the guards away, my people will steal the remaining tools, as we'd planned. You go rouse your people and get them out of the camp."

"But the trees—"

"Will not harm you. Trust me. In the dark, with Fatecarvers on your tail, the trees are one of your best friends—Fatecarvers aren't used to running through the forest." Hana encouraged the wood cutters to flee with her group—the canoes would be crowded, but they'd make it, even with the extra people.

Qin's answering whistle wafted through the trees. "Let's go." Hana's heartbeat pounded in her ears as they emerged into the clearing and jogged toward the camp. The wood cutters split off, and Hana's people converged on the storage tent. Hana ran her fingers along the bottom edge, rolling off the rocks and tugging up the bladestone pegs that held the edge down.

"Where are those people going?" asked one of her thieves.

"Slight change of plans," Hana said. "I'll explain once we're away. A bunch of folks from the camp will be joining us." She and Sendalee lifted the side of the tent and hauled out a saw, handing it to the first pair waiting. A dozen more saws were passed out, and then Hana straightened up. "That's it."

"I thought there were more," one of her people said.

"There were. Again, I'll explain once we're out of here."

A shout echoed from inside the camp. A moment later, pounding feet sped past the tent. A small group of wood cutters, pursued by a pair of Fatecarvers. The guards must not have all followed Qin's group.

"Go!" Hana hissed. Her people ran.

CHAPTER 6

Kalish paced through the Fatekeeper camp. Where was Hana and her group? Why had she not made their rendezvous yesterday? Dayo had urged her to be patient, but worry had Kalish's stomach tied in knots.

Kalissssh … Kalish's vision blackened as the hiss of her name skittered like rustling leaves through her mind. *Kalissssh* … She turned and sprinted back to where Dayo was tending a cooking fire.

"Iskra is calling me. Can you keep watch while I go to the Fatewalker Realm?" she asked as she skidded to a halt next to Dayo. Without awaiting his answer, she lay down and slipped out of her body.

Normally, Kalish would spend a moment relaxing when she entered the Fatewalker Realm—the spiritual realm exuded peace, calm and perfection, and it had always been a balm to her emotions. Today, however, she transformed immediately into her falcon form and raced toward the nalati grove on the other side of the mountains.

With falcon eyes, she saw the destruction from afar. At least a dozen of the giants in the grove had been felled. How had it happened so quickly? Where was Hana and why hadn't she stopped the cutting? Twin fears—for

Hana and Iskra—drove her harder. She pumped her wings with burning muscles, willing herself forward at Fatewalker-enhanced speed.

Reaching the grove, she swooped over the felled trees with a cry of dismay. The once cool and shady paths through the grove were baking in the sun now. She landed and transformed back to her human form, not caring if there were others here, knowing there would not be.

She pressed her hands against one of the remaining trees. "Iskra? Iskra, I'm coming. I'll stop the destruction of the grove."

A sigh rustled overhead. *Kalish. You are our hope. You must come into your full power. You must become.*

"Become what?" She could transform into a snake and a falcon. Is that what Iskra meant? Were there other things she could become?

Ignoring her question, Iskra continued. *You will not do it alone, but you are the key. When I am gone, you must find them. Choose wisely, my little falcon.*

Panic rose in Kalish's throat. "Find who?"

Death, Love, War and the Unknown.

Four of the five Fates. "What about Life?"

That is you, my falcon. It is what you must become. The others you must find when I am gone. I do not know how much time you will have. The spiritual realm will wither, and with it the real world. You must act before they fall into chaos.

"But we're going to stop the destruction of the nalati grove. We'll save you Iskra." They couldn't fail. How could she become a Fate? And how and where was she supposed to find the other Fates? They *were* Iskra—if Iskra was gone, the Fates would be gone. "What about the people?" Iskra had given her a task, to unite the Fatecarvers and Treekeepers and save them both from the forces of greed that were poised to devour them. Was she to abandon that task?

If the spiritual world crumbles, so will the people. Kalish. I feel your fear. Indeed, there is much to fear at this time. But you are my falcon, my lantan, my pebble. You are my Fatewalker. Only you can do this.

"But I don't know what I'm supposed to do!"

A shudder ran through the tree. "Iskra?" She held her breath, awaiting an answer. The god was silent. "Iskra!"

A whisper, barely perceptible. *Must become ... life ... start ... sunsinger ... see.*

Spines! "Iskra!" Kalish's heart pounded, and her hands were sweaty. What was happening in the real world? Were they cutting more trees? How much time was left to save the nalati grove, to save Iskra?

Overhead, a sunsinger bird sang, but the song was cut short, replaced by a clattering alarm call.

Sunsinger. "I must become life," she muttered. "Start ... starting with the sunsinger?" Realisation slammed into her. "I have to become the sunsinger bird. Because the bird is present both in the Fatewalker Realm and the real world at the same time. I'll be able to see what's happening."

How could she become the sunsinger bird? Was it like transforming into her falcon form? Logic suggested it was different, because her falcon form didn't exist in both realms at once—only the one she was in when she transformed.

Somehow she had to *enter* the bird's body.

How the Fates was she supposed to do that?

Another tremor ran through the tree. What was happening? Iskra remained silent. *Think!* When she travelled in the Fatewalker Realm, it wasn't the same as travelling in the real world. It was like she pushed herself forward with her mind, rather than her limbs. Could she push herself into the bird with her mind? What would it do to the bird to be invaded like that? What would it do to *her*?

The sunsinger bird called again, and Kalish peered into the branches. A flash of red feathers showed her where the bird perched. No way to know but to try. She took a deep breath and pushed her thoughts at the bird.

Nothing happened.

Did she need to be closer? She shifted into falcon form, pumped her wings, and joined the sunsinger bird in the canopy. Again, she pushed her mind toward the bird.

Again nothing.

She tried to get closer to the sunsinger, but the bird was wary of a falcon, and it flitted away every time Kalish moved toward it. But she was a falcon. With a dive and a swoop, she closed the distance between her and the sunsinger. The colourful bird dropped off its branch in an effort to escape, but Kalish snatched it out of the air, careful of her grip—it wouldn't help if she killed the bird. With the sunsinger firmly trapped in her talons, she pushed her mind toward it.

A flash of light, swirling green and blue. Disorientation made her stomach churn before the world snapped into focus. Well, sort of into focus. Is this what it was like to exist in both realms simultaneously? Light rain fell from a dull grey sky, but she could feel the warmth of sunshine on her back. Leaves flickered between the unreal vibrance of the Fatewalker Realm to their more natural green in a kaleidoscopic shimmer.

She sensed the sunsinger's terror and confusion. The falcon had vanished, and now something was wrong inside its body. It fluttered to a branch and shook itself, heart beating wildly with panic.

Sorry. I know how you feel.

She perched on the limb for a moment, stunned

and trying to make sense of the world around her, the sensations of this body which wasn't really hers. Then a noise below caught her attention. A rhythmic whooshing sound in time with the shivers of the branch beneath her feet. She turned the sunsinger bird's head so she could see, sensing its desire to flee. *Give me a moment, friend, and then I'll let you go.*

A man and a woman, each with the handle of a giant blade gripped in both hands, drew its serrated edge back and forth. The blade bit further into the bole of the tree with each stroke. Scanning the grove, she saw other pairs working on trees nearby. Each pair—composed of Treekeepers—was guarded by a Fatecarver. Norili was forcing them to cut the trees against their will. Because Treekeepers understood the importance of the nalati grove. Part of Kalish was relieved to know that the Treekeepers had to be forced into this action; maybe they would be able to resist and prevent the destruction of the entire grove.

A cry went up from one of the pairs. Instantly, all the blades stilled. Workers left them sitting in the trees as they scurried away. Another cry was followed by the crackling of snapping wood, the rush of leaves shaken violently.

The sunsinger was frantic to flee now, but Kalish held it on the branch, watching in horror as one, two, three giant nalati trees toppled in quick succession. Before the leaves on the fallen trees had stopped shaking, the workers were back, the whoosh-whoosh of the blade sending shivers through her feet.

She let the bird go and it streaked away, leaving her as a falcon in the Fatewalker Realm, staring at three nalati trees lying on the ground slowly dripping sap.

Kalish slammed back into her body with a gasp and scrambled to her feet. "We have to go now."

A hand gripped her wrist. "Kalish?"

She blinked. The camp was quiet, and in evening shadow. Had she been gone so long? She turned to whoever held her wrist. "Dayo."

"Sit down Kalish. We're going nowhere at the moment. You missed a meal. Eat and tell me what happened."

"I can't sit. We have to get everyone up. They're cutting the grove down now! There's no time to wait. We need to send a group across the mountains."

Dayo stood and grabbed Kalish by the shoulders as she tried to turn. "Kalish. Calm down."

"No. We need to gather a group—good fliers and good fighters. We have to *go*!"

Dayo pressed a hand over her mouth and spoke quietly, his tone deliberately calm, like someone soothing a child. "The snow is piled high in the mountains. No one is going to make it over them until spring. And even if we could, it would take days. Besides, it's getting dark. They won't be cutting the trees in the dark. Now sit, eat, and then we'll make a plan."

He was right. She seethed with impatience, but she nodded and he released his hold on her.

She related what she'd seen, what Iskra had said to her as the trees were falling.

"But how did you see what was happening in the real world from the Fatewalker Realm?" Dayo asked.

Kalish wasn't sure she could describe what she'd done, even if she wanted to. And she was reluctant to tell even Dayo that she could insert her spirit into another living thing. Every new skill she displayed pushed her further from the people she loved. At what point would Dayo start treating her like a god alongside so many others?

She hesitated, and Dayo's eyebrows rose in a familiar gesture. This was Dayo. She had to trust him.

"I sort of ... entered the body of a bird. They exist simultaneously in the Fatewalker Realm and the real world, so I could see through its eyes."

A beat of silence. "Did you know you could do that?"

Kalish sighed. "No. Look, the important thing is, they're already chopping down the trees, and if we don't get there in the next day or two, there will be no nalati grove left to save."

"We're not going to make it Kalish." Dayo's voice was low and apologetic. At least he wasn't so awed by her he was afraid to tell her the truth.

Especially when it was a truth she didn't want to hear.

"If we get an early start tomorrow, we might almost make it to the other side of the mountains. Then the next day we might be able to glide all the way to Council Island. I'm sure we can find a spot to land there."

"Glide all the way, without landing?" Because there was nowhere to land in the dense forest that blanketed the Treekeeper lands from mountain to sea.

"Well, we *might* be able to do it, if conditions are good." Never mind that conditions in winter were always marginal.

"And if they're not?"

They'd crash in the treetops. Kalish and Dayo had done that once. It wasn't pretty, and would destroy all their gliders, so they'd be stuck in Treekeeper lands until spring. If they survived the crash.

Kalish's shoulders fell as the weight of failure pulled her down. "What else can we do?"

"Have you talked to Hana today?"

Kalish shook her head. "She never showed up for our scheduled meeting. I'm worried about her, too. Obviously, her plan to take the saws failed—for all I know she could be dead." Kalish rubbed her face, trying hard not to succumb completely to the panic surging through her chest.

"So we need to find Hana. She's there, or at least close enough to possibly do something to save the trees."

"But what if she can't? And it's not just the trees, it's Iskra I need to save. They're counting on me. I need to go to Council Island. How can I just sit here and—"

Dayo gripped Kalish's arm. "Iskra is a *god*. What can you do that a god can't? You're just a person, Kalish. I don't care if you are a Fatewalker, and you can turn into a snake or a falcon, and inhabit other creatures or whatever. You're still just one person." His voice softened. "You're my favourite person, Kalish, and I don't want you to throw away your life and the lives of others on an impossible task."

Just a person. Dayo's favourite person. Which is all she ever wanted to be in the first place. She clung to him, the only stable point in her life for as long as she could remember.

Dayo rubbed her back. "Don't cry, Kalish."

Was she crying? "But I've failed Iskra."

"When you spoke to Iskra today, did they ask you to protect the nalati grove?"

She shook her head.

"They knew you couldn't help there. But they *did* tell you what to do after the grove was gone."

She nodded.

"We'll figure this out together. Please don't do something foolish. I couldn't bear to lose you."

CHAPTER 7

Hana and Sendalee dashed into the forest side by side. "The Fatecarvers?" Sendalee asked.

"Ahead and to the right." Hana could hear them stumbling and cursing.

Sendalee chuckled. "Shall we slow them down?"

"Absolutely." They angled toward the noise. Their steps were sure, having spent months living a mostly nocturnal life. The Fatecarvers, by contrast, were struggling.

Hana and Sendalee could have simply passed them and outdistanced them, but once they all reached the path, the Fatecarvers would speed up, and then their longer legs would give them an advantage over the Treekeepers, especially those laden with stolen saws. Better to lead these two on a wild chase and let the others escape.

"Remember, these men are fighters. We can't beat them if we attack directly," Hana reminded Sendalee.

"Trip them? Take their weapons?" Sendalee suggested.

"Maybe." Now she thought about it, she wasn't

sure what they should do. But the first thing they needed to do was get these fighters to follow her and Sendalee instead of everyone else. She began to shuffle her feet and make noise. Hopefully the Fatecarvers would hear her over their own ruckus.

"Shh!" said one. "Over there!" The fighters began crashing toward Hana and Sendalee.

"Uphill!" Hana changed direction, careful to not outdistance the fighters, but to keep them heading away from the rest of her people.

A strange call rang out from their left. The fighters behind Hana and Sendalee repeated it.

"More fighters." Sendalee's voice was tense and slightly breathless.

"Not far away, either." Within a few moments Hana heard the pounding of steps approaching from two directions. It was time for a different tactic.

"To the trees?" Treekeepers all climbed trees as children. Not all adults were adept.

"Sounds good. Next decent climber we come to," was Sendalee's reply.

"We'll take different trees, just in case."

A few moments later, the fighters coming from the left were nearly upon them. Sendalee leapt at a small tree and scrambled up, nimble as a squirrel. Hana took the tree next to her, jumping for the first branch and scrabbling with her feet on the rough bark. Ugh. It had been a while since she'd climbed a tree. She'd barely cleared head height when the Fatecarvers arrived. She froze on her perch, taking long deep breaths to calm herself.

There were four of them. Tall shadows on the forest floor. They kept their voices low, and Hana strained to hear their conversation.

"Lost them," said one.

"They're fast in the forest," said another.

"Go back?"

There was some shuffling of feet, and a few murmured words Hana didn't catch.

Then, "Yeah, let's go. I hate this place at night. Do you think it's true, what they say about the trees?"

"You've been on night-time guard duty for days, you seen any trees move?"

The men retraced their steps, muttering to one another as they went. Hana waited until she could hear nothing from them. Then she waited for another ten slow breaths. Finally she dropped to the ground.

She bent to retrieve her spear where she'd dropped it. "Senda—" Pain erupted in her side and she crumpled to the ground.

"Hey little Treekeeper. Thought you were being clever, eh?" The man cracked Hana over the head with his spear, and she cried out and covered her head with her arms. "You think we're stupid, don't you? Think we can't manage here in your Fate-cursed forest. Well, at least we're not afraid of the trees."

Hana couldn't move, couldn't think. All she could do was focus on taking a breath. Pain lanced through her side as she inhaled. Blood tickled her scalp as it dripped through her hair.

"You'll find that the trees aren't the most deadly thing in the forest tonight." The man took a step closer, and Hana knew without looking that the next blow would be the point of the spear sinking into her side. She needed to move now, no matter how much it hurt.

Gritting her teeth and hoping darkness hindered his aim, Hana hurled herself away from the man, rolling along the ground, fighting the scream that wanted to rise from her throat with the pain in her side and head.

As she rolled, she registered movement. The

Fatecarver lunged forward and toppled to the ground. Sendalee stood behind him, spear in hand.

After a moment, the spear dropped from Sendalee's hand. "I … I … did I kill him?" Horror laced her voice. "By Nalatassa, I've killed him."

Hana moved, groaning at the pain.

"Hana? Are you okay?" Sendalee's voice shook, and when the young woman touched Hana's shoulder, her hand was no steadier.

"I'll be okay." She wasn't sure of that, but Sendalee needed to hear it.

"Hana, what did I just do?"

Hana eased into a more comfortable position. "You did exactly what you needed to do. He would have killed both of us. We're lucky they didn't leave two men behind to ambush us, or we'd both be dead by now."

"But … but …"

"I need your help, Sendalee. Listen to me. I've been injured, and I don't think I can make it back to the boats on my own. You're going to have to help me."

With Sendalee's help, Hana got to her feet. Her head throbbed, and after a moment she vomited, causing the pain in her side to spike. Maybe she should send Sendalee back on her own.

But Sendalee wouldn't leave her. As Hana had hoped, caring for her was keeping Sendalee from thinking about the fact she'd killed a man. Allowing herself to be dragged to the boats would keep them both alive.

Sendalee pulled Hana's right arm over her shoulder, and then, gripping Hana's left hip, began inching them slowly downhill toward the path.

Hana shut her eyes against the pain, trusting Sendalee to guide them. Every time Sendalee stumbled, which was often with Hana hanging awkwardly onto her, Hana sucked in a breath. She began to count steps, and after every two hundred, she asked for a break, sinking gratefully to the forest floor and breathing with quick, shallow breaths to avoid aggravating the pain in her side.

In fits and starts, they slowly made their way through the forest. They encountered no one along the way, and Hana hoped her people had gotten away and the Fatecarvers had given up the pursuit.

When they reached the path, their pace remained slow, but it was less painful for Hana. She was able to go twice as long between breaks. Still, the sky was lightening before they neared the turn-off from the path to the canoes.

Waiting for them were Qin and five others.

"Hana!"

Hana finally let go of the thread of strength she was holding onto. She sank to the ground and passed out.

Hana awoke to the sensation of motion. She vaguely remembered being carried through the forest and being given a strong dose of banalem—a herb that drugged a person into a deep sleep.

She opened her eyes and found herself staring up at someone's knees. She lay wrapped in a blanket in the bottom of a canoe, like a sack of grain. She chuckled at the thought, but the stab of pain laughter brought on made her moan.

The owner of the knees peered down at her. It was Qin. "Hana! You're awake. How are you feeling?"

"Like I was beaten with a stick." But the truth was, the pain wasn't nearly as bad as it had been the last time she was conscious. "Where are we? Did everyone make it out? What about the wood cutters? Did Sendalee tell you what happened? Why are we travelling in daylight?"

"Calm down. We're on the river, not too far from home. Everyone made it, most in better shape than you. We rescued every one of the remaining wood cutters in camp, and Sendalee explained everything."

"How is she? Did she tell you she ..." Hana didn't want to say it if Sendalee hadn't told them.

Qin nodded. "She was pretty much babbling all the way to the boats—I think you were in better shape than she was. We gave her banalem too. She's in a different canoe, and I expect she's waking up about now. Hopefully the sleep will have done her good. Only two canoes are travelling by day—hers and yours. We thought we should get both of you home quickly, and two boats won't be noticed like a dozen would. We've been taking it in shifts to paddle and sleep, so we're making good time."

"How long has it been?"

"About two days."

Two days! "Is there any water?" Hana asked. She wasn't ready to consider food at the moment, but her throat was dry and scratchy.

Qin handed her a water skin and helped her sit up to drink. Sitting hurt enough that Hana settled back into the bottom of the boat afterwards and closed her eyes, letting the rocking of the canoe lull her senses.

They had failed to steal all the saws. A tree-felling crew had been on Council Island for ... it must be two days now. The nalati grove could already be gone. Did that mean Nalatassa—Iskra—was gone? Kalish would be distraught.

Her eyes flew open. Kalish! Hana had missed two daily check-ins with her. The woman must be frantic. "What time of day is it now?" It was difficult to tell, because the sky was overcast.

"Late afternoon. We should arrive home sometime in the night."

Not long until another check-in. Hana asked Qin to wake her at dusk if she fell asleep again.

Hana's usual Fatewalker Realm headache was nothing compared to the one she still had in the real world. She was relieved to discover that, once she adjusted to the transition, her real world pains nearly vanished. She could tell they were there, but they were mild annoyances, rather than debilitating pain. She took a few moments to breathe deeply and stretch her arms and legs without pain.

She was alone in the canoe as soon as she had crossed over. In the real world, the canoe would continue to make its way upstream, with her body on board. Qin thought they'd reach Upper Falls by the middle of the night. Hana agreed to meet them there to return to her body. Now she picked up a paddle and gave a tentative stroke.

Ouch. No, even in the Fatewalker Realm, paddling wasn't comfortable. She would have to walk. A few strokes brought her to shore, where she disembarked and began the hike to Market Rock to meet Kalish.

In the real world, it would have taken all day to walk to Market Rock. In the Fatewalker Realm, each step seemed to carry Hana twice the distance, and she reached the trading spot with time to spare. She sat on the rock with her face turned to the sun, basking in the warmth of the Fatewalker Realm. But her peace was fleeting, as thoughts of her failure surfaced. What was happening on Council Island? Had the nalati grove been destroyed already? How would Kalish react to the news?

No doubt Kalish had been keeping an eye on the nalati grove in the Fatewalker Realm. She probably didn't need Hana to tell her she'd failed.

The important question was, what should they do next? Norili was still in power. But after meeting the wood cutters, Hana was more confident that other villages would support an assault on Norili. With numbers on their side, surely they could overpower even Norili's seasoned fighters.

The screech of a falcon overhead caught Hana's attention. Kalish. The bird plummeted from the sky, and Hana couldn't help but smile and shake her head—Kalish loved flying and seemed to have no fear whatsoever of falling. Fifteen paces from where Hana sat, the falcon swooped to a halt, hovered for a moment, and then transformed into Hana's friend.

"Hana! Thank the Fates you're alive!" Kalish rushed to Hana and wrapped her in a fierce hug. When Hana winced, Kalish pulled back. "You're hurt. What happened?"

May as well get the worst over with quickly. "We failed, Kalish. We didn't get there in time."

Kalish nodded. "I know. The grove is half gone already." She blinked rapidly and her voice hitched. "When you didn't show up for two days, I thought … I thought you were dead."

"Not dead, but injured." Hana related what had happened.

"You were lucky. Most Fatecarvers would have gone for the killing blow first."

Hana nodded. "We should have suspected they were waiting for us to come down from the trees. But Kalish, I think we've got a lot more support among the Treekeepers than we know. Talking to the wood cutters made me realise that Norili has made enemies everywhere, not just among the bladestone mining villages. If we can organise a coordinated attack, we can overpower her with our numbers. Her fighters are good, but there simply can't be that many of them on Council Island."

"That's good to know. We're going to need as many supporters as possible. But I'd like to try to topple her without bloodshed, and sending a whole lot of Treekeepers to Council Island would be devastating, even if you did overpower Norili's people in the end. Besides, we need to not only plan Norili's fall from power, but also what comes after—we've made that mistake once, and I don't want to do it again."

"But we could save the nalati grove."

Kalish shook her head. "It's too late. By this time tomorrow, it will be gone."

Chapter 8

It was torture, but Kalish felt compelled to watch as the last of the nalati trees crashed to the ground with a thunderous roar. The tiny mouse she had entered quivered in fear. It had babies in a nest nearby, and its thoughts were focused on the safety of its young.

It was strange, inhabiting another creature. Different from her transformations, she wasn't alone in the body. She sat alongside the creature's own consciousness, and sometimes had to fight its will to make the body do what she wished. It wasn't much of a fight in a mouse—she was by far the stronger of the two—but she felt a bit guilty about it. The mouse's fear was real, and she was making it worse by insisting on remaining where she could watch.

But now that it was over, she released the poor rodent to scurry back to its den. She stood in her human form in the Fatewalker Realm among the fallen giants and listened for Iskra's voice.

Nothing.

She pressed her hands against the scarred bark of the largest of the trees, but the tree felt cold, and the hum of life was gone. "Iskra?"

When there was no response, she transformed

into a falcon and soared across the bay into the forest beyond. There were other nalati trees. Maybe Iskra survived there. She would keep looking. For however long it took.

Kalish! Kalish?

The voice that interrupted her flight wasn't Iskra's. It was Dayo's. Something must be happening in the encampment, or he wouldn't disturb her in the Fatewalker Realm. She changed her course and headed for home.

The camp was unsettled when she returned. Tension vibrated in the silence around her. She opened her eyes, and Dayo leapt up from where he crouched. "Thank the Fates you're back."

"What's happened?" Kalish clambered to her feet, eyes scanning the camp for signs of trouble.

"Surefoots."

Kalish's pulse quickened.

"A scouting party found them. They claim to want to join us, that you invited them and Iskra guided them."

Kalish smiled. "They must be members of the raiding party we intercepted a few months ago." Had Iskra actually guided them? Could it be the god was still present, here in Fatecarver lands? Hope flared in her chest. "Let's go talk with them." She swirled her Fatewalker cloak over her shoulders, the feather-embellished hem swishing around her knees.

There were fifteen in the Surefoot group—most were men, but two women accompanied them, and a young girl pressed herself against one of the men's legs. They stood uneasily inside a circle of bristling Fatekeeper spears.

The spear holders parted to let Kalish through, and one of the Surefoot women stepped forward and bowed her head in acknowledgement. "Fatewalker."

They looked weary and a little frightened. Kalish wanted to reassure them, but until she was certain they weren't spies sent by her mother, she couldn't. She infused her voice with a touch of Norili's imperiousness when she spoke.

"I can think of only two reasons a group of Surefoots would be here—to attack and destroy us, or to gather information about us to take back to the Surefoots. Or perhaps you are merely lost."

"Not lost, Fatewalker." The woman kept her eyes on the ground, as did all the adults in the group. The only one who dared gaze at Kalish was the child. "We were seeking the Fatekeepers. Iskra guided us to you."

They knew Iskra's name. That was a point in their favour. If they had said the Fates guided them, she would have suspected a ruse by her mother. "Exactly what sort of guidance did Iskra provide you?"

The woman turned and elbowed one of the men, who spoke up. "I ... I'm not entirely sure. There was a humming. I was the only one who could hear it, but it ... drew me forward. I just ... knew where to go."

Kalish was familiar with Iskra's hum. It was how she sensed their presence when they were too busy or weak to speak to her.

"Why were you seeking the Fatekeepers?"

The woman spoke. "Semul returned from a raid describing an encounter with you, Fatewalker."

Kalish held up her hand. "Is Semul here?"

"I am, Fatewalker."

"Then speak for yourself. Among the Fatekeepers, you need not defer to a woman."

Semul's shoulders straightened. "After you spoke

to our raiding party, Fatewalker, I returned home determined to convince Yora" —he waved toward the woman who had spoken— "to leave the clan, to join you. Yora and I have always felt … dissatisfied … with our options. When we found that Yora was pregnant, we made our decision. Our baby, whether boy or girl, will not be bound by the restrictions under which we have always chafed."

The child piped up. "But Semul, you said the Fatewalker was taller than two men, with wings, and hair that crackled with lightning. But she's short, and has no wings at all. She's just a person."

Semul's face reddened. "Maybe I exaggerated a little?"

Kalish pressed her lips together to suppress a smile. "Would you like to see my wings?"

The child nodded, her eyes going wide. The man beside her, presumably her father, squeezed her shoulder, as if reminding her of her manners. "Yes please, Fatewalker."

Kalish was already transforming as the words left the girl's mouth. She pumped her wings and rose above the group to turn a few circles in the air. Then she dove straight at the girl. Many of the adults in the group gasped and stepped away, and the girl's father tugged at her arm, but she held steady, and Kalish pulled up to hover in front of the girl's open-mouthed gape before returning to her human body and dropping to her feet.

"You *do* have wings!" The girl's eyes narrowed. "And the lightning?"

Kalish allowed her smile to emerge. "Semul's imagination."

The girl shot Semul an offended look, then returned her gaze to Kalish. "Well, at least you're taller than me."

Kalish stepped back so she was flanked by Dayo and Yinlan. "Fatekeepers all take an oath confirming their loyalty, their commitment to change among our people, their commitment to seeking a path of peace and equality."

"We are ready to take the oath, Fatewalker." Semul fell to his knees, head bowed.

Kalish's stomach squirmed. She much preferred the girl's response over Semul's.

"You will not take the oath today. Zev, was it your scouting party who found the Surefoots?" At Zev's nod, she continued. "You six will take the Surefoots to the cooking fires for a meal. I'll send Kofri and Umbel to them to explain the rules they will need to live under if they choose to stay with us." Zev would be kind to them. He had shown up at their encampment in similar fashion not long ago, and knew how it felt to be mistrusted and surrounded by hostile spears.

"And their weapons?" Zev asked.

"You can return their weapons to them tomorrow, after they have taken the oath."

The newcomers proved their worth within days. Kalish assigned a trusted Fatekeeper to take each new member under their wing, teaching them how things were done, and also gently probing them for as much information about the Surefoots as possible.

And when Semul mentioned that the Surefoots used the Fatewalker Realm to help track the Fatekeepers, Kalish called her advisors together to discuss how the information changed their outlook for winter.

"So many of us are using the Fatewalker Realm now, I can't believe we didn't consider it as a point of weakness," Tili said. "I'm afraid I'm part of the problem." Her eyes flicked to Fino, sitting next to her.

Kalish raised her eyebrows. If anyone was in the Fatewalker Realm too frequently it was her, not Tili.

Fino grasped Tili's hand. "Tili and I meet there regularly. I don't think any Surefoots have seen us there, but ... well, we aren't always paying attention."

"So, you and Fino?" Kalish smiled at Tili. She'd been so busy, she'd barely had time to talk to Tili lately. Not outside of advisory meetings and planning.

Tili blushed. "We've decided to proof."

Kalish squeezed Tili's hand. "Congratulations!" Proofing was the step before marriage. Couples moved into small 'proofing rooms' set slightly apart from a terrace. They stayed there for a month to determine if they were compatible. If they proofed well, they'd then marry. Where Tili and Fino would proof was uncertain— life on the run didn't lend itself to the practice—but Kalish wasn't going to diminish the glow on Tili's face by questioning her about it.

"I'm sorry we've been sneaking away to the Fatewalker Realm and maybe causing trouble," Tili said.

Kalish shared a smile with Dayo. All through their childhood, Kalish and Dayo had met in the Fatewalker Realm. For them it had been an escape from Kalish's mother and her disapproval of Dayo. For Tili and Fino, she imagined it was a chance for privacy, completely lacking in their nomadic camp life. "You're not the first ones to use the Fatewalker Realm ... recreationally."

Yinlan hung his head. "I go there a lot too. To meet Sendalee. I never even considered covering my tracks."

Ah! So those two *were* still interested in each other. Kalish was thrilled for her friends who had found partners to share their lives. She hoped at some point

Yinlan and Sendalee could get together in the real world. They'd have a hard time of it, though. Not many people would look favourably on a marriage between a Treekeeper and a Fatecarver. Hopefully it would be different in the future, but that sort of social change would take time.

"I suppose we're going to have to limit people's access?" Wathi directed the question to Kalish, pulling her from her reflections.

"No. In fact, I think we need to step up our use of the Fatewalker Realm." Kalish glanced at Jenti, Umbel and Kofri. "You have all said we need to find better shelter and food sources before winter sets in, and you suggested taking back the Flintcrag Prime Terrace."

"And you pointed out the Surefoots would follow us there, as they have every time we've moved," Wathi replied.

Umbel's lined face cracked into a smile. "You want to use the Fatewalker Realm to lead them away from where we're actually going."

"Exactly. What if Tili and Fino, Sendalee and Yinlan, and everyone else who is using the Fatewalker Realm for ... recreational purposes ... keeps on doing it, but spends their time here. Meanwhile, in the real world, we can be moving south toward Flintcrag. We may be able to trick them into thinking we're still somewhere around here."

Dayo nodded. "We could even make them think we're moving north, back toward Point Clan—it would make sense if we did that, because our access to Treekeeper lands is easier there."

"If we're going to do it, we should move quickly, before the weather gets worse," Umbel said.

"Yes. And I can check the Flintcrag lands in the real world to make sure there aren't Surefoots guarding the terraces. I can also search for grain the Surefoots might have missed when they razed the fields," Kalish added.

Umbel frowned. "Kalish, you can't fly all that way in your falcon form in the real world. It'll kill you. We'll have to take our chances."

"I'm not going to fly there in the real world. I'll fly there in the Fatewalker Realm." Why was it so hard to tell people about her growing powers? These were her advisors. They needed to know what she could do, and she trusted them to treat her like a person. "The last time I spoke to Iskra, they encouraged me to … try something new."

She told them of her last discussion with Iskra.

"Why didn't you tell us this when you returned?" Kofri sounded hurt.

"I've barely seen any of you since then. I slept for half a day, spent half of a day in the Fatewalker Realm trying to find Iskra, was immediately called back to deal with the new Surefoots, and by the time that was all taken care of, I forgot about it, and you were all busy settling in the newcomers."

And now she would need to spend even more time in the Fatewalker Realm. While the rest of her advisors rushed around getting ready to move the camp, Kalish steeled herself for a trip back to Flintcrag's prime terrace.

"Are you sure you're okay watching over me? I could ask someone else to." She hated that Dayo spent so much time performing the mind-numbing task of watching her inert body.

"No. I'll do it." There was a possessive note in his voice.

Kalish smiled. "Maybe we should be meeting in the Fatewalker Realm like Tili and Fino, and Yinlan and

Sendalee. We might see more of each other."

He rubbed her arm. "You're as busy there as you are here. We still wouldn't have much time together."

A group of men and women jogged by the clump of bushes Kalish was using for shelter at this camp, clearly on an urgent errand. "At least we'd have more privacy."

"Maybe not, with Tili and the rest of them there already." Dayo sighed dramatically. "Ah for the good old days when you and I were the only ones sneaking into the Fatewalker Realm."

Kalish chuckled. "Speaking of which. I should go." She squeezed his hand, and then lay down and closed her eyes.

When she stepped out of her body in the Fatewalker Realm, she took a moment to centre herself. Five deep breaths, soaking in the peace. Except it was too peaceful. Iskra's pervasive hum was missing. *I'll find you*, she promised the god. *I'll bring you back*. How, she had no idea.

She pushed that worry away for the moment to focus on the task at hand. Closing her eyes again, she imagined her arms as wings, her feet as talons. Her skin rippled and prickled as she took on her falcon form.

As a falcon in the Fatewalker Realm, it took almost no time to wing her way to Flintcrag's prime terrace. In the real world, their glider pilots would need a few days, taking a circuitous route to avoid Surefoot notice. The majority of the Fatekeepers, travelling on foot, would take nearly two five-days, carefully covering their tracks as they passed.

A summer of growth had softened the scorched earth the Surefoots left behind. Shrubs and tussocks had put out new leaves, frosting the ground with a hint of green. Maybe some sugarspike had survived the fires—

they could spend the winter replacing damaged glider wings.

The terrace itself was still a wreck—walls collapsed, grain stores charred—but there was probably enough intact to house them all. It would be cramped, but warmer and safer than their current nomadic existence.

The grain stores teemed with mice and rats, who apparently didn't mind burnt grain. She took control of a fat male rat and sidled into the real world on his furry feet.

No wonder the rodents were so bold—the silence of the terrace told her it was deserted. She scampered along the paths through the main part of the terrace to what was once the central gathering place for her clan, around the Fatechamber, which had collapsed entirely in the Surefoot raid. There, she picked up the smell of humans. Tuning into the rat's thoughts, she was surprised to note he wasn't at all concerned about the smell. It was old and faint, and its presence triggered memories in the rat of a brief encounter with a pair of warriors passing through.

Satisfied the terrace was not being heavily guarded, Kalish released the rat and arrowed back to the encampment in her falcon form.

Returning to her body, Kalish heard a woman's laughter, then Dayo's voice. "Honest, it looked like it was sleeping."

She opened her eyes and smiled at Dayo and Benut sitting nearby, mending torn glider wings. "Is he telling you about the goat I killed that he tried to take credit for, Benut?"

They both turned, and Dayo put on a shocked

face. "I didn't try to take credit for it."

"No, you just couldn't imagine that a little six-year-old me could have possibly killed it," she teased as she rolled to her feet. "Never mind that the dart in its chest was clearly mine." She fake-whispered to Benut, "I was always the better shot."

Dayo set aside the fabric on his lap and stood to hug her, something he did every time she returned from the Fatewalker Realm. She knew the sight of her inert body bothered him a little. His hugs must have reassured him—just as they reassured her—she had really come back, and he was there for her.

"Well?" He held her gaze, asking a multitude of questions with his eyes.

"Let's gather all my advisors—they should all hear what I found out, and then we can make a plan." Glancing at Benut, she apologised. "I'm afraid I'm stealing him away from the mending. Is there a lot to do?" Benut had taken charge of glider wing maintenance, which was a never-ending task that she farmed out to a small team on a daily basis.

"No." Benut held up the fabric she was working on. "This is it for today."

Kalish nodded. "Good. We'll need all the gliders fully functional as soon as possible."

CHAPTER 9

"She's replaced *all* the male Speakers with women?" Hana asked. As Speaker of High Reaches, Benha was in regular communication with Norili. And everything she learned, she communicated to Hana to help in the resistance.

Benha nodded. "Do all Fatecarvers believe men are inferior to women?"

"No. You've met Kalish and Dayo, and there are hundreds of Fatecarvers who have joined the Fatekeepers—they all take an oath to uphold gender equality."

"Well, to hear Norili talk, men are good for nothing but meeting the needs of women."

Hana snorted, then regretted the motion as the injury in her side twinged. Rubbing the sore spot, she said, "So she's replaced all the male Speakers. You're still in her good graces?"

Benha put on a sugary voice. "Oh yes. The mighty Norili amply rewards her most ardent followers." Wrinkling her nose, she added, "I was promised thirty baskets of grain and a selection of bladestone tools in return for resuming bladestone production. She's offering similar things to the other mountain villages, too."

"I suppose you're going to have to accept."

"To keep up the ruse. I can't think of any other way. I did point out that we couldn't produce the quantity of bladestone she demanded—it's not physically possible."

"And her response?" Hana couldn't imagine Norili caring if she worked people to death.

"She's sending us a machine to help break up the rocks and make it easier to extract the bladestone." Benha's tone was sour. "It's like the catapults the Fatecarvers use. She's modified the design and is using bladestone balls instead of rocks as the missiles. She thinks we'll be able to fire a bladestone ball and crack the rock, although she hasn't tried it yet. If it works, we'll have no excuse for not sending her all the bladestone she wants."

Hana smiled with grim satisfaction. "Ask for two or three of the machines."

"What?"

"Tell her it will take that many of them to produce the bladestone she wants—she knows nothing about mining. It will make you look eager to please, and we'll take the extra machines and use them against her."

Benha laughed. "Now you're thinking like a Fatecarver."

"We're going to have to in order to beat Norili at her own game."

A few days later, Hana and Boluso were strolling through the Fatewalker Realm. It was something they'd begun doing recently when they were struggling with troubled thoughts. The Fatewalker Realm was so peaceful, so perfect; thoughts were clearer there. Problems seemed to sort themselves out when discussed in the Fatewalker Realm.

Maybe it was Iskra's influence, although the god's hum within the trees was gone now. Hana could feel the difference—something vaguely missing. She might not have noticed if she wasn't acutely aware of Kalish's failed attempts to find Iskra since the nalati grove had been felled.

But that worry would have to wait. At the moment, she and Boluso were discussing the issue of rebuilding the houses of Upper Falls.

"You know the villagers want to rebuild in the same place," Boluso said as he stopped to watch a bright sunsinger bird swoop through the trees.

"And I agree it's the best place for the village. I'm eager to get out of the cave too, especially since our numbers have grown so much with the addition of the wood cutters, but don't you think Norili's people will be watching? Waiting for us to show ourselves?"

The sunsinger bird landed on a low branch and let out its musical song. Its mate answered from high in the forest canopy.

"I do. So how do we convince people to abandon their village?" Boluso began walking again.

"Especially when they're all itching for a fight anyway—most of them haven't thought through the possible consequences of being attacked by Norili's people. If they think she'll stop with the destruction of their houses like the council's fighters did last time, they're sadly mistaken. If she finds us—"

The harsh chi-chi-chi of a sunsinger warning call froze both of them in their tracks. Someone else was here. Boluso pointed the way, and they both crept off the path and into the dense brush growing up in a former house clearing nearby.

Hana held her breath, straining her ears. Soon, footsteps padded down the path.

"You mustn't let them see any sign of you." Norili's voice. "When they return, they will no doubt be wary."

"And you think they use the spiritual realm for communicating with Kalish?" The second speaker's voice was familiar, but Hana struggled to place it.

"I'm certain of it. Kalish has a bad habit of introducing people to the Fatewalker Realm. It is one of the practices we must stop before it gets out of hand."

"So, if I find the villagers—"

"*When* you find the villagers." Norili's voice cut sharply, and Hana winced, even though it wasn't aimed at her.

"When I find the villagers, I'm not to tell you immediately? Are you not going to destroy them? They attacked the former council. And you believe they are responsible for the rebellion at the forestry camp? I would think eliminating the threat they represent would be more important than finding this rogue Fatecarver."

The footsteps stopped close by. "Well, you would think wrongly then. *Nothing* is more important than finding Kalish. *She* is our main threat. Who do you think goaded the people of Upper Falls into rebellion in the first place? She is driving all of our problems."

Hana wanted to point out that *she* was the main person encouraging rebellion on this side of the mountains, not Kalish. It stung her pride to be dismissed as unimportant. Boluso squeezed her hand—he must have caught her scowl and understood. She squeezed back.

"So, when I find Kalish?"

"You will likely see her first in the Fatewalker Realm. You will follow her back to her body."

"You don't want me to kill her in the Fatewalker Realm? She won't survive the experience in the real world. I've learned that first hand when one of our council leaders was killed."

"No! Whatever you do, do not kill Kalish. I have plans for her. Once you find her, report the exact location to me, and I will have others deal with her."

"What if she turns into a falcon and I can't follow?"

"You will find a way to follow her. Is that clear?"

"Yes, Exalted Norili."

Exalted? Hana was so busy chewing on Norili's new title she nearly missed the other woman's next words.

"And once I've found her, I can move my children to Council Island? Surely that level of service should get me and my family out of Weaver's Retreat."

Hana glanced at Boluso, and he mouthed, "Sintala." Of course it was Sintala, the scheming snake. She was drawn to power like wasps to ripe fruit. Being Speaker of Weaver's Retreat would never be good enough for her. No doubt she was fomenting a plan to eliminate Norili herself someday, once Norili had done all the hard work of consolidating power.

The footsteps resumed, passing close to where Hana and Boluso crouched. "We will discuss your role once you have accomplished this task. It might be better if you found a man to care for your children. An ambitious woman like yourself doesn't want to be tied down with menial childcare."

Sintala was silent for several steps. "But they are my children." At least the woman had the decency to love her children, unlike Norili.

"And they should have a competent man to look

after them. Honestly, you Treekeepers are so backwards. One day you'll understand. Women were meant to rule. Now, let me show you the extent of the village. I have no doubt the people will try to return here."

The footsteps faded. Hana and Boluso remained hidden and silent for a long time. When it was clear Norili and Sintala were gone, they quickly returned to their bodies and left the Fatewalker Realm. Hana was glad they had a meeting with the Fatekeeper advisors the following day—Kalish needed to know about her mother's plans.

CHAPTER 10

Exhaustion dogged Kalish in the real world. Escaping to the Fatewalker Realm was a respite from it, but also one of the causes. She wasn't sleeping enough. Coordinating the movements of the Fatekeepers, the complete overhaul of Fatecarver society, and the downfall of her mother by day, and then spending most of each night in the Fatewalker Realm searching for Iskra was wearing her ragged.

But she didn't feel it in the Fatewalker Realm. Under the warm sun there, she could fly in her falcon form forever. Unfortunately, she was beginning to worry that she *would* fly forever before finding Iskra. The gentle buzz of their presence was gone. Kalish had scoured the Treekeeper lands for nalati trees, pressing her hands against every tree, hoping to feel the god's life force. She'd returned to the one lonely nalati tree in Fatecarver lands—at Lone Tree Terrace—and run her fingers over the bark of the stunted plant. She'd begun touching every living plant she could find—surely Iskra's presence was around somewhere.

But there was no hum underneath her palms, no whisper in her mind.

The plants weren't cold and inert—the quiet hum

of their own life tingled when she touched them—but the life force that was Iskra had vanished.

Still, she searched. Today, she spiralled down into the headwaters of the Flintcrag River, far above any of the former Flintcrag terraces. The spring where the Flintcrag River arose spilled down through a narrow channel in the rock to a shallow, gravel-bottomed stream hemmed in by cliffs taller than three men. Ferns grew thickly in the narrow, shady chasm. For the Flintcrag Clan, this place was one of life and renewal. Perhaps Iskra sheltered here.

She transformed back to her human form, bare feet bathed in the clear cold flow of the stream. Returning to her human senses, she felt the profound silence of the place. The ferns were still and silent. An underlying vitality was gone. She stepped slowly along the stream, brushing the ferns with her hands, listening with her whole body for the missing god.

When a shimmer of energy downstream danced in her chest, she picked up her pace. The hum grew more distinct. Could this be where Iskra had retreated to?

A rock shifted, rattling in the stream bed ahead. A moment later, a figure appeared, picking its way upstream toward her. Kalish sucked in a breath.

"Grandmother Ma?"

The old woman raised her eyes and smiled. "I thought I felt you here. You have a distinct energy, did you know that?" She opened her arms and Kalish scrambled forward and embraced her.

"It's so good to see you, Grandmother."

Grandmother Ma, Kalish's father's mother, had died years ago, leaving a huge hole in Kalish's life. It had been Grandmother Ma who taught Kalish how to enter the Fatewalker Realm when she was a small child. Grandmother Ma who loved Kalish after her father had died. Grandmother Ma who encouraged her to pursue the things she loved.

When Grandmother Ma was dying, she fled into the Fatewalker Realm to escape the pain. And there her spirit remained, long after her body had perished. It comforted Kalish to know she was still around, looking after the people she loved in life. She had seen Grandmother Ma only once since her death. That time, the woman had sought out Kalish to warn her of her mother's treachery.

"Were you looking for me?" Kalish asked, pulling away from the embrace and examining her grandmother's weathered face.

Grandmother Ma nodded. "The Fates have vanished."

Kalish sighed. "I know. And my mother is to blame."

They found a broad, sun-warmed rock to sit on while Kalish shared all that had happened in the real world since they last met. Grandmother Ma knew some things and had deduced others.

Kalish finished her tale in tears. "I don't know what to do—Iskra is gone, Mother has even more power than before, and I'm so tired. All I want is an ordinary life." She laughed bitterly. "My friend Tili is talking about proofing with Fino once we arrive at Flintcrag's old prime terrace. I'm so happy for them, and so jealous, because there's no way I can proof with Dayo. No one would let me disappear like that, without guards, to let me be an ordinary person for a moon cycle."

Grandmother Ma patted Kalish's shoulder, then gripped hard as she levered herself up. "Come on. There's someone you should meet."

Who was here with Grandmother Ma? Kalish followed as the old woman picked her way downstream.

"I've found the perfect spot up here—a little ledge just right for one person." She flashed a smile back at Kalish. "Of course, it never rains here, or gets cold, so I don't need much in the way of shelter. And I find I don't need sleep or food, but they're habits I still enjoy. The ledge is quite homey. I like it."

The chasm widened as they clambered downhill, and the ferns gave way to sugarspike and tussock as the riverbed grew more exposed and dry.

When Grandmother Ma turned away from the stream, Kalish scanned the steep slope ahead until she spotted Grandmother's ledge. They climbed a well-worn path from the stream, and as they stepped onto the small space, Kalish said, "You're right. It *is* homey. Did you construct the room yourself?" It was tiny, to fit on the ledge, with a low, narrow door and adobe brick walls that curved inward at the top to meet the natural rock.

Grandmother Ma nodded and waved a hand toward a pair of flat-topped rocks next to her little cooking fire. "Have a seat. I'll brew us up some sugarspike tea."

Two seats? "Does someone else live here with you?"

Grandmother Ma chuckled. "So you noticed. You have always been clever." She pulled a small, lidded crock from a storage area chipped from the rock and sniffed the contents before dropping a small handful of dried sugarspike leaves into a pot of water. "I mostly live alone, but have a regular guest." She raised her voice. "Tensa, are you awake?"

Tensa? Surely not ... Kalish glanced at Grandmother Ma's face, and then followed her gaze to the door of the room.

A moment later, the curtain swished aside and a woman who looked a decade younger than Grandmother

Ma stepped out. She wore finely woven sugarspike fabric clothes embellished with beads in traditional Fatecarver patterns. Her hair was spiked with rare dark red clay, and Kalish scanned the storyscar on her face for a clan mark—there was none.

Then the woman swirled a long cloak around her shoulders, and Kalish knew. Worked into the cloak in tiny beads were a large black mountain cat and a golo beetle. "Tensa the Mountain Cat. Tensa the Golo Beetle. Fatewalker Tensa." She stood and offered her hands, palms up, in the traditional gesture of greeting.

Tensa smiled and placed her hands atop Kalish's. "Fatewalker Kalish. It is good to meet you."

Kalish stared, frozen by awe. This was *the* Tensa of legend, who saved the Fatecarvers by leading them from the dying plains to the buttes and teaching them to live in terraces, spin sugarspike, hunt goats—

A slap to the back of her head broke the trance.

"Quit gawking, girl. She doesn't like it any more than you do."

Tensa snorted a laugh. "I love your grandmother." And like that, Tensa was just a woman in a fancy cloak. Older than Kalish, but the lines that uncertainty, fear and responsibility had etched in her face were clearly visible.

"Sit down, both of you."

Grandmother Ma had never been overawed by power, and to hear her ordering two Fatewalkers around made Kalish smile. She waved a hand toward the rocks. "Please, take one of the rocks. I'm the youngest—I'm happy on the ground." Sitting at the feet of these two incredible women—women she never expected to be able to talk to—was better than the most luxurious seat imaginable. She *belonged* in this very spot. The unfamiliar and long-sought feeling made her dizzy, and for a moment she closed her eyes and simply soaked it up.

Then the questions pushed themselves to the front of her brain. All the questions she had wanted to ask Tensa but thought she never could. All the questions she wanted to ask Grandmother Ma if she ever found her again.

But one question overrode them all. "Have you seen Iskra lately?"

Tensa shook her head. "I felt them vanish. How could I not? It reverberated in every living thing in the Fatewalker Realm. It shook me out of a stupor I'd been in—after so long by myself here, I'd sort of stopped ... everything. Iskra was the only being I spoke to, and they had grown so weak in recent years, I'd stopped trying to reach them. It took too much effort, and I'd stopped caring about anything—there didn't seem to be much point in caring." She accepted the cup of tea Grandmother Ma handed her. "But when they vanished, I knew something was terribly wrong."

"Why don't you tell Tensa what you told me," Grandmother Ma suggested.

"All of it?" She'd poured her heart out to Grandmother Ma earlier.

Grandmother Ma nodded. "All of it. If we're going to find Iskra, she needs to know what we're up against. And I think it will help Tensa to hear of your own struggles."

Kalish hadn't considered the idea that she might be as much a comfort to Tensa as Tensa was to her. Tensa had been alone here in the Fatewalker Realm for how many years? It must have been horrible.

They each drank three cups of tea before Kalish was finished with her tale—Tensa had many questions, and Kalish sprinkled in some of her own as she wondered aloud whether she'd made the right decisions over the past year.

"I can hear that you want to know how to move forward, how to change the Fatecarvers, unite the Fatecarvers and Treekeepers," Tensa said, even before Kalish could ask. "But I don't have any answers. All I can say is keep listening to the good people around you, and be patient. You've been at this for a year. Do you know how long I struggled to move the stubborn Fatecarvers?"

Kalish shook her head.

"Twenty-five years."

"Twenty-five!" Kalish's heart fell. "You mean I'll be forty-two before I can have a real life? I may not even live that long."

Tensa's expression was pained. "Kalish, you'll never have a normal life. You're a Fatewalker. If you succeed in your role, the people will treat you as a god until you die."

"And if I don't succeed, they'll kill me." Kalish was accustomed to that grim thought, after multiple attempts on her life. She wasn't afraid of death—she was afraid of a life alone.

"The important thing is to keep working toward your goal, and make sure that lots of other people are involved. By the time I died, I wasn't doing much of anything to help the Fatecarvers adapt to their new home—the young people had taken over. I'd encouraged innovation and experimentation, because I didn't have a clue how to live among the buttes when we first arrived. But I set contests and challenges—who could create the most efficient water collection device, who could grow the best crops, who could construct the most durable and comfortable dwellings. The actual solutions to our problems were nearly all formulated by other people—all I did was supply the motivation."

"*You're* responsible for our culture of

innovation?" Somehow that was more inspiring than if she'd worked out all the problems of shifting the Fatecarvers off the plains by herself.

Tensa smiled. "And someday a young woman will say something similar about you. *You're* the one who established trade with the Treekeepers? *You're* the one who unlocked the potential of our men?"

Kalish sighed. "Maybe."

Grandmother Ma spoke up. "You are on the right track, Kalish. I have no doubt about that. Unfortunately, Tensa and I can't help you in the real world. But we can help you here. I'm worried about the loss of Iskra."

"I am too," Tensa said. "The absence grows."

Kalish ran her fingers through her hair in frustration. "And Iskra themself told me the Fatewalker Realm would fade without them. We *must* find Iskra. But I've looked everywhere I can imagine them being and found nothing."

Tensa gazed into the distance. "I seem to remember a story from when I was a child. It was an ancient story then, and probably vanished under the weight of all the tales of me. I don't remember much about it, but it involved the disappearance of the Fates."

Kalish leaned forward. "How did they get them back?"

Tensa turned to focus on Kalish. "I don't know. I'm not sure the story even mentioned it."

"Well, that's not very helpful, is it?"

"No. But I think I should make a trip back to our old home."

"Back to the plains?" Kalish asked.

"Yes, and maybe even to the coast. We were a coastal people once upon a time. Maybe I can find clues there."

CHAPTER 11

"Spines!" Benut jerked back from the pot she'd been stirring, rubbing at her hand.

Tili leaned forward, taking up the spoon Benut had dropped and stirring. "You've got to keep stirring or it will burn."

"It splashed—the stuff is hot."

Tili rolled her eyes. "Of course it's hot—it's over the fire." Then she flinched as a splash hit her arm. "Ow!"

"See!"

Kalish schooled her face, wiping the smile off as she approached. Dayo didn't bother. His grin was broad as he said, "Having fun?"

Both women scowled at him, and he chuckled. "If you take it off the fire now, it will keep cooking without splashing. By the time it's cool enough to eat, it'll be done cooking."

"Why didn't you tell us that before?" Tili used a pair of sticks to lift the pot and set it on the ground.

Dayo shrugged. "It's second nature to me—I guess I didn't think of it."

"I had no idea cooking was so hard," Benut said. "You men make it look easy."

"You'll learn, and then it'll be easy for you, too. Wait until we get to Flintcrag's prime terrace—then I'll teach you how to make bread in the ovens there." He turned to Kalish. "If the ovens survived the raids."

"One did. The one by the elders' compound was smashed, but the main oven is intact." Kalish's mouth watered at the prospect of bread. "But we won't be baking bread if we have no grain." So far, Kalish hadn't found any Flintcrag crops that had survived the destruction the Surefoots wreaked on the Flintcrag Clan. She'd been searching in her falcon form in the Fatewalker Realm whenever she got a chance. Unfortunately, it wasn't often she got a chance—there was too much to do.

"Are you certain you don't want to take over the cooking again?" Benut asked jokingly as she stabbed at the pola in the pot. "I'm pretty sure this is burnt."

Dayo laughed. "I can't. I've got gliders to organise and launch." The pride in his voice warmed Kalish from head to toe. Under the old Fatecarver ways, Dayo had been relegated to the fields and the fire, too small in stature to gain a more prestigious place as a fighter. And of course, as a man, he would never have been given the leadership role of coordinating a glider fleet, even though he'd proven his skill in designing and flying gliders.

He stood taller now, freed from an oppression Kalish hadn't entirely understood until she'd experienced Treekeeper culture, where men and women were considered equal halves of a whole, where children weren't even assigned to a gender until their coming-of-age ceremony, when they were allowed to choose which they would be. All tasks were shared in Treekeeper culture, and that's what Kalish aspired to for the Fatecarvers as well—a culture in which anyone could pursue their passions, where everyone shared in the menial tasks, and everyone was valued for themselves.

Her Fatekeepers had bought into the idea, even if some were reluctant to learn new things—women in particular. There was a reason there were more men among the Fatekeepers than women. Extending the cultural shift to all Fatecarvers was far more challenging.

"We should go," Dayo said. "I want today's first group well away from camp before that scouting party you saw gets near."

Kalish had scoured the area in her falcon form to make sure the gliders would be unmarked by Surefoot scouts and raiders. They'd send small groups of gliders to Flintcrag's prime terrace, each group taking a different route, so that if they were seen, the location of the main party, going on foot, wouldn't be obvious. They were also careful to have groups loop back on themselves, so their destination wasn't clear, either.

No doubt the Surefoots would eventually find them, but if they could get to the terrace and reinforce its fortifications before then, they stood a chance of survival. Out here in the open, they were doomed.

She and Dayo climbed the hill next to their camp, where the gliders and pilots were waiting. Dayo walked down the line of gliders, checking each one, while Kalish joined the cluster of pilots.

The group was a mix of men and women—Dayo was careful to balance his pilot groups. As she approached, their conversation halted, and a chorus of greetings was followed by dipped heads. Sighing inwardly, Kalish smiled. "Good flying today." Launching the glider fleet was less of a production than it was the first couple of times, so there were no rousing speeches, but Kalish made a point of seeing off each group and giving them encouragement. Today, one of her advisors, Wend, was among the pilots. She glanced at him now. "You'll let us know how things are going?" They'd arranged for him to meet the advisory group in the Fatewalker Realm in three days, during their regularly scheduled five-day meeting.

Wend nodded. "And I'll be extra careful getting there, so no Surefoots can track me."

"Can I come to the meeting too, Dad?" Wend's son Ino stepped forward.

"Ino, are you piloting a glider today?" Ino was small for his fourteen years, and Kalish thought of him as a child. But of course Dayo had been designing and piloting gliders from age ten—he wouldn't have seen Ino's size and youth as a problem. But Kalish was ultimately responsible for all her people's safety, and she worried about the boy's lack of experience.

Ino straightened his shoulders and pushed out his chest—a move so like Dayo's at that age, it brought a smile to Kalish's face. "I am. Dayo said I was ready."

Smiling fondly, Wend added, "As long as I was here to keep an eye on you."

Ino rolled his eyes.

"Well, I'm impressed. You might be the youngest glider pilot we have. I'm afraid you can't come to our meeting, though. We don't want to attract too much attention in the Fatewalker Realm. Besides, I'm sure someone as hard-working as you will have plenty to do at the terrace to get it ready for the rest of us when we arrive."

Dayo joined them, his inspection finished. "Okay, let's get you into the air."

"Fly well. May the Fates be with you," Kalish said, her heart heavy, because the Fates would not be with them. Iskra was still missing.

"And also with you," the pilots chorused in return before scattering to their gliders. They were all eager to go, and it wasn't long before they began peeling off the hill into the air. Dayo came to her side. "Two more groups to send off. If the weather holds I'll get them in the air today."

"Are you disappointed to not go with them?" Kalish felt guilty because she'd asked him to travel with her and the rest of the Fatekeepers on foot.

"My place is with you, Kalish." He clasped her hand. "Would I rather fly tandem with you to Flintcrag? Yes. It would be safer for you. But I understand why you want to travel with the majority of the Fatekeepers."

"I just don't want to be seen putting myself above—"

"Shh." He silenced her with a kiss. "I agree with you. But I worry about you, too. One of these days your mother is going to find you and" —his voice hitched— "I don't want to lose you." He pulled her into his arms, and for a moment she forgot she was Fatecarver Kalish. She was simply Kalish. Dayo's friend and lover.

It didn't last. A runner came puffing up the hill. "Kalish? Tili is asking for you."

Spines. She pulled away from Dayo. "Tell her I'm on my way." Tili was carving a storyscar today on a young former Flintcrag woman. Someone Kalish hadn't known growing up, because the girl grew up in one of the outlying terraces. Tili liked Kalish to 'bless' each storyscar she carved. "It makes it more special for the women, and it calms them," she'd told Kalish.

It calmed Tili, is what it did. She'd carved several storyscars now, and she was good at it, but she was still nervous before each one.

"I suppose that was our private moment for the five-day," Dayo said, pressing his forehead against Kalish's.

"I'm sorry. If it could be any different ..." She let the thought trail off. Dayo knew her heart.

"I know. Now go. Bless Tili's work. And I'll see you this evening, if not before." He kissed her once more, and then gently turned her away.

Two days later, the entire camp was on the move. They'd sent most of their supplies and their young warriors ahead by glider, so they travelled light, but not quickly, their pace matching the slowest of the elders and young children. They also needed to obscure their tracks, so in addition to picking their path carefully, a team followed behind to wipe out or confuse any sign of their passing.

Kalish was surrounded by a guard composed of Dayo, Benut, Tili, Fino, Yinlan and Zev. Zev's brother, Nenu, also joined her, but not because he was a good fighter. He simply refused to be parted from Zev and Kalish.

Kalish didn't mind Nenu's presence. He was a child-man, permanently gifted with a child's happiness. He had been a member of a Surefoot hunting party that had captured Kalish shortly after she was banished from her clan. In a strange twist, she'd saved his life when he was attacked by a mountain cat. He'd adored her ever since. And Kalish envied his simple, childlike joy in life. He reminded her that there was beauty and joy to be had, even in their dire situation. So she'd made certain he was properly outfitted as one of her guard, with a spear and atlatl. He carried himself proudly, and Zev, who always looked after him, squeezed Kalish's arm and whispered, "Thank you."

Kalish took regular scouting flights in her falcon form to ensure they weren't stumbling into Surefoot raiding parties. Whenever they stopped for a break, she slipped into the Fatewalker Realm, soaring back toward Point Clan territory in falcon form, and then walking around in her human form, in the hope some Surefoot spy would notice and think they were headed in the opposite direction. It was also a good chance to keep searching for signs of Iskra.

When she wasn't scouting or misdirecting, she moved up and down their straggling column of travellers, chatting with people, encouraging those who were lagging, and generally being seen.

By the end of the first day, she was exhausted, and they'd barely gone any distance.

"At this rate, it will take two full five-days to get to Flintcrag's prime terrace," she said to Dayo that evening.

"That's fine. Better to get there undetected than to get there quickly and risk being seen," he assured her.

She nodded, not mentioning that she wasn't certain she could keep up her level of activity for ten days. It was the real-world scouting flights in falcon form that wore her down most—transforming in the real world drained her like nothing else. Unfortunately, those scouting flights were the most important thing she could do to keep her people safe. She could see much further than the scouts on foot, and as long as she behaved like a falcon, soaring lazily and diving at birds once in a while, the Surefoots couldn't tell her apart from any other falcon in the sky.

The camp was cold and silent that night—they lit no fires, in order to avoid detection. Feeling slightly guilty that her guards would be on watch half the night, she wrapped herself in her bedroll and fell into an exhausted sleep.

She woke before dawn to the sting of rain on her face.

"Spines," she muttered.

At her back, Dayo stirred. "I suppose we may as

well get moving."

Others stirred around her, wakened by the rain. By the time the sky eased to grey, the entire party was ready to go, with packs shouldered and hooded capes making them look like a strange procession of hump-backed animals.

The wind picked up through the morning, and rain came down in great, blowing sheets. In the arid Fatecarver lands, rain was largely a winter phenomenon. Fatecarvers rarely had need to be out in the rain, and they didn't enjoy it.

Kalish hated the rain as much as anyone, but she remained outwardly cheery all morning as she moved among her people. She reminded them that they'd be out in this rain, no matter what, and the quicker they moved, the sooner they'd have a nice dry terrace to live in. She wasn't certain her pep talks helped much, but everyone kept moving and they took fewer breaks, because the children got chilled when they stopped. Kalish worried about how they would fare overnight and hoped the rain would stop before then.

The only positive aspect of the rain was that it appeared to slow the movement of the Surefoot scouting and raiding parties. Kalish had kept tabs on two parties the previous day, one small group of scouts moving quickly, who crossed their path without detecting them late in the day, and one large and heavily armed group moving more slowly in the direction of their old camp.

Today, the large party was taking shelter under a rock overhang when she made her first scouting flight. It looked like they were arguing about what to do for the day. With luck, they'd simply stay put in their little shelter.

The scouting party had clearly been on the move before dawn. It took her some time to locate them—they'd turned and were heading back toward her people.

At their current rate of movement, the scouts would meet up with them by midday.

Kalish arrowed back to the Fatekeepers and gathered her advisors together to tell them what she'd seen.

"If they come across the whole lot of us, they'll know what we're doing," Wathi said.

"We should split up," Kofri suggested. "If the scouts find a small group, they might think we're simply out hunting."

Kalish raised her eyebrows at Kofri. "When was the last time *you* went out hunting?"

"Sending elders out to hunt is the act of a desperate people," Kofri pointed out. "And there's no point in attacking a group that's already on its last legs, right?" The woman was shrewd. It was a good thing she didn't have the ambition Kalish's mother had—those two would have been scary together.

"What if they come across more than one group and work out what we're doing?" Dayo asked.

"What if they decide to wipe out the pathetic hunting party instead of letting them die on their own?" Tili added.

Kofri acknowledged the questions with a nod. "Each group should have at least one decent fighter among them. Kalish, you'll go with your guard."

"You should transform into a falcon if we're attacked," Dayo said.

"I will not fly away while you are fighting." Kalish glared at Dayo.

"But Norili's after *you*."

"That doesn't mean the Surefoots won't kill everyone else," Kalish shot back.

"Stop!" Umbel's voice silenced them. "If Kalish is right, we don't have time to argue. A scouting party is unlikely to engage in fighting. When they find us, they'll assess our strength, and then scurry away to report to the raiding party. Kofri is right—we should split up. The smaller they think our group is, the better."

"It will be harder to disguise our tracks," Wathi said. "What if they see more than one group?"

"I can keep an eye on them from the air," Kalish offered. "If they're on track to encounter a group, I can warn the group." She smiled. "I'll have to come to you as a falcon, so if you're attacked by a bird, you'll know why."

Breaking into groups of fewer than ten meant Kalish had almost twenty moving targets to keep track of. It also meant their forward progress would slow to a crawl, because they'd spend time scattering in different directions before resuming their trek.

"We *could* let them find us. There are eight of them and over a hundred of us," Yinlan suggested. "If they never reported back, the raiding party would be none the wiser."

"If they don't return, it will be clear where we are," Kalish argued. "Besides, we don't kill unless we have to. If we can avoid a confrontation, that's what we'll do."

Yinlan dipped his head in acknowledgement. "I just thought we should consider all our options."

Whether they agreed with her or not, her advisors accepted her word. In short order they broke their party into groups and sent them in all directions. With Kalish's help, they'd regroup after the scouting party had moved on.

As Kalish's group began to move, Dayo gripped her arm. "Don't spend too long in your falcon form today. Even if a group is in danger of being discovered. It's okay for them to find a group, or even two."

"I know. But the fewer of us they encounter, the better."

"If you collapse somewhere out there because you've overdone it—"

"I won't collapse. I know my limits."

She knew her limits, but when push came to shove, she knew she'd overstep them. Dayo knew that, too. She'd have to carefully hide her exhaustion from him.

They marched in silence through the driving rain. Kalish's cape, made of Treekeeper barkcloth, was mostly waterproof, but it had no hood, and water streamed from her neck and trickled in icy rivulets down her back.

She spent as much time in falcon form as in human form. Twice, the scouting party came close to one of her small groups, and she swooped down to lead them off in another direction.

By mid-afternoon, she was swaying on her feet. The first time she tripped on a rock, Dayo cast her a glance, his brow furrowed.

The third time she stumbled, he grabbed her by the waist. "Don't you dare transform again today," he muttered into her ear.

She didn't have the energy to argue. Slinging her arm around his shoulder, she shut her eyes and let him take her weight.

CHAPTER 12

The rain continued to fall heavily all day. Even the ever-cheerful Nenu was sullen and quiet by afternoon. Despite Dayo's protests, Kalish insisted on one final flight before dark to touch base with all the groups and set a rendezvous point for the following day. By the time she landed among her guards, she was unable to stand, crumpling in a heap at Dayo's feet.

"Spines! What did I say about flying again?" Worry sharpened Dayo's tone, and Kalish wanted to reassure him she'd be fine after a little rest, but even her voice wouldn't work. Her eyelids felt glued shut and her arms were as heavy as boulders. Her guards lifted her, and she vaguely registered the sensation of movement before she lost consciousness.

She woke to the same rocking sensation. Her entire body ached, and for a moment she lay still, gathering strength, assessing her situation.

She was being carried in a blanket sling by swiftly moving people. A second blanket had been thrown over her—both blankets were sodden and cold. The sound of wind and rain formed a backdrop to the wet footsteps around her. Nenu hummed a tuneless melody somewhere nearby.

Cold and pain were her overriding sensations. *I need to move, warm up, ease my muscles.* How long had they been carrying her? She opened her eyes. Pale light filtered through the blanket over her face. So it hadn't been long. It was just beginning to grow dark when she'd returned.

She'd recovered quickly, then. Maybe she hadn't overexerted herself as much as she thought. Raising an aching arm, she flipped the blanket off her face.

"She's awake!" Tili, jogging near Kalish's hips, looked bedraggled. Her spiky hair was limp and plastered to her head; the clay she used to stiffen it streaked her face in muddy stripes. Her guards slowed, lowering Kalish to the ground.

"Kalish!" Nenu's face lit up. "You've been sleepy."

"Thank the Fates." Dayo crouched beside her and brushed a hand over her face. "How do you feel?"

"Cold and sore. But not as bad as I expected. I told you I just needed a little rest."

Dayo and the others shared a glance.

"What? It hasn't been that long—it's not even dark yet."

"Kalish, it's been a whole day."

"What?"

Tili nodded. "We've been so worried. We deliberately missed the rendezvous with the others, because we thought they'd freak out. You looked …"

"You looked dead," Yinlan said.

"Spines!" Kalish rubbed her face with her hands. "I'm not dead. But I need to move before I freeze to death."

Dayo helped her to her feet, and Zev bundled the blankets away into his pack.

"Is there food?" Kalish hated to ask, hated to slow them down even more, but she was ravenous. Dayo handed her a couple of strips of dried goat meat and a water skin. She took a swig of water. "My pack?"

"I've got your stuff," Fino said.

She held out her hand for it, but he shook his head. She huffed. "Well at least let us walk while I eat. I'm fine, really. And walking will warm me up."

She wasn't fine. She was sore and weak, cold and wet. She pulled her cloak tightly around her and clamped her teeth together to keep them from chattering as she shivered.

The rain was relentless, but eventually Kalish warmed up and her muscles eased. When she felt comfortable enough to open her mouth without complaining, she asked, "Where are we in relation to the others?"

"We don't know," Dayo admitted. "Hopefully they continued onward today, even though we didn't show up last night."

"Kofri and Umbel would have kept them moving," Kalish agreed.

"We should be ahead of them," Benut said. "We carried you all night, and then jogged once it was light again."

"You mean you haven't slept at all? You could have set me down and rested—what difference did it make whether I slept on the ground or in the sling?"

"We hoped to find some shelter from the rain." Dayo shrugged. "We didn't, so we simply kept moving."

Kalish shook her head. "You're all going to let me take first watch tonight."

The sky cleared late in the day, bringing the smell of winter. To the west, the mountains were laden with snow.

"I should go up and look for the others."

"You will not," came the chorus from her guard. "But—"

Dayo gripped her arm. "No. You try it, and I'll sit on you so you can't fly."

She raised her eyebrows. "You know, I do have another form, and I'm pretty certain you don't want to be bitten on the butt by a lantan."

"You wouldn't!"

Kalish smiled. "No. I wouldn't. But don't you think they're worried about us? Aren't you worried about them?"

"We are," Tili said. "But you are our priority. Besides, they have Umbel and Kofri—and Wathi, who brought all the Flintcrags safely to us. They're fine."

"Your mum will be worried." It wasn't an attempt to convince Dayo she should fly, just an observation.

Dayo nodded. "She knows I'll look out for you."

Kalish rolled her eyes. "I mean, she'll be worried about *you*."

"You are every bit her child as I am, Kalish. And she has always worried more about you." He wrapped an arm around her shoulder and kissed her cheek playfully. "Because you were always getting into more trouble than me."

"Oh, Kalish is a troublemaker—naughty, naughty," Nenu sang.

Everyone laughed, and the cold and damp was forgotten, at least for a while, as Dayo launched into a litany of stories about getting into trouble with Kalish when they were children. While he spoke, they ate a cold meal and rolled themselves into wet blankets and furs to stay warm through what promised to be a frosty night.

No one told stories like Dayo. And no one loved stories more than Nenu. As the light faded, Kalish took pity on Nenu, who fought to stay awake to hear the next story. "Enough stories. You all need sleep. I've got first watch. I'll wake Fino when it's time to switch."

Before long, the even breathing of the others surrounded her, and Kalish was alone in the night. The half-moon was just beginning its downward arc, sinking slowly as the stars spilled across the sky. She breathed deeply, reaching for a calm confidence she longed for. It was out of reach, thoughts of the seemingly insurmountable obstacles before her pushing away the peace she sought.

Would they all make it to Flintcrag's prime terrace? Would they be able to gather enough food there over winter to support them all? How were they going to unseat Norili? Would any of it matter, if they didn't find and restore Iskra to the world?

A swish of grass and the clack of a shifting stone tore Kalish from her musing. She strained her eyes and ears. The sounds could have been fox, goat, or human, but she couldn't distinguish between the three. And she couldn't see much of anything. She cursed her dull human senses. In her lantan form she could easily smell what lurked out there in the darkness—it would only take a moment to taste the air.

She stilled her thoughts and imagined her skin as smooth scales, her teeth sharp and deadly. She shivered as she shifted—the rock felt like ice. She understood now why lantans hid away underground during the winter. Fear gripped her as the cold invaded her body.

It would only take a moment. She flicked out her tongue, gathering the scents of the night on the forked tip and bringing them back to the roof of her mouth to taste.

Not goat. Not fox. *Spines!*

By the time she shifted back into her human form and shouted a warning, the raiding party was upon them.

Kalish, visible on a tall rock, took the first blows. She slid off the rock, dodging a spear thrust, only to parry a second thrust with her own spear. The brushy area they'd taken shelter in crackled with the blows of weapon on weapon, and Kalish was thankful for her lightly sleeping friends, able to roll out of bed with spear in hand.

How many had there been in the raiding party she'd seen before? Fifteen? Twenty? Spines! There was no way they could hold their own against that many.

A form loomed in front of her—tall, braids clacking as he moved. She knew that sound. Tana—no one else had hair that clacked like that. No one else had so many human teeth laced through their braids. Anger burned in her chest. Tana had been in the Surefoot hunting party that had caught her shortly after her banishment, and she'd had a run-in with him at the Assembly a few moon cycles ago. His pleasure in making human kills was unsettling, and when he joined forces with his bully of a friend, Riven, he could intimidate anyone.

Well, almost anyone. Last time she'd tangled with Tana and Riven, she'd turned into a snake and bitten them both. She was afraid to do the same tonight—the cold would slow her snake form down, and she'd be lucky to get one strike in before she was either trampled by someone in the dark, or froze to death.

Tana lunged, and Kalish slipped sideways, toward her guards. Did he know who she was? She hoped not. She imagined that revenge would only fuel his blood-lust. She jabbed at his face, and then whipped her spear downward to strike his leg while he fended off the high blow. He grunted and staggered sideways. Kalish grinned.

But her blow only made Tana angry. He came at her with a flurry of jabs that had her dodging and dancing backwards into the melee behind her.

Her guards had gathered back to back, and she slotted herself into their circle, swatting down a strike from the side as she wedged herself between Tili and Yinlan.

They could hold out like this for some time, but as she stabbed at Tana, missing again, she knew that eventually they would tire, and the Surefoots would pick them off, one by one.

"Zev?" Nenu's voice carried over the scuffle. Kalish's heart squeezed in fear—Nenu shouldn't be here. He wasn't a fighter. "Where is Kalish?"

Tana paused. Zev and Nenu were from his terrace. They had been part of his hunting party when they captured Kalish. Would he stop fighting, knowing who they were?

Kalish wasn't about to wait to find out. She lunged forward, aiming for Tana's chest. He dodged the blow, only to end up on the point of Tili's spear. He cried out and staggered into the darkness, to be replaced by another form materialising out of the shadows.

Kalish jabbed, dodged, jabbed again and again, losing her thoughts for a time in the fight.

A voice rang out through the darkness. "Give us the Fatewalker, and we'll let you all go on your way."

"Never!" Dayo shouted.

"Who says she's even here?" Yinlan added.

"Where *is* Kalish?" Poor Nenu. Kalish wanted to tell him she was here, but didn't dare.

Between spear thrusts, Tili muttered, "You should go, Kalish."

"Not until there's no other option," Kalish muttered back. "We need all the spears we can get." But she knew her spear wouldn't change the outcome. Her friends would all die. She could either choose to die with them, be captured, or escape. It was a choice she didn't want to have to make. No one should have to ever make that choice. Anger ballooned inside her chest, and she jabbed savagely at the opponent in front of her.

Yinlan grunted as a spear point sliced into his leg. He fell back into the middle of their circle and Kalish stepped sideways to plug the hole, stabbing Yinlan's opponent in the shoulder as he lunged forward for another attack.

"Nenu? Nenu!" Zev's anguished cry made Kalish falter, and a spear tip slipped through her guard and grazed her arm. Then Yinlan was back beside her, breathing hard, but reinforcing their shield.

Zev howled, and Kalish knew Nenu was dead. When Zev's howl turned to a snarl, she nearly threw down her spear and gave herself up to save Zev, who was, no doubt, about to rush out into the Surefoots to avenge his brother—and be killed.

But as she pulled back from her last spear thrust, the man in front of her suddenly collapsed with an atlatl dart in his temple.

Another opponent fell, and then a third. Soon the Surefoots were in disarray. Zev charged into the scattering Surefoots, stabbing furiously at backs and legs, taking down three before shifting his grip on his spear and launching it through the air at a figure darting away through the tussocks. The spear soared past its mark, landing with a thud in the grass.

And then her people were around her. Dayo, with his hand on her arm, her guard close around them both. Through the brush came a phalanx of Fatekeepers—the elderly, the youths, parents carrying babies in slings on their backs. At their head was Umbel, spear in hand, cape fluttering in the breeze, looking like the Fate, War, striding across the threshold of the Fatewalker Realm into the real world. Flanking her were Kofri and Wathi—not quite as imposing as Umbel, but every bit the warrior goddesses.

Umbel marched directly toward Kalish. "Where the *Fates* have you been? We've been looking all over for you."

CHAPTER 13

They farewelled Nenu where he fell, raising a cairn over his body. Kalish stood beside Zev, Boled and Lofi—Nenu's only clanspeople present—while the air vibrated with the death chant, performed by the travelling Fatekeepers. When Zev sniffed and swiped a hand across his eyes, she wrapped an arm around his back. "You were the best brother to him," she murmured. "You were his favourite person. I'm glad you were there with him at the end."

Zev responded with another sniff. Nenu had been Zev's favourite person, too. He'd poured his whole heart into caring for his brother. What would he do now?

Travel had kept them busy in the days since then, prevented Kalish from thinking too much about Nenu's death, Zev's sullen silence, Iskra's absence, and Norili's influence. As they finally neared their destination, Kalish steeled herself for the work ahead.

The glider crew had been busy in the ten days before the rest of the Fatekeepers arrived at Flintcrag's prime terrace, now dubbed Fatekeeper Prime. The largest of the room complexes had been repaired, rubble had been cleared and put to use to enhance the fortification of the terrace, and the most sheltered of the rooms in the elders' compound had been repaired for Kalish's use.

"And look at this," Ino said proudly, drawing Kalish through a doorway. Inside the tiny storeroom were dozens of tall storage urns brimming with grain. Kalish's spirits rose and her mouth watered at the thought of bread. "Where did you find it?"

Wend, following close on his son's heels, said, "Enothe, one of the former Flintcrags took us to her old terrace—Marginal was I think what they called it." He laughed. "It certainly was marginal. It was a wonder the rooms hadn't tumbled off the cliff. And the valley was so narrow, the terrace was barely visible until you were inside it. The Surefoots hadn't touched it."

"Yet they left?"

"When they got the news that Prime Terrace had fallen, they fled, like everyone else, assuming the worst."

"The crops were still standing in the field, and the grain stores were full," said Ino, excitement in his voice.

"It won't feed us all through the winter, but it's a good start. Once all the former Flintcrags have settled in I think we should do some reconnaissance to all their former terraces to see what else the Surefoots might have overlooked."

"Good idea." With luck, someone else would take charge of organising it, and she could rest. All she wanted was to crawl into a corner and close her eyes for a few hours, shut out everything. After the Surefoot attack, she'd insisted on regular surveillance flights, although she agreed to keep them short. It was exhausting, but she didn't collapse again.

Unfortunately, now that they had shelter and a modicum of safety, her mind churned. She wasn't certain she could rest, even if she got the chance.

Nenu was dead. Would he have survived if she'd given her warning more quickly? If she hadn't transformed into a snake? If she'd roused the others the moment she heard a noise, without ascertaining what it was? Unlikely, but it didn't stop her from feeling the weight of his death on her shoulders. She should have refused to let him join her guard, should have insisted he travel with a different group when they split up. He would still be alive, begging her for a story, tagging along beside Zev.

"Kalish?" Dayo poked his head into the storeroom. "There's food, if you want some."

She followed Dayo along the eerily familiar pathways of her youth. The terrace's destruction was still visible in the ragged edges of walls half caved in, the burnt ends of roof beams, the broken ladders littering the ground. Memories of the past leapt out and accosted her with every step. They passed the children's sleeping room where she'd first met Dayo, where he'd first taken her under his protection. They passed the room where Dayo's parents, Wathi and Jenti, had lived—the only room in which Kalish had ever felt completely welcome. Both were currently crammed with Fatekeepers claiming sleeping platforms and floor space as their own—it was going to be tight this winter. Like her, though, most of them were simply grateful to have any sort of shelter in a fortified and defensible location.

The cooking fire had been set up inside the half-destroyed walls of the former Fatechamber. Kalish's mother would have freaked out at the sacrilegious act. Strategically it made sense—with the walls around it, the fire was less visible to Surefoots. They'd be found eventually, but the longer no one knew they were here, the better.

Dayo collected two bowls of stew and led Kalish to the far edge of the terrace, where the ledge on which the terrace was built narrowed to a goat path leading to the proofing rooms. A small hollow beside the last room caught the sun. Tucked into the space with their bowls on their laps, Kalish and Dayo were shielded from the buzzing activity of the terrace. Kalish shut her eyes for a moment and relaxed her shoulders, mentally shrugging off her Fatewalker cloak for a moment.

"Thank you," she said to Dayo. "For everything."

He bumped her shoulder with his and took a bite of stew. "Eat. It's the first warm meal you've had in two five-days. It'd be a shame to let it get cold."

Kalish smiled and focused on her meal.

She was scraping the last bits of stew from the bowl when two people rounded the corner of the last room.

"Oh!" Tili jumped in surprise. "I didn't know you were here."

Kalish raised an eyebrow at her friend. "And where are you and Fino headed, looking so guilty?" She knew exactly where they were going, and she couldn't help cracking a smile.

"The proofing rooms. I hope nobody has claimed them already." Tili frowned. "Do you think they'll be needed for ordinary use, with so many of us here?"

Dayo grinned. "I think that if you claim a proofing room, no one is going to barge in on you and insist on sleeping there, no matter how crowded the terrace is."

"Go on." Kalish shooed the young couple along with a smile.

They picked their way along the path, and Kalish watched until they were out of sight around the curve of the butte. A sigh escaped her lips.

Dayo wrapped an arm around her. "You know, it doesn't matter if we never have a chance to proof. You're stuck with me. Besides, we spent nearly a moon cycle travelling together from the Treekeeper lands to Point Clan—surely that counts as proofing."

"It's not the same, and you know it. Proofing is supposed to be a time when you can focus on one another—we were barely managing survival on that trip."

"But it did prove we're compatible. I mean, we managed that whole trip without murdering each other—how more compatible does it get?"

Kalish slapped him playfully, and then her smile faded. "Someday, I want to proof with you. Properly. Without worrying that any lapse of attention on my part will lead to the destruction of the Fatekeepers. Without it being a big deal to hundreds of other people. Can you imagine if we snuck off to the proofing rooms now? People would be bringing us food, popping in to ask for advice, a boon, a blessing. Half the Fatekeepers would question whether you were worthy to proof with the Fatewalker, and the other half would be fawning all over you. Neither one of us would have a moment's peace."

"Nah, all you'd have to do is turn into a lantan and bite one person—everyone would stay away after that."

"Dayo!"

He turned her by the shoulders so he was looking into her eyes. "You will always have me, whether we proof or not, whether we marry or not. I know the ceremonies are important to you, but they don't change anything about how I feel." He leaned in, but before he could kiss her, Yinlan appeared around the corner.

"Aha! There you are." His look of triumph turned sheepish. "Sorry. Advisor meeting. You're late."

With a sigh, Kalish scrambled to her feet, Dayo right behind her. "Thanks Yinlan."

"Guards are already stationed in the former elders' compound to look after our bodies while we're in the Fatewalker Realm."

Dayo took her hand as they followed Yinlan to the meeting.

Since they'd learned that Norili's people were using the Fatewalker Realm to spy on them, Kalish and her people had been more careful about entering and exiting the spiritual realm. They no longer travelled together to their meetings with the Treekeeper contingent of the Fatekeepers. Instead, Kalish flew as a falcon, some of the advisors flew gliders, and some walked. It didn't matter which transportation mode they used—speed was almost irrelevant in the Fatewalker Realm. If you knew where you were going and you willed yourself to move quickly, you did. So they all took circuitous routes to Market Rock, moving quickly and erratically to shake off any pursuit.

Kalish circled down to the rock and transformed into her human form. The Treekeepers had already arrived, and she embraced them in turn: Hana, Boluso, Sendalee, and Qin.

"How is the baby?" she asked Qin. His wife Rista had given birth in late summer.

"They are doing well. We've named them Mani."

"And Hana? How are you feeling?" Kalish asked.

"Much better. My side still aches when I twist the wrong way, but I'm on the mend."

Yinlan touched down in his glider, followed by Dayo, Wend, Tili and Fino. He greeted Sendalee with a kiss that inspired good-natured joking by the others about the pair's *private* Fatewalker Realm meetings.

Umbel, Kofri, Wathi and Jenti soon crested the ridge on foot, descending to the rock with stately, precise steps. One did not hurry elders.

Finally gathered together, they shared the news from both sides of the mountains.

"Norili has given herself a new title: Exalted Norili," Hana said with disgust. "She's replaced all the male village Speakers with women and is bribing Speakers with goods and newfangled inventions—your technology." She related Benha's story and how she encouraged the Speaker-spy to ask for extra 'mining' catapults they could then use against Norili.

Kalish and the other former Fatecarvers related their experiences with the Surefoots under Norili's command.

"I believe her hold on the Fatecarvers is tenuous," Kofri said. "Now that we are in a position of relative safety, we need to make a concerted effort to start undermining their loyalty to her."

"If she's treating them anything like she's treating the Treekeepers, it shouldn't be hard," Qin commented. "The only reason more Treekeepers haven't joined our rebellion is that they've been so abused by the previous council, they don't realise life should be better."

"Benha believes Norili is still feeling out who her key supporters will be," Hana said. "It would be best if we dealt with her before she consolidates support."

There was general agreement on that point.

"Does anyone know where, exactly, she is?"

"We think she's on Council Island," Boluso said. "Although no one we know has actually seen her in the real world. It's just a hunch."

Kalish nodded. "It's a good hunch—there is such a cache of resources amassed there, she'd want to be there to make sure no one else got their hands on them." Maybe Kalish would make a visit to Lela—Norili's 'apprentice' fatecarver should be able to ferret out where the woman was.

The discussion soon turned to their next moves on both sides of the mountain. The general agreement was that they didn't yet have the resources or support to directly confront Norili. They needed to focus on fomenting discontent with Norili and the old ways of doing things, and promoting the Fatekeeper alternative.

"I think there could be strong support among the Treekeepers, but we need you on this side of the mountains more often, Kalish," Hana said. "Not physically—in the Fatewalker Realm is fine—but people need to see your power. They need to see you're the better alternative to Norili, not just because of how you'll care for the people, but because you're more powerful than she is."

"I am not the alternative to my mother. I'm not a *ruler*. I want the people to decide how to govern themselves. I want councils of ordinary people making decisions for their peers. I'm not—"

"We know that," Hana said. "But we need to show anyone wanting to follow in Norili's footsteps that the post of *ruler* isn't vacant."

"No one else has the power you do, Kalish," Umbel said.

All eyes were on Kalish, as the young woman in her—who wanted only to *belong* somewhere—warred with the Fatewalker, who knew they spoke the truth. If she didn't play the part, they could end up fighting this battle over and over with a succession of ambitious, selfish dictators.

It would mean going head to head with her mother. The thought made her palms sweat.

But who else *could* go head to head with Norili?

She counted breaths. One. Two. Everyone waited.

What would Iskra have said?

She swallowed the lump in her throat and nodded once. "What would you like me to do?"

Kalish left the meeting on foot, with Kofri, Umbel, Wathi and Jenti. She wanted the ballast of their wisdom right now. She worried that if she transformed into a falcon at the moment, she might fly away and never return.

"Nenu was a special friend for you, wasn't he, Kalish?" Kofri said, surprising Kalish because it had nothing to do with the meeting that had recently transpired.

It was a stab to her already aching heart. "He was."

"What you did for him was magnificent."

"What? Saving him from the cat?"

Kofri shook her head. "Giving him a place, an important job to do. You saw him. You saw what he needed, and you offered it without question, despite the fact you would have been safer without him in your guard."

"And look where that got him. He's dead."

"The moment he learned he would be in your guard, he began bragging about it. Everyone congratulated him, told him how jealous they were of the trust you'd placed in him. He was the happiest person in camp."

"He was always the happiest person in camp."

Kofri chuckled. "He'd found his place. The place where he was loved and respected. The place where he belonged. You gave that to him. You have given that to all the Fatekeepers. If you let them, they will give it back to you in return."

Kalish blinked, and her steps faltered. The quiet clink of a shifting rock behind her tore her thoughts from

Kofri's words. Listening carefully, she sped up, then suddenly stopped. Ha. Again a slight shift of rock on rock. She didn't second-guess her senses this time; she hurried to catch up with Kofri and the others.

"Kofri, I've gotten something in my eye. I can't seem to blink it out. Can you have a look?"

The old woman turned, and Kalish let her grip her face in her hands.

Kofri frowned at her eye. "I don't see—"

"Someone is following us," Kalish whispered. "I'm going to turn off in a different direction. No doubt they'll follow me. I can easily lose them later."

Kofri's glare said, *don't do anything stupid*, but she only said, "Ah, there it is," before flicking at Kalish's eye with her thumb.

They continued on for a few moments, and then Kalish announced her departure from the group. "It was so good to see you all. Maybe someday we'll be able to see each other in the real world again."

Umbel, Wathi and Jenti looked confused for a moment, but Kofri's raised eyebrows had them playing along after the briefest of pauses. Kofri held out her hands. "May the Fates be with you."

"And also with you." Kalish placed her hands atop Kofri's and squeezed.

They parted, Kalish turning north, away from the Fatekeepers. She was pleased to hear the follower tracking her and not the others. *So, mother, you think you can track me in the Fatewalker Realm? Think again.*

She could transform into either a lantan or a falcon and vanish without too much trouble, but whoever Norili had sent to follow her would know those forms. Maybe it was time to try a new trick.

When one of the ever-present sweat flies landed on her arm, Kalish shoved her spirit into its body.

It was a tight squeeze, but the fly had no choice but to make room for her. Its startle was momentary, before she was in full control, buzzing away from the spot where her human form had simply vanished.

The fly's eyesight was atrocious—she couldn't see where her follower was—but its sense of smell led her directly to the woman, not far behind, still creeping forward without a clue that Kalish had slipped away.

Sintala. No surprise. I'm beginning to think I should have let you die after I bit you. She and Sintala had fought in the Fatewalker Realm when the former Treekeeper Council sent Sintala to find her. Kalish had transformed into a snake and bitten Sintala, but gave her the antivenom before she left.

Sintala would be one of those lined up behind Norili when they finally ousted her. But she wasn't in Norili's league.

And she had come in handy during the ousting of the Treekeeper Council. Let her keep remembering that Kalish *hadn't* killed her.

Kalish buzzed away in her cramped, six-legged body. It was going to be a long flight back.

CHAPTER 14

"And what, exactly, do your … Fatekeepers … intend to do about this woman, Norili?" The former Speaker of Upper Swampland handed Hana and Boluso each a cup of water.

Hana met Boluso's gaze, her eyes inviting him to speak. She thought this man might respond better to him.

Boluso took a sip. "The Fatekeepers are led by Fatewalker Kalish. She has a bold new vision for the unification of Treekeepers and Fatecarvers, and the governing of all our people by the people. Would you be willing to meet with her? And then, if you think the village would be interested, we'd like for everyone to meet her."

"Why are you coming to me with this? I'm not Speaker any more." His tone was bitter, like most of the former male Speakers.

"We'd prefer if the new Speaker not hear of this just yet," Hana explained. "Having been appointed by Norili—"

"You mean *bribed* by Norili?" the former Speaker interrupted.

Hana inclined her head. "As you say. We think the new Speaker wouldn't be receptive to the ideas we're promoting." Hana didn't know how much of the former council's bribes this man had taken—many old Speakers were as corrupt as the new ones—but as long as he was unfriendly to Norili and willing to arrange a clandestine gathering of the villagers, it didn't matter.

"I can't believe this! It's ... it's so ..."

"Perfect!"

Hana smiled at the exclamations of the villagers entering the Fatewalker Realm—what Treekeepers simply called the spiritual realm—for the first time. People always marvelled at the sense of perfection. Hana's smile dimmed slightly. That perfection had slipped. Ever since Iskra had vanished, there was something missing from the Fatewalker Realm. She couldn't pin down exactly what it was, but somehow the colours weren't as bright, the sounds not as clear, the smells not as sharp as they had once been.

Boluso's touch brought her back to the present, and she raised a hand for quiet. "Welcome to the Fatewalker Realm. This is the place Norili and your Speaker would like you not to know about. They want to prevent you from experiencing its perfection, keep you from the powers that all of us possess in the spiritual realm."

"What? Powers of spectacular vomiting?" There were always a few who struggled to make the transition. It was disorienting, and not everyone handled it well. The young man who spoke up, however, did so with wry humour in his tone. He'd lost his lunch upon entering the Fatewalker Realm, but appreciated the place nonetheless.

Chuckles rippled through the gathered villagers,

and Hana continued. "In the Fatewalker Realm, you will find that travel is swift and safe. The weather is always mild, the sun always shines. It is in this realm that Treekeepers and Fatecarvers have been meeting regularly. It is here we have forged bonds of friendship, of kinship. Those bonds would not have been possible without the help of a remarkable Fatecarver named Kalish. I've asked her to join us today." She glanced into the trees, spotting Kalish in falcon form, perched on a branch overhead. "Kalish?" she called.

The falcon dropped from the branch, hovered momentarily between Hana and the assembled villagers, and then transformed to her human form with a swirl of feather-embellished cloak.

There was a collective intake of breath, and the villagers all took a step back. Kalish's tattooed face, short hair and strange clothing, combined with the dramatic entrance, had the same effect on every group they'd visited so far. Hana knew Kalish hated that look on their faces—the one that was half awe, half fear. But the Fatekeepers needed Kalish to inspire awe in order to convince people that she—and by extension the Fatekeepers—could oust Norili and improve their lives.

Whether she knew it or not, Kalish was a natural at both inspiring awe and dispelling fear. She turned to Hana and embraced her warmly, a move Hana knew was calculated to make Kalish appear less frightening.

"Hana, good to see you." Addressing the villagers, Kalish said, "Thank you for welcoming me to Upper Swampland. I am honoured to be here."

Kalish told them a brief, highly selective account of her life and how she and Hana met, focusing on her status as an outsider among all people, her desire to build a world in which she and *everyone* who felt marginalised was loved, cared for, and played an important role. Hana liked to think she had at least a little hand in teaching Kalish that she wasn't the only one who felt different in some way, that most people struggled for a sense of belonging, and that even those who had been marginalised, like herself and Boluso, could provide love and acceptance to others.

Kalish spoke of Iskra, of how the god had tasked her with re-establishing contact between the Treekeepers and Fatecarvers, how they'd challenged her to bring people back into the Fatewalker Realm, wresting the spiritual world from the corrupted hold of their leaders.

Then she outlined the values by which the Fatekeepers lived, by which they hoped to remodel the cultures of Fatecarvers and Treekeepers—equality, inclusion, innovation, respect, love, responsibility, community.

From fear to suspicion and disbelief to acceptance and hope—Hana watched the emotions wash across the faces of the villagers. The transformation sent shivers down her spine every time she observed it. She knew Kalish didn't crave power for its own sake, but this—the power to inspire others—was heady stuff. Even Hana felt it, and she wasn't the god-like inspiring figure Kalish was. It brought out a different Kalish from the one Hana knew—a confident Kalish who commanded respect, who didn't hide the shame of her clanless storyscar that branded her a snake and a traitor, who radiated power with every word and gesture. This Kalish embraced all that she was, and celebrated every bit of her power as Fatewalker. At times, Hana was frightened by this side of her friend—if Kalish desired her power at all, she would make Norili look like a harmless child. But in their advisory meetings, and as they interacted in friendship, it was clear Kalish was more frightened by her own power than anyone else.

Coming to the end of her speech, Kalish encouraged action. "What my Fatekeepers and I strive for is a change in our thinking, an overhaul of our cultures and our ways of doing things. It will not happen overnight, and it will take all of us working together to make it happen. I'm asking you to join us. I'm asking you to make a commitment, not to me, not to Iskra, but to yourself, your family and those you love. I'm asking you to strive for something better—for yourself, your children, your people." Kalish paused for a moment, letting her request sink in. "Hana and Boluso are part of my group of advisors." She smiled at the villagers' surprised faces. "Yes, I have advisors. I listen to people just like you, to be certain that what I and the Fatekeepers do benefits everyone."

Another pause. Kalish was a natural at oratory, and Hana carefully studied her techniques, employing them herself when she needed to talk to villagers. It struck her that Kalish had likely learned from her mother how to project power when speaking. She liked the idea of Norili's own teachings being used against her.

Kalish concluded with, "Hana and Boluso are spearheading and coordinating Fatekeeper activities in Treekeeper lands. They are your point of contact if you choose to join us."

A few more words of farewell, and Kalish transformed into a falcon and vanished into the forest canopy, leaving Hana and Boluso to answer questions and coordinate the village's resistance efforts.

They slipped back into the real world, and Hana and Boluso chatted with the villagers about how Upper Falls, High Reaches and the other bladestone mining communities had become more self-sufficient, formed support networks to ensure everyone was properly fed and supplied with goods outside of the official channels, and limited their supply of bladestone to Council Island.

"Some communities are in open rebellion, but others pretend to support Norili while secretly spying for the Fatekeepers and resisting her efforts to consolidate power. Our rebellion works best when entire communities work together. And when Norili's hand-picked Speakers are on board, we can have a huge impact. One of the key things you need to decide is whether to attempt to bring your Speaker into the rebellion. I can't advise you on this—you know your Speaker. You must decide whether it's possible to engage her against Norili."

Hana spoke as if it was a given the community would join the Fatekeepers. They hadn't yet agreed to, but she'd learned that by speaking as though the villagers were already part of the Fatekeepers, they soon came to accept it. Was it manipulative? Yes, but it really only hastened the inevitable—they had yet to fail at convincing a village to join them. Speakers were another matter—few were willing to risk their own good fortune by becoming spies within Norili's regime or leaders of openly rebellious villages.

"I don't see why we should rebel at all. I don't see Upper Swampland suffering under Norili," said a young woman with a pair of children playing at her feet.

"Well, of course you wouldn't see it, being the Speaker's daughter," replied an older man. "I'm sure Lensil passes on plenty to her own family."

"What are you lacking?" Her tone wasn't angry, more curious.

The man snorted. "Let's see ... bladestone tools for the increased grain production this Norili has demanded, dried fish for our winter stores, barkcloth for new clothing—"

"Medicines from the uplands, baskets for grain shipping and storage, pitch for boat repairs," added a woman sitting near the Speaker's daughter. "Pretty much everything we don't supply for ourselves is in short supply."

Another woman leaned forward to look at the Speaker's daughter. "See. It's like I've been trying to tell you."

The Speaker's daughter frowned. "I had no idea. I thought you were jealous or something."

"Well, I suppose we are," said the man who first spoke, "but we're actually suffering here."

"And don't forget that we men without families are even worse off than the rest of you," said the former Speaker. "She didn't just strip me of my Speaker role; she essentially cut me and any male without a wife or female child off from support. She's barely allocated us enough to survive."

"Does Mother know?"

An elderly woman spoke up. "She's providing her own children and grandchildren with everything you need, while short-changing everyone else. Of course she knows."

The Speaker's daughter pressed her lips together for a moment. "I'll talk to her. I'll convince her we need to join the Fatekeepers. She's a good person." She cast her gaze around the group, a desperate look in her eyes. "Honest. You all know her too. Don't you think she'll want to do what's right for the village?"

The elder nodded her head. "I think she deserves to know there's an option other than agreeing with whatever Norili decrees. No doubt Norili's threatened her in some way. That's what she did to you, didn't she, Das?"

The former Speaker nodded. "Threatened to either haul me to Council Island to cart bladestone and stoke the furnace for the bladestone smiths, or slit my throat."

"Let me talk to my mother." The Speaker's daughter turned to Hana. "Tell us how we're going to overthrow Norili."

CHAPTER 15

Returning to her body after another Treekeeper village meeting, Kalish lay still, savouring the brief respite before she faced more of the day's challenges. Dayo and Benut—her regular guards for her forays into the Fatewalker Realm—chatted quietly nearby. The walls of the former elders' compound muffled the sounds of the busy terrace beyond. It was peaceful here. Maybe she could steal a few more moments.

"Kalish?"

Of course Dayo would notice the change in her breathing when she returned to her body. He was well attuned to her. So much for a rest. She opened her eyes and smiled.

"How did it go?" Benut asked.

"I'm pretty sure I convinced them to join us. I think we're lucky the former council was so awful to the Treekeeper villages—Norili's getting blamed for years of oppression, even though she's merely doubled down on what the council was doing. Makes it easy to convince them to rebel."

"If only it was as easy to convince the Surefoot terraces," Dayo said. "Are you ready to go?"

"Is everyone else prepared?"

"Everyone except Zev. Do you want to talk to him? Maybe he'll listen to you."

Zev. Ever since Nenu was killed, he'd been angry and sullen. He begged to go after the remainder of the raiding party and kill them. When Kalish told him she couldn't find any survivors of the raid, he grumbled that he would find a Surefoot terrace to attack. She reminded him of the Fatekeeper pledge he'd taken that promised non-violence whenever possible. It had silenced his grumbling, but hadn't improved his mood.

"No. If he's going to be antagonistic, I don't want him with us. We have Lofi and Boled as our Surefoot ambassadors, right?"

Dayo nodded.

"Then let's go. Leave Zev to stew until he decides to let it go." Maybe she'd ask Kofri to talk to him. No doubt he blamed himself for Nenu's death—maybe Kofri could give him the same speech she'd given Kalish.

With some covert Fatekeepers among the Surefoots, they were slowly making inroads. A five-day ago, they'd visited a tiny Surefoot terrace—twenty residents—and convinced the entire population to join the Fatekeepers. The people of that terrace were now funnelling information to the Fatekeepers and reaching out to other Surefoot terraces for more converts. In return, the Fatekeepers folded them into their supply network and provided them with one of their superior gliders. Food was tight, but with Norili now demanding outlying terraces supply Surefoot Prime Terrace with goods, supplies, and even workers to construct some sort of religious centre there, many of the terraces were in bad shape.

Today Kalish was headed to a former Flintcrag terrace that was now occupied by Surefoots. They'd been invited by one of the terrace's elders, which was a good sign that they'd be able to win over the entire terrace—nearly seventy strong.

In addition to Dayo, Lofi and Boled, her travelling party included Benut and Yinlan. It was hunting-party sized in order to avoid any appearance of a raid. No one would attack a terrace with only six warriors.

Though their party was small, their goal was to project the appearance of strength. Flying in on gliders, with Kalish circling down in falcon form was a surefire way to get their attention. Besides, glider flight was fast. Walking to the terrace would take several days, but with gliders and favourable weather, they could get there and return on the same day.

Dayo, Benut and Kalish found Yinlan, Lofi and Boled waiting for them in the central courtyard of the terrace with a group of others all fashioning catapult parts to replace the ones destroyed along with the terrace. The Fatekeepers weren't going to initiate violence, but they would defend the terrace in whatever way necessary.

"Looks like a good day for flying," Boled said as they made their way around the base of the butte to the access point to the top. Hand- and footholds chipped into the rock and worn smooth by generations of Flintcrags led to a grassy, windswept plain above the terrace. Cairns marked the graves of former clan leaders along the sacred western edge of the butte. The eastern side, overlooking the approach to the terrace, held more strategic value. It had been used as a glider launch pad for years. The Fatekeepers maintained a permanent presence here—five warriors with gliders, ready to launch at any time if the terrace was threatened. During an attack, they would pepper the invaders with pebbles, distract them from the terrace, and if the worst happened, escape with Kalish in falcon form.

Not that Kalish had any intention of fleeing if it came to it.

Today, there were an additional five gliders perched on the edge of the butte. Kalish and Dayo would fly tandem, as they often did, so Kalish could transform into her falcon form on the approach to the Surefoot terrace.

The majority of their glider fleet was currently dismantled and stored in the terrace, or stationed at outlying terraces and nearby buttes occupied by small teams of Fatekeepers whose main job was to provide backup in case of attack. Because at some point, Surefoot would attack. The Fatekeepers needed to be ready to defend themselves when the time came.

Kalish and her party exchanged pleasantries with the on-duty glider team before launching into the blue sky. The day was crisp and clear. The cold air rushing across Kalish's hands soon numbed her fingers, but she didn't care. Flying next to Dayo, she felt like her younger self, before the tumult of the past year or so, free of the responsibilities of Fatewalker. Dayo shifted beside her, and she instinctively moved with him, turning their glider into a wide spiral, riding the valley's familiar thermal upward, as they'd done countless times as kids.

Hours later, as they came within sight of the Surefoot terrace, her nerves returned. Every time she had to display her power, she grew nervous. Presenting herself as a strong leader able to command warriors was critical in gaining support, especially among the Fatecarvers, whose politics were based heavily on physical superiority. Plenty of men would join her based solely on the equality she promised them, but to sway the women, she needed to appear more powerful than Norili.

What if they saw through her to the uncertain teen underneath the Fatewalker facade? With the

Treekeepers, she needed to show a little of the teen—a little friendliness. Among shrewd Fatecarver women, she couldn't reveal a single crack in her armour.

I am Fatewalker Kalish, and I am surrounded by my people.

It had become her mantra whenever she entered 'enemy' territory. She repeated it over and over to herself until it was time to transform.

In falcon form, Kalish had few doubts about herself. She was the wind, perfection in the air. As the gliders circled down to the hill above the Surefoot terrace, she peeled away, swooping out from under her glider's wing with a wild cry and buzzing the terrace guards before swinging upward while the gliders landed.

When a flight of ten gliders breached the ridge behind them, her wing beats faltered. With her falcon eyesight, she couldn't mistake them for anyone but her own Fatekeepers. Why were they here? Had the terrace been attacked? Had it fallen?

She scanned the pilots. All men from Flintcrag Clan, except Zev, at the head of the pack.

What the Fates do you think you're doing Zev?

The gliders were coming in fast, not aiming for a gentle touchdown on the hill, but racing toward the terrace.

No. No. No!

The gliders carried nets filled with rocks.

They had come to attack the terrace.

Kalish screamed and hurtled toward Zev. At first he didn't notice her, his eyes glued to the terrace. When she swooped up, flipped upside down, and sank her claws and beak into his arm, his eyes went wide.

"Get off me, Kalish!" he growled, shaking his arm. "You're not going to stop me." He shook his arm again and dragged it across the bar of the glider, forcing her to let go. She tumbled for a moment toward the ground before righting herself and aiming for his net full of rocks. This was a manoeuvre she'd done before. Clinging to the net, she tore at the rope connecting it to the frame of the glider. Zev batted her away. "If you drop mine, the others will do the job. You can't take us all out in time."

He was right. If the others were as determined as Zev was, she had no hope of stopping their attack this way. She broke away from the glider, powering ahead of Zev and then diving straight for the terrace. He'd have to hit her if he wanted to hit the terrace.

She landed at the edge of the terrace, transforming back into her human form as the first of Zev's men released their missiles. The guards nearby cried out, but Kalish wasn't certain if it was in surprise at her sudden appearance or in warning of the attack. A rock shattered at her feet, sending stinging shards into her legs.

"Come on Zev. Do you want to kill me, too?" she muttered.

A second shower of rocks pounded the guards as they lunged for Kalish, obviously deciding she was part of the threat. Both fell, one with a blow to the head, the other with a leg obviously broken. Kalish swore and raced toward the guards to drag them to safety, but was pulled up short when someone tackled her around the legs. She hit the ground with a thud, and then twisted to try to break the hold of the person gripping her.

Another shower of rocks. Obviously, Zev didn't care if they killed her. One bounced and slammed into the side of the person holding her legs. She kicked when his grip slipped, and scrambled to her feet, only to have the skin on her legs shredded by a spray of broken pottery dropped by one of the gliders.

She heard steps behind her and turned just in

time to see someone lunge at her with a spear. *Spines!* With no time to dodge, and a terrace full of Surefoots lined up to run her through, she transformed into her falcon form and dove off the edge of the terrace.

Where were Dayo and the others? Could they see what was happening?

A glider swished by beside her—Dayo. His gaze was locked on one of Zev's band, lining up for a shot at the terrace. Kalish held her breath as Dayo manoeuvred his glider between the attacker and the terrace, forcing the other glider to veer away. They were dangerously close to one another. If they clipped wings, they could both go down, to splinter on the rocks below.

Dayo soared up, and the other glider swerved aside, spilling its load of rocks harmlessly onto the hillside.

Several of the gliders were fleeing, pursued by Lofi, Boled and Yinlan. Benut swooped toward the glider Dayo had just diverted, driving it further from the terrace. Dayo hung back, circling.

Looking for me.

She pumped her wings and rose to meet him. She landed on the glider bar in preparation for transforming, and Dayo gave her a nod when he was ready.

She returned to her body with a curse. "Did you see who it was?"

"Zev," Dayo growled.

"With a bunch of Flintcrags, who've probably been itching all this time to get their revenge on Surefoot. Spines! How are we going to convince the Fatecarvers to follow us if Zev's attacking them? I'm sure they think I was responsible."

"Why the Fates did you land on the terrace?" Dayo steered them after the others.

"I thought they wouldn't attack if they risked

hitting me. Obviously I was wrong." She glared at the wayward Fatekeepers ahead of her. "We cannot let them get away with this. Especially not Zev—I have no doubt he's the instigator of the attack. He's going to have a lot of explaining to do when I get hold of him."

"I think you'll need to get in line. The way Boled and Lofi were cursing him, they've got a few things to say about his actions too. And they're ahead of us."

"Well, let's hurry up, then. Because I'm not sure I have the patience to wait."

As Kalish and Dayo approached Fatekeeper Prime, Kalish's impatience got the better of her. "I'm transforming," was all the warning she gave Dayo before she dropped off the glider and powered her way toward the top of the butte. Boled and Lofi had flanked Zev, but Kalish worried he might give them the slip at the last minute and fly off somewhere else. She swooped up under his wings to perch on his glider's bar, giving him her most scathing falcon glare as he brought the glider down.

The instant he was on the ground, Kalish transformed again. "What the *Fates* do you think you were doing, Zev!"

He refused to meet her eye as he worked on the knots of his harness. "They killed Nenu."

"They had nothing to do with Nenu's death. They were considering joining us—they were potential allies. But you've just turned them into enemies. You've handed them over to Norili, to the ones who are actually responsible for Nenu's death."

Zev shrugged out of his harness. Lofi and Boled drew up beside Kalish, arms crossed. "If you want to kill those responsible for Nenu's death, you can start with Lofi and me," Boled said. "Lofi taught him how to handle a knife, and I taught him spear work."

"Is that why you were content to launch rocks at me, too?" Kalish asked. "Because I'm the one who appointed him as one of my guards—I'm responsible for his death, too."

"I didn't want to hurt you. I just—" he turned his face to the sky, blinking hard. "Nenu was my brother. I was supposed to keep him safe and I didn't. It's my job to avenge his death."

Kalish's heart hurt for Zev. As responsible as she felt for Nenu's death, he must feel it ten times more. She gentled her voice. "No one needs to avenge his death. Part of being a Fatekeeper is letting go of destructive ideas like that—you'll kill someone to avenge his death, then their loved ones will kill someone else, and on and on. It doesn't end unless we stop it."

"Well, maybe I'm not cut out to be a Fatekeeper then." Zev pushed Boled aside and stomped away.

Kalish swallowed the lump in her throat. "Is there anything we can do to help him?"

Boled put his arm around Kalish's shoulders. "He loved Nenu more than anyone in the world. Give him time."

But Kalish didn't know if she could afford it, if he was going to promote violence. It wasn't simply that Zev had sought vengeance for Nenu's death—he'd dragged nine other men into his plot. What if the thirst for violence spread? It wasn't hard to imagine—even Kalish had struggled not to strike Zev in her anger— Fatecarvers learned to fight from infancy.

Her worries were reinforced later that evening, when she called a meeting of her advisors to discuss the matter.

"Reducing inter-clan violence was the initial reason for forming the Fatekeepers in the first place," Tili said. "We can't be seen turning a blind eye to it, especially when it was aimed at a terrace who had invited Kalish to talk to them."

Umbel nodded. "If we are trying to bring about societal change, we must live the changes we want to see. Fatecarvers are accustomed to living with firm rules. We must show them that our rules are every bit as firm as Fatecarver rules. Otherwise we're nothing but a new rival clan."

Boled's face was grim. It must be hard for him to consider punishing Zev—he treated the young man like a son. "Death or banishment would be the traditional Fatecarver response to this sort of blatant disregard for rules, particularly since it has political ramifications and put Kalish's life at risk."

"But death and banishment, which generally leads to death, are both forms of violence. Are these appropriate punishments for the Fatekeepers?" Kofri asked.

"Besides, if we banish them, it might simply unleash their fury onto others," Yinlan suggested. "Wouldn't be the first time a group of banished men went on a killing spree."

"Well, when I got into trouble, my mother always put me on latrine duty until I behaved," Kalish half-joked.

"Hmm. Maybe not latrine duty, but perhaps some other form of service would be appropriate," Wend suggested.

"They could cook for everyone for a five-day," Tili suggested.

"Or do double guard duty," Fino said.

Kofri shook her head. "I think we need to look at this differently. Zev is emotionally in pain. The men who followed him are, too. Is punishment what they need? Aren't they already being punished by their own thoughts?"

"But we can't simply do nothing but pat them on the hand and say we're sorry they're unhappy," Kalish insisted.

"No, of course not," Kofri agreed. "But what if we considered how we can help them rather than how we can punish them."

CHAPTER 16

In the end, it didn't matter what they decided to do to Zev and the nine former Flintcrags who attacked the Surefoot terrace. During the night, they vanished. Kalish searched for them in her falcon form, and others tried tracking them on the ground, but they were gone.

Kalish sat on the sleeping platform in her room, head in her hands. "I was so angry with him yesterday. Was I too hard on him? Why couldn't I control my temper?"

Dayo, sitting next to her, squeezed her shoulder. "You were no harder on him than any of the rest of us were."

Zev had been her friend. He'd protected her, probably saved her life more than once. What had happened to change that? Was he bitter she'd chosen Dayo? He'd certainly been interested in her as more than a friend at some point.

It was because you became a god.

The thought came unbidden, followed by Tensa's words, *you'll never have a normal life. You're a Fatewalker. If you succeed in your role, the people will treat you as a god until you die.*

No. It didn't have to be that way. She had friends who didn't treat her as a god. Zev didn't treat her like one, either. Not all the time. Maybe he simply didn't care about her that much. Maybe his attention to her was based on Nenu's adoration of her. And maybe he did blame her for Nenu's death, but was enough of a friend not to kill her for it.

She sighed. It didn't matter. He was gone, and there was nothing she could do about it now. What she *could* do was keep trying to figure out what her mother was up to and how to ultimately break her hold on the Fatecarvers.

She lifted her head. "I'm going to Surefoot's prime terrace today. I want to see this big religious centre Mother's building."

Dayo frowned. "Won't you risk running into Norili in the Fatewalker Realm there?"

"Yes. That's why I intend to go in as a rat."

Finding a rat at Surefoot Prime Terrace was easy. The large store rooms at the top of the butte, where grain was winched from the valley below in giant pots, were crawling with them. Kalish muscled her way into a young male rat.

His surprise at the intrusion made him shake his head. He scratched his ear. Was that a flea bite? Kalish felt his mind probing her own, curiosity taking over from surprise.

Come on my friend. We're going on an adventure. Kalish pushed her awareness fully into the rat and slipped back into the real world.

The terrace bustled with activity. No surprise—the population must have swelled, with the influx of people from other clans that had been taken over by Surefoot recently. Maybe she should have come at night-time, when it would be easier to sneak around unseen.

Even a rat would struggle to remain hidden, travelling across the terrace at this hour.

But the rat was eager to explore, and it knew the cracks and crevices of the terrace. Kalish barely had to give it a nudge before it was off, scurrying up the wall to the roof, where it scampered brazenly, unconcerned by the bustle below.

Huh. I would never have thought to use the rooftops.

When the rat dropped down into the main part of the terrace, where the walls rose all the way to the roof of the shallow cavern in which the terrace sat, it skirted the back wall, where the natural curves and indentations of the rock left gaps between raw rock and constructed rooms. Back here, away from the main thoroughfares, they encountered few people. Those they did see paid little attention to them—rats were common inhabitants in the terraces. Children hunted them for sport, and occasionally those in charge of the grain stores would make an effort to reduce their numbers, but most of the time, their presence was simply taken for granted.

It wasn't long before Kalish was poking her whiskered nose out of a small hole halfway up the wall of a room on the edge of the main courtyard of the terrace. In the centre of the courtyard stood the fatechamber.

The last time Kalish had come through here, she'd been a prisoner, so she hadn't exactly been paying attention to the fatechamber, but there was no question it had changed. Instead of occupying the centre of the main courtyard, the fatechamber now filled the entire courtyard, with only a narrow avenue separating it from the surrounding rooms. The walls were twice the height of an ordinary fatechamber, and appeared to still be under construction. The five doorways, each representing one of the Fates, were likewise enlarged. Elaborate designs around each doorway had been created with brightly painted clay tiles. Workers hauled rocks through the narrow avenue, disappearing around the side of the structure.

Kalish scampered along the avenue, pressed closely to the walls opposite the fatechamber. The rat resisted her now that she forced him into the open. But again no one paid any attention to the rodent in the corner.

Rounding the side of the fatechamber, she came to the cliff edge. The enlarged fatechamber reached right out to the drop-off, extending the line of the cliff upwards three storeys above the ground. Why would a fatechamber need to be that tall?

There were no cracks in the newly laid masonry, so Kalish scampered back toward one of the doorways. She crouched next to a stack of rocks, waiting until a worker passed before skittering into the building.

The shadow of the old fatechamber remained in the form of the original sunken floor. The new area hadn't been lowered, and one side of the chamber—the side along the cliff edge, with no doorways—was slightly raised. A cushioned seat occupied the raised side. The wall behind the seat had been painted with what Kalish recognised as images from her mother's storyscar. This chamber was a shrine to Norili. No doubt she would conduct five-day ceremonies and weddings from the raised platform, and sit on the cushioned seat to receive the unsubtle bribes from mothers and grandmothers whose daughters and granddaughters were soon to have their fatecarving done.

A larger fatechamber was probably necessary, with the growth in the terrace. Of course, her mother would take the opportunity to make it a showcase of herself.

What occupied the other storeys? A ladder to the

second floor was in heavy use by men hauling stones and mortar. The rat could easily shimmy up it, but there was no way to do so without being noticed. She could probably scale the outside wall, but a rat climbing the outside of the fatechamber in broad daylight was bound to draw attention. She crouched in a shadowy corner and watched the workers come and go.

There wasn't enough time between people to make the sprint up the ladder. It appeared they were hurrying to finish—what punishment had Norili promised if the work wasn't done on her time schedule?

Her nose twitched as the rat's brain registered the smell of food nearby. Something left here for the Fates, no doubt. Every fatechamber included alcoves beside each doorway where supplicants could leave gifts for the Fate of their choice. The rat tugged her in the direction of the food. *Oh no you don't.* Then she reconsidered. A rat zipping up the ladder might be strange, but one scurrying along the dimly lit floor in search of offerings wouldn't raise any concerns. Unless, of course, it scurried right by your feet, startling you into dropping your load of mortar.

Kalish pushed the rat directly into the path of a worker, racing across the floor and over his feet. As the man jumped in surprise, she darted away from the falling pot of mortar and spiralled around to the back side of the ladder where she'd be less visible. Racing upward, she registered the rat's disappointment at the lost meal. *Sorry.*

With the flow of workers temporarily stalled, there was just enough time to reach the second floor and skitter to the nearest dip in the floor, where she pressed herself flat, vanishing into the shadows.

A worker with empty hands descended a second ladder from the top floor, crossed the room, and went down the ladder Kalish had climbed, without even glancing her way.

This room was divided down the middle. The side Kalish sat in was outfitted as a fatecarver's work room. A stone table against one wall held pigment pots, several mortar and pestles, and baskets of dried herbs. A clever rack held fatecarving tools, and bunches of freshly picked herbs hung in the window over the table.

In the middle of this half of the room sat a low sleeping bench, but Kalish knew this bench wasn't used for sleeping. It was where storyscars were carved. The young woman would lie on her back on the bench while an older woman held the teen's head steady. Norili would ink the girl's future in painful lines and swirls on her face that would determine the course of her life.

The memory of her own fatecarving, and the storyscar that caused her to be banished, pushed at her consciousness. She shoved it away. Now was not the time for bitter reminiscing.

Like the room below, this one's walls were decorated. In addition to the symbols for each of the five Fates, the walls had been adorned with blatant displays of wealth—rare beads and colourful rocks pressed into the adobe plaster, a white fox pelt, a mural painted on fine sugarspike cloth. And among all the Fatecarver trinkets were Treekeeper items—a display of colourful bird feathers, a Speaker's tunic covered in nalati pods and an intricately designed bladestone medallion, polished to a high sheen.

A display of power. An indication of the calibre of bribes necessary to sway her, a reminder of the breadth of territory over which Norili held sway.

Not for long. Kalish scurried into the other half of the room. It was a proper sleeping chamber. Rooms this size normally slept fifteen people, but this was outfitted for one. Thick furs softened a large sleeping bench, and wooden shelves held Norili's clothing, hair stiffening clays and jewellery.

She was clearly separating herself entirely from the rest of the terrace. No surprise.

A ladder in the corner led upward, and Kalish scampered to the top floor.

She blinked in the bright light—there was no roof yet. As her eyes adjusted, she understood why. There would be no roof here. This wasn't a room, it was a defensive battle station.

Three catapults were already stationed here, their arms aimed to sling rocks over the head-high walls. Correction, they were aimed to sling spheres of bladestone, which were piled at their bases. Atlatls and spears leaned against the front wall, and several clay crocks bristled with darts—all of them tipped with bladestone.

The work was nearly done—the walls all topped out at head height, with slits for launching darts, rocks and spears through. With a lurch of her gut, Kalish realised that the fortifications—and the slits—faced into the terrace as well as out to the valley below. This building was designed to defend against enemies and residents of the terrace. It wasn't a religious centre, it was a fortress.

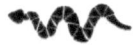

Kalish returned to her body with a sense of relief. As usual, Dayo recognised her return before she'd even opened her eyes.

"Kalish?"

She scratched her side. "Do you have any idea how irritating fleas are?" The rat she'd inhabited had been teeming with them, and she itched with the memory.

"Um ..."

Kalish opened her eyes and smiled at Dayo. She

143

sat up and scratched again. "Sorry I was gone so long."

"Not a problem. Benut and I made good use of the time, spinning some sugarspike thread." Dayo turned to Benut, who was already gathering up a bundle of fibre and a pair of spindles. "Thanks for keeping me company."

"Thanks for doing some spinning—I can't believe how much fabric it takes to keep these gliders in the air." She gave a wave encompassing them both. "See you later."

The moment she was out of the room, Dayo's smile vanished.

"What's wrong?" Kalish asked.

"Benut says that Zev talked to her before he and the others left last night. Apparently, Zev told her you had banished them—told them they needed to be gone before dawn or risk death."

"What? I never said that."

"I know. I was there. But Benut says Zev claimed you came to him later and gave him the ultimatum."

"But I didn't."

"I know. I've asked her not to repeat what Zev said, but" —he shrugged— "you know what terrace gossip is like."

Was Zev really so angry at her he would seed a rumour like that? Well, he picked a good person to tell—Benut loved gossip. No doubt word was all over the terrace that Kalish had condemned ten men because they attacked an enemy terrace. In Fatecarver culture, attacking an enemy terrace was something to be celebrated—Fatekeeper vow of nonviolence or not, these people weren't going to look kindly on deadly punishment for the deed. They'd use the vow against her, say she had a double standard, was putting herself above everyone else.

"I hope you told her the truth. That we decided their punishment should be accompanying the outreach missions, talking to other young men about gender equality issues."

"I did. But banishment is the more interesting story."

Yes. And no doubt that's the story that had already made its way, like wildfire, through the terrace.

CHAPTER 17

Winter days were short and cold. The terrace was crowded, but at least the Fatekeepers weren't camping in the open somewhere. Kalish and her advisors sent out regular envoys to small Surefoot terraces and kept in touch with their supporters embedded within the Surefoots through the Fatewalker Realm.

Every other five-day, she visited Lela at the former Point Clan Prime Terrace.

"Norili thinks she controls this terrace because she controls our food, but the moment she shows her face here for real, the terrace is going to explode with anger," Lela said. "I just hope I can coordinate all the different assassination plans people have, so we're effective."

"She'll arrive prepared for a fight," Kalish warned.

Lela nodded. "I know. If I can funnel all the anger into one plan, we'll be able to overpower her people."

"Please be careful. If you try, but don't kill her, she'll destroy you all."

"It might be better than the gradual starvation she's subjecting us to."

Kalish's visit to Lela had both bolstered her spirits and depressed her. She could count on Point Clan to help her, but at what cost to the people?

The former Point Clanspeople weren't the only ones suffering, either. Life in some of the Surefoot terraces had gotten downright desperate as Norili syphoned off food for her own stockpiles or destroyed the stores of terraces who resisted her rule.

The Fatekeepers managed. They might be reduced to eating mice and rats by springtime, but for now the hunting parties were successful frequently enough that their stores were holding out.

Life in the terrace felt almost normal—like they weren't hiding out waiting for an attack, gathering themselves for an overthrow of the most powerful leader ever to arise among the Fatecarvers.

They even celebrated a wedding.

Tili and Fino finished their proofing determined to marry. In Fatecarver society, marriage ceremonies were performed in the fatechamber by the clan's fatecarver.

Tili had essentially become the Fatekeepers' fatecarver. But she wasn't the Fatekeepers' spiritual leader in the same way a traditional fatecarver was. And she couldn't perform her own ceremony, even if she was the spiritual leader.

"You should do it, Kalish," Tili declared during an advisory meeting.

Kalish nodded. "But we can't perform the traditional Fatecarver ceremony."

"No," Dayo agreed. "We can't have Fatekeeper men pledging to serve, honour and care for their wives, and the wives promising to bring strength and cunning to the family."

"What do the Treekeepers do?" Tili asked, turning to the Treekeepers in the group.

"Well," Hana began, "like you, we have vows, but the man and woman both say the same vow."

Boluso wrapped an arm around Hana. "We both promise to care for and support the other, to love our children, and to remain together always, facing hardships as a team."

With a grin, Sendalee added, "After the vows, the village blindfolds the bride and groom, ties their left ankles together and takes them into the forest, turning them round and round so they have no idea where they are. The couple must find their way home, blind and tied together so they have to either walk sideways, or with one of them going backwards."

Tili's eyes widened. "How many couples die on their wedding day?"

All the Treekeepers laughed, and Qin spoke up. "Well on my wedding day, I know people watched the whole drama of me and Rista stumbling through the forest together. We could hear them laughing every time we ended up on our butts on the ground. If we'd gotten into real trouble, someone would have helped us out."

Sendalee laughed. "Every time you fell, it took you longer to get up again. I didn't think you were going to bother the last time."

Qin shrugged. "Why get up when all we wanted to do was lie together anyway?"

"What's the point of the blindfolded stumble through the forest?" Kalish asked.

"The idea is that if you can work together to get home, without cheating by removing your blindfold or untying your legs, you can face any challenge as a team," Boluso explained.

"I like the idea," Kalish said. "But isn't that essentially what our proofing custom is?"

Kofri shook her head. "Not really—proofing is a

test of compatibility, but not a test of teamwork. It would be fitting if the Fatekeepers had a test of whether a couple could work together as equals, and we'll need vows to match."

On the day of the wedding, Kalish wasn't certain whether she or Tili were more nervous. This event would establish new customs that blended Treekeeper and Fatecarver traditions and reflected Fatekeeper values. How would people react to it? Would they embrace the new tradition, or would they find it too strange, too foreign?

"It's a celebration," Kofri reminded her as she settled Kalish's cloak over her shoulders and brushed a hand over a few wayward feathers on it, coaxing them to lie flat. "If you, Tili and Fino all treat it that way, everything will go fine—people will have fun, and it will reinforce why they became Fatekeepers."

They cleared the communal fire pit out of the fatechamber, because in spite of its half-crumbled walls and missing roof, it was still the most sacred place in the terrace. People could have entered by stepping through one of the many gaps in the wall, but they all filed in through the intact entrance dedicated to the Fate, Love.

Kalish stood in the centre of the fatechamber with Tili and Fino, both of whom wore garments of sugarspike embroidered with the symbols for the Fates Love and Life. Tili was resplendent in a beaded capelet that mixed Treekeeper and Fatecarver imagery, given to her by her mother, Jalen. On her face, her storyscar—the first storyscar ever chosen by the woman herself—reflected Tili's strength and energy and expressed her dreams for the future. Fino's capelet was pieced from fine, thick white rabbit fur and smooth black goat fur, its edge fringed with brilliant red sunsinger feathers.

When everyone had assembled, Kalish raised her hand for quiet. She experienced a moment of panic when everyone was looking expectantly at her. Looking for leadership and authority.

I am Fatewalker Kalish, and I am surrounded by my people.

She took a deep breath and began the ceremony the advisory group had hammered out.

"Friends and family, fellow Fatekeepers. We gather here today to celebrate one of the fundamental tenets of Fatekeeper society—Love. While we recognise all the Fates today, all the faces of Iskra, we acknowledge that Love is the most important. It is the Fate that brings us happiness, prosperity, and peace. It is the Fate that brings us light during the dark of winter and sustains us through difficulty."

She shifted her focus from the crowd to Tili and Fino. "Today, Love is the Fate that brings Tili and Fino here with us. Tili and Fino, the marriage vows of a Fatekeeper are distinct from those of a Fatecarver." Tili and Fino were well-versed in the vows they were about to take, having helped devise them, but most of the gathered Fatekeepers had no idea what to expect. "As Fatekeepers, you are expected to uphold Fatekeeper values of equality and respect within your marriage, as they are upheld within our community. Fatekeeper marriage vows reflect this expectation.

"By agreeing to be bound to one another, you also agree to respect each other's skills, opinions, likes and dislikes. You agree to listen to each other, even when your opinions differ. You agree to strive toward dialogue and understanding of one another at all times, recognising that the strength of your union relies on mutual respect and care for one another. You agree to approach all the challenges you face together as equal halves of a whole."

The entire crowd hung on her words in utter silence. Focused on Tili and Fino, she couldn't sense what the rest of the Fatekeepers thought of the new vows. She didn't dare glance up, lest she falter based on what she saw.

"Tili, Fino. Do you agree to be bound together by Iskra, to uphold the values of equality and respect, to support one another in all things, to become equal halves of one love?"

Without hesitation, both answered, "We do."

"You have passed your proofing, establishing your compatibility. Today you will prove your ability to uphold Fatekeeper values within your marriage. Fatekeepers believe in celebrating our diversity, and so there is no single way for couples to prove they can act as a team, with mutual respect. Each couple must prove it in their own way. To that end, your friends and family have chosen a task for you that they believe is appropriate for you, one that requires equal sharing of responsibility and effort."

Tili's eyes sparkled, and Fino grinned. The idea was that couples wouldn't know their task until the wedding day, but since Tili and Fino had been in on the planning of this first wedding, they knew.

"In front of your assembled kin and clan, you will cook a meal together. Fino, during this task you will be blindfolded and are not allowed to speak. You are the only one who may touch the food or utensils. Tili, your job is to direct Fino. You may not touch Fino or anything else. Do you accept this challenge?"

"We do."

Kalish lifted her eyes to the gathered Fatekeepers, relieved to find smiles on most of the faces. Kofri and Umbel pushed through the crowd bearing vegetables and a cooking pot. They were followed by the remainder of

Kalish's advisors, who remade the fire pit. Kalish handed Tili the blindfold, and Tili secured it over Fino's eyes.

"Everyone is welcome to witness the proof of Tili and Fino's union," Kalish said.

"If you laugh, you have to eat it afterwards," Tili said with a smile.

The excited chatter from the assembled crowd settled as the advisors stepped away from Tili and Fino. Fino rubbed his hands together. "Okay, what are we making?"

"Shh! You're not allowed to talk," Tili said to laughter from the watching people. "Let's see. We have a mixed selection of roots and" —she cast an accusatory glare at Kalish— "an entire rabbit?"

"I'm going to have to skin and gut a rabbit blindfolded?" Fino cried.

"Shh!" Tili covered his mouth with her hand before snatching it back. "Oops! I'm not supposed to touch you. Let's start with the vegetables."

Tili clumsily directed Fino's hands to the knife and the pile of roots. He followed her directions, but shook his head repeatedly as Tili gave him further directions.

Finally, Tili stopped. "What?"

"You have to—"

"Shh!" The crowd silenced Fino.

Fino pressed his lips together and waved his hand toward the fire pit.

Tili frowned. "Yes, we'll need to light a fire, but let's get the vegetables cut first."

Fino shook his head and waved toward the fire again, sending laughter rippling through the crowd.

"But we don't need the fire yet. Come on Fino, cut the vegetables."

Fino's shoulders slumped, but he began on the

vegetables.

Then she directed him to the rabbit. Taking pity on him, she told him to simply remove one of the hind legs and ignore the remainder of the animal. She frowned at the poorly cleaned leg, but forged ahead. "Now we put it all in the pot with some water—oh!" She laughed. "I suppose we should have started the fire earlier so our water would already be hot."

Fino nodded emphatically, and the men in the crowd laughed. "Listen to your man, Tili!" someone called.

Tili talked Fino through lighting the fire, then told him to put the pot on the fire. He shook his head again.

"Now what? By the Fates, I'm bad at cooking." Tili laughed at herself, but in spite of Fino's gestures, she couldn't work out what he wanted her to do next. Finally she said, "Just put the pot on the fire."

Once the pot was in place, she directed Fino to pour water into it. Unable to see, Fino missed and doused the fire instead, leading to more laughter from everyone.

"Oh! We should have put the water into the pot first!" Tili was shaking with giggles as they finally managed to fill the pot with all the stew ingredients and set it on the fire.

The crowd cheered, and Kalish stepped forward. She tugged the blindfold from Fino's eyes and waved him and Tili up to face the assembled people.

A hush fell over the crowd, and Kalish raised her voice. "Fatekeepers, what say you? Do we bless this marriage and agree to love and support Tili and Fino through their journey together?"

"We do!" the people chorused.

The knot of stress in Kalish's stomach eased as people laughed and milled around chatting and congratulating the happy couple. Dayo appeared at her side and slipped an arm around her waist. "Well done. It was perfect."

The rest of the day was given over to merrymaking. Though food was tight, they allowed excess today. Kalish wanted everyone to remember this as a special day—the first Fatekeeper marriage.

While everyone relaxed in the afterglow of plenty of food, Kalish slipped away to find some solitude. Performing Tili and Fino's marriage ceremony had been more stressful than she wanted to admit. It wasn't just the fact she was establishing new traditions for her people. It was the fact she wanted Tili and Fino's happiness for herself. She was jealous. Plus, she was physically and emotionally exhausted. She needed to be alone for a bit.

Ducking away from the party, Kalish climbed the ladder to the upper terrace and padded past the bread oven to what had once been the room she and Dayo shared with eight other teens. It was the last place in which Kalish had a normal life. She stepped inside. The room had survived the Surefoot attack and was filled with bedrolls now. Kalish sank onto one of the sleeping platforms, scooted back to the wall and pulled her knees to her chin.

Benut, Meech, Tino, Fala, Seeda … Some of the children she'd shared this room with were already dead. Others had turned on her when she was declared a traitor. And some were still with her now. All of their lives were changed, not what anyone could have expected. Is that the way life always was? Did her mother sometimes wonder how she'd gotten to where she was now?

A deep gash in the wall opposite Kalish brought

a smile to her face. That gash was the result of a dare between Dayo and Arnot to see who could twirl their spear faster. Who had lost control of their spear first? Kalish couldn't remember, but Dayo's had slammed into the wall and created that gash. Arnot's had hit the floor and the stone tip had shattered. The adults in the room next door had stomped in and told them all off.

Voices approached from outside the room. Kalish pressed her back against the wall, hoping it was no one looking for her. She wanted a few more moments to sit here with her memories.

"Why are we wasting our time with weddings when we should be overthrowing Norili?"

Kalish didn't recognise the man's voice. She had enough followers that she didn't know everyone well.

"It's winter. Do *you* want to go raiding in the cold and wet?" That voice was more familiar. Was his name Rone? The conversation continued.

"But we're just sitting here, doing nothing, waiting to be attacked by the Surefoots. With the Fatewalker's power, why can't we simply take Surefoot's prime terrace and be done with it?"

"Maybe she's not as powerful as she makes out. Norili's her mother, after all—maybe Norili's more powerful."

"Norili's not a Fatewalker. If she were, she wouldn't make a secret of it."

"So why doesn't Fatewalker Kalish do something? Fatewalker Tensa gathered every Fatecarver together and marched them over the plains, built the terraces, taught us to hunt and farm. What has Fatewalker Kalish done? Made some pretty speeches about *equality* and *respect.*"

Kalish bristled. Tensa worked for twenty-five years to accomplish all she did. Did they expect Kalish to simply snap her fingers and change every Surefoot's attitudes, convince her mother she didn't want to rule the world with a tight fist, and create an idyllic society in an instant?

"At least she had some backbone and banished Zev and his lot."

"But they were doing something productive, fighting back against Norili's minions. Isn't that what we're *supposed* to be doing? When are we going to stand up for ourselves?"

Spines! Did all her people think she wasn't doing enough? Did they all think she'd banished Zev? Kalish spent most of her time with her advisors. Maybe she needed to spend more time with everyone else.

Maybe you need to make a move, now that your Fatekeepers are settled somewhere. It's what they expect of you.

The men continued to chat. Kalish figured they must be standing beside the bread oven. It was a popular place to congregate in winter, because it was usually warm, even if there wasn't an active fire in it. She couldn't leave the room without being seen, and if she walked out, the men would know she'd overheard them.

"Have you noticed it's all men cooking the meal today?"

"They all volunteered for it."

"But why didn't the women volunteer? If we're supposed to be equal and all, there should be some women sweating over that stew, burning their fingers turning meat in the fire, feeding everyone else before having a bite to eat."

A laugh. "Would you want to eat their cooking? We're lucky the women didn't volunteer."

"Yeah, wouldn't have been much of a feast—raw stew, burnt meat." The men laughed.

Discouraged, Kalish wished she hadn't come to

this room and overheard the men's conversation. Was she too timid? Was she going about this cultural shift in the wrong way? Should she have allowed for more violence among Fatekeeper values?

If only Iskra was still around to advise her. The god remained distinctly absent, however. Kalish had noticed more and more imperfections in the Fatewalker Realm as the days had gone by without Iskra. The sun felt weak, and the wind carried a chill. The russets and ochres of the cliffs and canyons she loved so much had become muted, their colours washed with grey. It was as if the life were slowly draining out of the Fatewalker Realm.

Had Tensa found anything yet? The former Fatewalker had not appeared since their meeting almost two moon cycles ago. Another worry to add to the weight Kalish carried. Would any of her efforts in the real world matter if the Fatewalker Realm vanished? Iskra had implied that the health of the real world was linked to that of the Fatewalker Realm. How long before the real world suffered?

Don't think about it. Tensa and Grandmother Ma were tackling that problem at the moment. Her job was to make progress against Norili in the real world.

She wasn't doing very well at that. The rumblings of these men told her she needed to step up her game. She needed to do something dramatic, display her ability to confront Norili and enact real and lasting changes to Fatecarver culture.

She had to act more like her mother in order to beat her.

"Speaking of food, do you think there's any left?"

"Let's go. I could use another flatbread."

Finally! Kalish hurried out of the room and back to the party, where she was determined to mingle with people and make sure they knew of the progress she *had* been making, so they didn't focus on what she hadn't yet accomplished. And maybe it was time to chat about what had really happened with Zev.

CHAPTER 18

Hana was impatient. She wanted to descend on Council Island and physically kick Norili out.

But Norili had apparently left.

"She meets with us regularly, but only in the spirit realm," Benha reported. "Sintala still hasn't found Kalish, by the way."

"How do you know that?" Hana asked.

"Norili only meets with the Speakers as a group, rarely individually." She snorted. "I don't think she even knows any of our names, other than Sintala's."

"Didn't she appoint you all?"

"Yes and no. Female Speakers like me were basically left to get on with it, provided we did what she told us to. Male Speakers were replaced, but by women chosen by the villages, not by Norili. She's got minions to relay regular demands, and teams of fighters to visit villages that aren't toeing the line. She doesn't do the hard work, and only sees us as a group, mostly to impress upon us how great she is and how wonderful the changes she's making are." Benha snorted in disgust.

Later, Hana brought this information to a Fatekeeper advisory meeting, along with an idea.

"If we can secretly replace Norili's Speakers—the

ones we haven't convinced to join us—with our own, then we've severed her connection to the villages."

"Do you think that's possible?" Umbel asked.

Hana nodded. "Many of the villages we've visited are now working against their Speaker to thwart Norili. If they simply changed Speakers, they could act more decisively."

"But how simple is changing Speakers?" Kalish asked. "Wouldn't an ousted Speaker simply tell Norili what happened?"

This was the part of the plan Hana was a bit nervous about. "Speakers wouldn't be able to physically go to Norili at the moment, because Norili's not on Council Island. And Norili has refused audiences with individual Speakers in the spiritual realm, saying she doesn't have time to speak with them."

"And if the the new Speaker went to one of Norili's collective Speaker meetings and the old Speaker also showed up in order to denounce the new one?" Kofri asked.

Hana smiled. "Two things work in our favour. First, anyone who has learned to enter the spiritual realm from the old council or Norili will not know how to do so without piromanga leaves, which are strictly managed and rationed. The new Speakers should be able to ensure the old ones have no piromanga. Second, Norili is paranoid. She keeps strict control of Speaker meetings, because she's worried about infiltration. If a new Speaker shows up at the meeting early and provides the old Speaker's name to gain entrance, the old Speaker won't be allowed in."

"And what if the guard at the entrance knows the old Speaker?" Trust Kofri to find all the strategic holes in a plan.

Boluso spoke before Hana could. "The guard is a

Fatekeeper."

"My only worry is that we don't know where Norili has gone," Hana said.

"We do," Kalish said. "She's at Surefoot's prime terrace. Flew a glider over the mountains along with a team of bodyguards."

Sendalee's eyebrows rose. "In the middle of winter?"

Kalish nodded. "Apparently, she felt the need to shore up her support over here. She's holding great ceremonies in the new fatechamber, and with the backlog of fatecarvings to do, she's taking massive bribes from women to jump to the head of the line."

Hana's silent coup happened with little effort on her part. She was in regular contact, through the Fatewalker Realm, with all the villages who had joined the Fatekeepers, and once she told them the plan, they were quick to enact it.

By the time Norili met with her Speakers again, every one of them except Sintala was a Fatekeeper. Then Hana called them all to a meeting.

"The first thing we need to do," Hana began, "is to make sure every village has what they need. I know that not every village can be self-sufficient, or even wants to be, but the village of Upper Falls has made significant progress toward self-sufficiency and there are plenty of people there who would be happy to come to your villages and teach some of the traditional hunting and gathering methods many of us have lost. We'll also want to organise trade so that we can all share the things our villages do best."

"Will we be distributing goods from a central location, like the old council did?" asked one Speaker.

"We'd like to avoid the problems of the past. By centralising the distribution of goods, we create an opening for the likes of Norili and our previous council to take control. If villages work with each other to determine what they can share with one another through trade, then each village can both negotiate what they receive and what they must produce in return, maintaining control of the entire process."

"Seems like a lot of work," another Speaker said. "I don't even know what each village produces. It was easier to simply produce what the council told us to and accept what they gave us."

Hana smiled. "That's why we're here. In the Fatewalker Realm, we can meet easily, discuss what we need, and make plans for trade."

The notion that they were being given real power to improve the state of their villages injected energy into the group. Women began introducing themselves to each other, discussing their villages' products and needs, making deals to exchange fish for grain, baskets for barkcloth. Before long it became clear that the burdens the council and Norili had placed on them were artificial—there was more than enough to go around, without anyone having to struggle.

The only difficulties were faced by the bladestone mining villages. Raw bladestone was useless without a furnace in which to refine it, and the only furnace was on Council Island. Hana thought she might have to step in to negotiate the provision of those villages, but once the Speakers accepted their new role, they embraced it fully.

"We *will* take back Council Island at some point, right?" asked the Speaker of Lost River Village. At Hana's affirmative response, she concluded, "Then the bladestone producers can trade bladestone. We'll stockpile it until we regain control of the furnace." After that declaration, accepted without argument, trade negotiations proceeded smoothly.

Hana regretted that the group was entirely women. It was wrong not to include men in this exchange, but until they ousted Norili, they had to maintain some level of cover. She also regretted the exclusion of Weaver's Retreat—Sintala's village—in the negotiations.

Hana had excluded Weaver's Retreat from all her schemes—unlike other villages with Speakers loyal to Norili. She didn't think the village would be receptive to her or Kalish, given that they had condemned both of them, and Boluso, to death in the past.

But her parents still lived there, and the knowledge that they were struggling under Norili's abuse, had no idea there was a rebellion under way, and didn't even know their daughter and grandchildren still lived, was a stone in her stomach.

She silently promised her parents she would release them from Norili's grasp. It wouldn't be long now.

CHAPTER 19

Caverna and Southcrag Clans had not yet fallen to Surefoot, though Kalish was certain Norili was trying to weasel her way into those clans. Her Surefoot spies reported that Norili was promoting herself as the great unifier of the Fatecarver clans. Norili argued that only unified could they take full control of Treekeeper lands as well, bringing untold riches from Treekeeper lands to enrich the Fatecarvers.

Not surprisingly, Norili hadn't mentioned those plans to the Treekeepers.

Kalish hoped to acquire by negotiation what her mother wanted to take by force, so she paid a visit to Farlin, Caverna Clan's fatecarver, in the Fatewalker Realm.

As a falcon, she flew into Caverna's prime terrace, a deep cave with a narrow entrance. Fatecarver terraces were usually built in shallow caves—not much more than ledges with overhanging rocks above them. These terraces caught the sun, warming up in winter, and making all but the rooms furthest back light and pleasant.

Caverna lands were studded with deep caves, and this is where Caverna built their terraces. Flintcrags had always joked that you could tell a Caverna clansperson by their pale skin and eyes that squinted in the sunlight.

The truth was, Caverna terraces were simply used differently than other clans' terraces. Most Caverna terraces were at ground level, and the area in front of the terrace was used for most of the daily activities of the community—cooking, pottery, spinning, weaving. The rooms within the terrace were for storage and sleeping. When a Caverna terrace was raided, the residents could quickly slip inside, and easily defend the narrow entrance. Caverna would be the last to fall to Norili.

Caverna's fatechamber was situated inside the cave. In the Fatewalker Realm, Kalish shed her falcon form at the mouth of the cave and entered in the form most suited to the dark—a lantan.

Guided by smell, she slithered along the floor, worn smooth by generations of feet, toward the reek of burning piromanga leaves. Kalish was in luck—Farlin was in the Fatewalker Realm. She paced back and forth within the fatechamber, and Kalish slithered along the wall, listening before she announced her presence.

"Life, Death, Love, War, Unknown. Guide my steps and let the path be shown." The fatecarver's chant called the Fates to provide guidance for a fatecarving. Farlin's voice held a note of desperation. No Fates had answered her call.

No Fates would.

Kalish transformed while Farlin had her back turned, so that when she rounded to pace the other way, she came face to face with Kalish.

Farlin shrieked. "What are you doing here?"

"Farlin. It's good to see you again," Kalish replied calmly. She and Farlin had met at the Assembly last summer. Farlin had been reluctant to accept that Kalish was a Fatewalker. She had refused to allow the young women with her to learn how to enter the Fatewalker

Realm without piromanga leaves, but had requested Kalish teach her how. In the short time they'd spoken, Kalish got the impression of a woman who wanted proof of a clear benefit before she did anything.

"Fatewalker. What are you doing here? Can you not see I'm busy with a fatecarving?"

"You were calling the Fates. They will not come." This couldn't be the first time she'd done a fatecarving without the Fates to advise her. "I have come, instead, to offer you guidance."

"Have the Fates entrusted this task to you, then?" Her tone was dismissive.

"In a fashion. The Fates are unavailable at the moment, and I am here. What do you need to know for your fatecarving?" It was presumptuous, but Farlin would be swayed by power, by what Kalish could offer her. To offer power, Kalish had to display it.

"Are you saying the Fates speak through you?"

Kalish inclined her head. "I *am* a Fatewalker."

Farlin pressed her lips together for a moment, then huffed. "Fine, then, tell me what I should carve on this girl's face. She has no prospects—she is the youngest in a long line of weak women with no ambition."

"What does she enjoy?"

Farlin snorted. "Flowers, bugs, plants … She brings them back to the terrace and, I don't know, looks at them. She could at least bring back edible things, but no—she finds bizarre stuff of no use. I've tried to send her out to pick useful herbs, gather materials for my pigments—she comes back with half of what I asked for and an armload of rubbish."

Kalish couldn't help smiling. This girl sounded like a version of herself. Not that Kalish had been interested in bugs and flowers, but that she had always gotten distracted from what she was supposed to be doing. For Kalish, that distraction had been glider design, and look what it had produced—a fully steerable glider that was the envy of all the clans, and the key to her ability to unite Fatecarvers and Treekeepers.

"Her storyscar should include images of the flowers and bugs she loves. It should include the symbol of the Unknown and that of Life." Kalish didn't know all the symbols fatecarvers used, but she knew the ideas they tended to embody. She also knew the fatecarver was free to interpret the future the Fates predicted for the young woman in the designs she created. "This young woman will give birth to understanding and innovation. Her children will be ideas and new ways of thinking." The more she considered the young woman's obsession, the more she wanted to encourage her to follow that passion and to connect with like-minded people. "Her partner will not be of Caverna, and they will be connected in body and mind." Was that sufficiently vague and encouraging? Would it give the girl scope to pursue whatever she wished? Did it sound like something the Fates would say?

"And clan?" Farlin asked. Her tone indicated she'd love to boot this girl out of Caverna with the mark of another clan.

Kalish would be happy to call her a Fatekeeper, but having another clan's mark—or worse, no clan mark—in your storyscar was distressing for most women. "Caverna."

Farlin nodded. "Thank you. I believe I have enough to go on." She turned, as if to leave.

"Wait." Kalish had planned on asking Farlin if she could visit Caverna with a delegation, but she changed her mind. It was going to take more of a display of power to sway Farlin and the Caverna Clan. "Tell your elders that I require an audience with them. I will arrive with a delegation of Fatekeepers in three days' time. You and the elders will make yourselves available and guarantee our safety."

"I can't simply—"

Kalish raised a hand. "You are Caverna's fatecarver. Would you ignore the gods in order to not ruffle the feathers of your elders? Do I need to remind you of what I am?" Kalish flickered briefly into her falcon form and then her lantan form before returning to herself.

Farlin bowed her head. "Fatewalker. I will tell the elders. We will be waiting to receive you, and look forward to your arrival. Until then, may the Fates be with you."

"And also with you." Kalish shifted once more into a falcon and shot out of the fatechamber and the cavern.

Three days later, Kalish approached Caverna's prime terrace flanked by Dayo, Umbel, Yinlan, Benut and Jenti. Mixed genders, clans and ages—a delegation certain to offend the Caverna elders. Negotiation would be easier if Kalish had brought an all-female delegation of elders.

But that would miss the point.

They had come by glider, but the closest landing spot was some distance away. They approached the terrace on foot and armed—the risk of attack by Surefoot or Caverna was too high—but laid down their spears when they were within hailing distance of the guards.

Five guards met them a hundred paces from the bustle of daily activity going on in front of the cavern entrance. Kalish held out her hands, palms up, in a sign of friendship.

The guard in front glanced at her hands, her delegation, and then her face. "You are Fatewalker Kalish."

"I am." She kept her hands resolutely out. To greet a guard, especially a male guard, with open hands, rather than a perfunctory word, implied he was someone valued, someone important. She watched as his eyes darted to the group behind her. What did he think of her choice of ambassadors? What had he heard about the Fatekeepers, and the society they were striving for? Did he long for an escape from the constraints of Fatecarver culture, or was he content with his life? His face gave nothing away, but after a moment of indecision, he handed his spear to the man next to him and placed his hands on Kalish's.

"Greetings, Fatewalker Kalish. Welcome to Caverna Clan."

Kalish let a small smile lift the corners of her mouth. "Thank you."

"The elders are expecting you," the man said, lifting his hands.

"Well, then. Let's not keep them waiting." She lifted an eyebrow, and the guard's eyes crinkled with a suppressed smile at the implication that the elders could get cranky. His shoulders relaxed somewhat as he retrieved his spear. "We'll look after your weapons while you are here." Nodding toward the spears they'd surrendered, he added, "We'll need the others you're carrying."

Kalish nodded. Their knives weren't visible, but no Fatecarver over the age of about six went anywhere without one strapped to their leg. They deposited their knives with their spears, and two of the guards collected them all.

"This way." The guard who'd spoken turned and

led them toward the cavern, and the other guards fell in around them.

Kalish's palms grew sweaty as they entered the cave. Stepping into an enemy clan's prime terrace was always risky—and in Fatecarver culture, any clan not your own was an enemy clan. She hoped that, by the time they left, she could count Caverna Clan as an ally.

The elder council—fifteen women—was seated not far inside the mouth of the cavern, and Kalish was thankful they weren't meeting in the depths of the cave. Most elder compounds were located at the back, in the most protected part of the terrace, but she supposed here in Caverna, light was at a premium, and the elders would get the brightest spot.

Farlin was with the council, and she stood as Kalish and her delegation entered. She made frantic eyes at the elders, but none of them rose. Turning back to Kalish, she said, "Fatewalker Kalish. Welcome to Caverna." She held out her hands, and Kalish placed hers on top.

"Thank you." Kalish's nervousness increased. For a delegation from another clan, the entire council should have risen. For a Fatewalker, the entire council should have risen. The Caverna elders were treating them as a motley assortment of people that included only one elder female. That needed to change, if they were to make any progress here. "Let me introduce you to my delegation."

She introduced each member of her group, elaborating their roles and value among the Fatekeepers. Then she introduced herself. "I am Fatewalker Kalish. Falcon, lantan, and chosen by the god Iskra." She shifted into her falcon form, hovering in mid-air for a moment before transforming directly to her lantan form, hitting the ground with a thud and hiss, a slither of scales calculated to intimidate. She flicked out her tongue and smelled their surprise, tinged with apprehension. Good.

Transforming back into her human form, she flashed one of her mother's predatory smiles, trying not to think about how easy it was to fall into her mother's patterns of behaviour—power displays, subtle threats. "Thank you for receiving us."

Slowly, the elders rose and nodded respectfully to her and her delegation. The most wrinkled of the elders invited them to sit and explain the purpose of their visit.

Dayo gave her a reassuring touch on her arm as he settled on her left. Umbel anchored her right, her solid presence a comfort. As the rest of her delegation fell into place, she acknowledged each one with a look that she hoped conveyed her thanks that they were here with her, supporting her. She may find it frighteningly easy to fall into power displays, but only because she had the support of the Fatekeepers, only because they understood the need for such displays.

"As you no doubt are aware, Surefoot Clan, under the direction of Norili, has taken over Flintcrag and Point Clans. I suspect you also know that Norili is my mother."

Oh. They hadn't known. Shrewd as elders were, they couldn't hide their surprise. Good. A little off-balance, they might be easier to push. Kalish continued. "Yes, my mother gave me the storyscar that led to my banishment. Do not, for a moment, think I aim for anything but my mother's downfall. As her daughter, I know she lusts for power. She will not rest until she has taken control of all the Fatecarver clans, squeezing them in her greedy fist. I'm here today to propose an alliance. One that will protect Caverna Clan from Norili, and improve the lives of all your clanspeople."

She had their attention. Now she had to deliver a compelling reason Caverna Clan should join the

Fatekeepers. She hoped the guards, standing nearby at the cave entrance, were all listening. Even if she didn't sway the elders and Farlin, if she started discussions among the ordinary people of the terrace, she might gain traction here in time.

She explained her goals and the tasks set forth for her by Iskra. With the members of her delegation chiming in, she explained the society the Fatekeepers were creating, and how Iskra had shown her the need for such change, so the Fatecarvers didn't destroy themselves.

The Caverna elders asked many questions, some curious, others aggressive. At some point, an elder with sparkling eyes who had so far been silent spoke up. "When you transform, do you take on the senses of the creature you become? What's it like?"

The other elders stiffened. Kalish glanced at Farlin, eyebrows raised. The fatecarver rolled her eyes, telling her what she needed to know. This elder was kin—grandmother, probably—to the young woman Farlin had tattooed three days ago.

Kalish smiled at the elder. "You are grandmother to a young woman who recently received her fatecarving."

The woman's eyes lit up. "I am! How do you know Glinha?"

Kalish stretched the truth slightly. "The Fates brought her to my attention, asked me to attend her fatecarving and relay their best wishes for her future."

"Oh! Can you give me an inkling of what we'll see when she comes for her reading?"

Kalish smiled a genuine smile. "No, but I hope she will be happy with it, and I would encourage her to make the most of what her future holds. Indeed, I expect great things of her." Hopefully, Farlin had carved what

Kalish recommended. And hopefully the elders would read the storyscar in the right way. Farlin's face gave away nothing.

Glinha's grandmother sat straighter. "You hear that?" she said to the woman next to her.

"And to answer your question, yes, in my alternate forms, I acquire the skills and sensory abilities of the animal I become. It is …" *Disconcerting? Occasionally nauseating? Scary? Euphoric?* "Enlightening, and quite handy at times."

When the discussion wound down, the most senior elder invited Kalish and her delegation to exit the cavern. "We have arranged a meal for you. Please enjoy our hospitality while we discuss your proposal."

Kalish desperately wanted to discuss with the others how things had gone, but under the wary eyes of a team of guards and what appeared to be the entire population of the terrace, there was no privacy for conversation. Instead, she accepted a flatbread wrapped around a chunk of roasted rabbit and tried to calm her stomach enough to eat it.

Dayo, with the social ease she'd always envied, fell into conversation with the man who served their food, joking and laughing as though they were old friends. Other members of Caverna edged closer as they spoke, and Kalish caught some of the women eyeing him up. Dayo was short, but his magnetic personality, and the dimple that appeared when he smiled, drew women to him wherever he went.

"Fatewalker." She turned toward the voice of the guard whom she'd first spoken to. He was obviously off duty now, and he cradled a baby in his arm. He stepped up to her with a dip of his head.

"I never had a chance to ask your name," Kalish said by way of greeting.

He smiled. "Wex."

"And who is this?" she asked, glancing down at the child.

"She has yet to be named. I was wondering if you would be willing to bless her so she will grow into a strong woman."

Kalish's smile froze. He wanted her to bless his child? She bit her tongue to avoid blurting out the first thing that came to mind—that a blessing from a teenager banished from her own clan and sentenced to death by several others would be a curse.

Umbel appeared behind her, peering over her shoulder at the babe. "Ah, a beauty, she is, just like her father. It seems to me she has already been blessed by her parents."

Kalish relaxed somewhat. If Umbel could deflect this request …

But Umbel continued. "I'm certain Fatewalker Kalish would be honoured to bestow a blessing on such a perfect child, just as she does for all the Fatekeeper children."

What? She had never blessed a child. She wasn't a god. "Umbel, I—"

Umbel clapped her hands together. "Oh, I'm so glad you'll do it." Then she sucked in a breath. "But do you think it's appropriate for a Caverna baby? I mean, the blessing is very much rooted in Fatekeeper values."

"Fatekeeper values?" Wex asked.

Clever Umbel! One day Kalish hoped to be as cunning and confident as her. She jumped in, as Umbel had intended, explaining with enthusiasm the values the Fatekeepers lived by. The rest of her delegation joined into the conversation, and before long they had an audience with the entire population of the terrace.

"Well," Wex said. "If those are Fatekeeper values,

then I *would* like you to bless my daughter, Fatewalker."

Spines. There was no getting out of it. And the opportunity to explain the Fatekeepers to the people of Caverna was well worth the cost of a hastily invented blessing.

What would Norili do in this situation? Make a show of it. Was she willing to go to those lengths to win support? Against her mother, she'd have to.

She held her arms out for the child. Cradling it close, she intoned, "Fates, bless this child with the love of family and friends, with strong men and women by her side to work with her in adversity. Bless her with understanding, compassion, and respect for all those who walk the earth beside her. Bless her with the wisdom to listen to her enemies before lifting a weapon. Bless her with the peace to walk among the Fates themselves in search of happiness."

She crouched and set the baby on the ground. Here came the show. "I, Fatewalker Kalish, promise to watch over this child, adding my own blessing to that of the Fates."

When she transformed into a lantan and circled the sleeping child, the surrounding people gasped. Wex tensed and lunged forward, but Umbel held him back. "Watch."

Kalish transformed into a falcon and mantled over the babe, as falcons did to protect chicks or a kill from other predators. Then she plucked out one of her own breast feathers and laid it gently on the girl's chest before transforming back to her human form.

She picked up the child and handed her back to her wide-eyed father amidst the stunned silence of the crowd.

Just then, Farlin emerged from the cavern. "The elders have made their decision."

Kalish glanced at Umbel, raising her eyebrows. *Is that what you expected of me?*

Umbel chuckled and threw an arm around Kalish's shoulders. "Let's go hear what the elders have to say."

Chapter 20

"We're bound to have better luck with Southcrag," Dayo suggested as he strapped himself into the glider next to Kalish a few days later. "They're not nearly as well-protected as Caverna Clan is."

The bubble of hope Kalish held as they left an awed crowd and re-entered the cavern to speak with Caverna's elders had popped when the elders' decision was explained.

"We acknowledge your offer and recognise the value of inter-clan cooperation in the face of a common enemy. We are no ally of the Surefoots. But we are well protected in our terraces, even against a strong enemy. We do not need your help. And we have no desire for the upheaval your Fatekeeper rules and values would cause. We are quite comfortable here, with traditional Fatecarver values," the elders' spokesperson had said.

They had parted peacefully. Their weapons were returned, and the people lined up to farewell them.

Her only solace was the hope that her little blessing of Wex's child had created a desire among the people of Caverna's prime terrace to join with the Fatekeepers. That desire would form a rift between the people and their elder council that would put pressure on the council to reconsider their position.

Now, the same group of delegates was on its way to Southcrag Clan's prime terrace. As at Caverna, Kalish had visited the clan's fatecarver in the Fatewalker Realm first, to advise the elders of their arrival. They were expected, and hopefully they'd be well received.

Kalish worried that Southcrag might not yet feel threatened by Norili and the Surefoots—Caverna stood between them and the Surefoots, and until Caverna fell, the Surefoots were unlikely to attack.

But this wasn't solely about defeating Norili and the Surefoots. It was about all Fatecarvers. Surefoot aggression merely provided a convenient rallying point.

Southcrag's prime terrace was open to the sky—a sharp contrast to Caverna. It sat on a high cliff above the Southcrag River, and the broad upland behind it provided the perfect glider landing site. Kalish and her delegates circled over the terrace before touching down amidst the stubble of grain fields. By the time they had secured their gliders, the elders and Southcrag's fatecarver, Margali, were there to greet them.

It was a better start than they'd had at Caverna. Kalish smiled and placed her hands atop Margali's outstretched palms.

"Welcome to Southcrag, Fatewalker," said Margali. She introduced the elders—ten in number—and Kalish introduced her delegation, and then together they descended the slope to the terrace.

The elder compound occupied the centre of the terrace—a ring of rooms surrounding a small central courtyard with a vibrant roof of vines. Kalish gaped at the lush foliage, so out of place in the dry landscapes of Fatecarver lands. "How do you keep it alive?"

Margali chuckled. "There is a spring in the hillside behind the terrace. Clay pipes carry water from the spring to multiple points within the terrace, one of which is the elder compound. That vine is rooted in the basin where the water collects, on the other side of the courtyard. When it first sprouted there, one of the elders, a woman long gone now, thought to train it up the wall and across beams over the courtyard to provide shade. Apparently this space used to feel like an oven on summer days. The beams are long gone, but the vine supports itself now, crossing from one side of the courtyard to another and crossing the roofs of the elders' rooms."

"It reminds me of Treekeeper lands," said Dayo as they all found seats around the sunken centre of the courtyard.

"Now, tell us why you are here, Fatewalker," said one of the elders.

Kalish launched into the same explanation she'd given to the Caverna Clan, with the same arguments for why Southcrag should make an alliance with the Fatekeepers. The elders, in their turn, asked many of the same questions Caverna's elders had asked.

As their conversation wound down, Margali stepped out of the courtyard, returning a moment later followed by two men bearing food.

"The elder council will now retire to discuss your proposal. Please, stay and enjoy the courtyard while you wait." Margali motioned for the men to serve the food, and then followed the elders out.

Kalish was simultaneously disappointed they didn't have an opportunity to interact with the people of Southcrag, and relieved she wasn't going to be put on the spot again to perform a hastily invented ceremony. She nibbled on a flatbread, growing more nervous as the time passed. None of them spoke as they waited. How long would it take the elders to decide?

Not too long. Kalish hadn't finished her bread

before a stream of armed men poured into the courtyard through the doorway. Twenty strong, to Kalish's delegation of six. There was no point in resisting as the men bound them all, taking extra care with Kalish— leather thongs tight around her wrists, ankles and knees, as opposed to ankles and wrists like the others.

Well, spines. Now what?

Margali entered the courtyard once all of Kalish's delegation were secured. She ignored everyone else, and strode to Kalish. "Fatewalker Kalish. Your mother told me you were too trusting."

My mother? Spines!

"Don't even think about transforming in order to slip out of those bonds. You escape, and the rest of your group dies."

"And what has the great Norili promised to Southcrag in exchange for me?" Kalish spat.

"Quite a large quantity of bladestone weaponry." The fatecarver slipped a bladestone knife from the sheath on her leg. "It's lovely stuff, this bladestone."

"Norili only wants me. Let the others go." She knew it was a long shot—anyone who had the chance would keep hold of her delegation in order to try to squeeze more out of Norili or maybe force something from the Fatekeepers.

Margali ignored Kalish and spoke to the men who had bound them. "I'll take the Fatewalker. Put the others in the storeroom near my quarters." She pointed at two of the men. "You, come with me. Carry her."

One of the men slung Kalish over his shoulder like a dead goat and hauled her out of the courtyard. She raised her head and mouthed to Dayo, "Wait for me." Hopefully he would understand.

Margali spoke to the men as she led them around the circle of elders' rooms. "It will take Norili some time to get here. All the prisoners are to be unharmed when she arrives. I don't expect the others to give you too much difficulty—they're a sad-looking lot. This one, however, needs to be watched at all times. She can change form, into a falcon or a snake."

The man carrying Kalish tensed. He clearly didn't like snakes. At least he didn't drop her. If she bit him in human form, would he freak out? It was tempting, but it wouldn't help her situation. As long as the others were patient, she could free them all … probably.

Margali kept talking. "Two men will stand guard. Do not take your eyes off her for a moment. If she transforms, one of you will contain her, and the other will report immediately to me, and then kill all five of the others."

Yes, yes. That was clear. But Kalish had no plans to transform. Not yet, anyway.

She wasn't worried for herself. She wasn't worried that Norili would actually succeed in getting hold of her. Compared with the other times she'd been captured, threatened or chased, she had an excellent chance of escape—her powers had grown so much over the past year that she had multiple options to gain her own freedom.

Margali was wise to hang on to the others. Kalish wouldn't risk them. As long as she could convince them to escape first and leave her behind, they'd be fine.

Assuming they could escape.

The man dropped Kalish to the floor inside a tiny personal storeroom in Margali's quarters. Bunches of drying herbs hung from the ceiling, and the floor was fragrant with dropped leaves and petals. She sneezed from the smell and dust. Her wrists and ankles already hurt from the leather restraints. How long before she could feign sleep and slip into the Fatewalker Realm?

As she waited, she considered a range of options for escape. It was too much to hope that their gliders were still on the hillside. They'd probably been spirited away before she and her friends had even sat down in the courtyard. Their weapons, too, were as good as gone. They'd have to slip out unseen and be far away before they were noticed missing.

Or there would have to be a big distraction.

Her guards were wary of her. "Don't worry," she told them. "I'm not going to turn into a lantan and bite you."

The guards' eyes went wide. "You turn into a *lantan*?" It was the most deadly snake in Fatecarver lands.

"Yes. But as I said, don't worry." She yawned. "I'm too tired to do anything crazy, even if I didn't care about the friends I came here with."

After a few more yawns, and a long stretch of silence, Kalish allowed her eyes to close. Soon after, she slipped into the Fatewalker Realm.

She opened her eyes and sat up. "Spines."

"I knew you'd try the Fatewalker Realm." Margali stood in the doorway of the storeroom.

"You're going to all this trouble for some weapons? You realise that no matter how much bladestone Norili gives you, she has more—eventually, she'll take over Southcrag."

Margali laughed. "Your mother isn't immortal. At least under her leadership the proper social order will be preserved. Men as equals? You must be kidding."

If she transformed and slipped away, would Margali let her return to her body? She'd have to—Norili obviously wanted Kalish unharmed. But would she have the others killed in retaliation? That would be the obvious response. *Spines!*

Well, Margali couldn't spend all her time in the

Fatewalker Realm. Kalish would simply have to be patient. She hoped the others would be.

She made a show of frustration and slipped back into her body.

Several times over the course of the long afternoon and even longer night, she snuck into the Fatewalker Realm, only to find Margali still there, waiting for her. Didn't the woman have things to do?

What else can you do?

It was a question Kofri had asked her, one that Iskra had encouraged her to ask herself.

Her plan had been to enter the body of some rodent from the Fatewalker Realm, cross back into the real world, and chew her friends' bonds to release them. After they had escaped, she would simply transform into a falcon in the real world and fly away.

But if she couldn't use the Fatewalker Realm, what could she do?

Her transformations to falcon and lantan came naturally, without effort, in the Fatewalker Realm. She could transform in the real world, too, although it took far more energy and left her exhausted.

In the Fatewalker Realm, she could push her spirit into another living thing, then move back and forth between the Fatewalker Realm and the real world within the other animal. Could she push her spirit into another animal in the real world? And if she did, what would it do to her?

The storeroom's herb-strewn floor attracted mice after dark. Kalish had been listening to them skitter along the walls and scuffle among the drifts of leaves. She'd carefully kept herself away from them, but now she shuffled close to the wall. In the Fatewalker Realm, she had to be touching an animal to push her spirit into it. With her hands and legs tied, there was no way she could catch a mouse. But if the mouse crawled across her, maybe it would be enough.

Her guards' gaze never left her, but she knew that in the dark they would know only what their ears told them—that she was moving around, probably trying to get comfortable on the stone floor, hands and feet throbbing from the bindings on them. She'd been doing it all day.

This time, however, she scraped up some of the herbs from the floor and held them in her open palm, then lay as still as she could, thinking quiet thoughts.

I'm part of the floor, not a person. I smell like something tasty to eat.

In the Fatewalker Realm, thoughts like that might actually turn her into the floor or make her smell like a crust of bread. She'd never tried it, but the conviction that she *could* grew the more she considered it.

In the real world, the thoughts apparently weren't enough to entice a mouse to scamper across her. She lay still until the cold of the stones seeped into her bones, until her fingers grew numb, until she lost all sense of where her limbs were.

Cold grey light filtered into the storeroom. Kalish's stomach growled. She groaned as she rolled to her side and struggled into a sitting position. Leaves and dust drifted off her body, and she sneezed. When had she fallen asleep? Long before any mouse had decided to take a stroll across her.

Her guards had changed while she slept, but the boredom on these men's faces was identical to that on the previous guards'. Footsteps approached, then a voice said, "Go get yourselves something hot to eat—you look frozen. Cal and I are on duty here now."

The speaker stepped through the doorway carrying a steaming bowl of pola and a jug of water. He set them on the floor next to Kalish. She looked at the food, then up at him. "How am I supposed to eat with my hands tied?"

The guard crouched beside her and she leaned forward so he could reach her wrists. He began working at the knot of her binding. "Fatecarver Margali says that if you try to escape, the elder dies first."

Umbel. Kalish pressed her lips together and said nothing.

The man leaned forward, wrenching on the stubborn knot. He whispered close to Kalish's ear, "My sister is getting her fatecarving this afternoon."

Kalish's pulse kicked up.

The binding was off her wrists, and she sighed at the relief, rubbing the raw flesh and numb fingers before reaching for the bowl. "Thank you." She met his gaze for a second, hoping to convey the depths of her thanks.

He'd given her the information she needed—Margali would be busy this afternoon.

CHAPTER 21

When Kalish finished eating, she swiped the last of the pola out of the bowl with a finger and rubbed her hands together, spreading the grainy paste over both hands. Then she endured the indignity of being watched while she relieved herself in a pot they brought to her. When the guard bound her hands again, he whispered, "May the Fates be with you."

"And also with you," Kalish replied.

She remained alert, listening to every noise outside, doing her best to get a glimpse of any activity happening in Margali's room. Meanwhile, she spread her hands wide, holding as still as possible, hoping the smell of pola would attract a mouse. Her guards stood silent, bored. When the guard changed again, she reckoned the time had come, mouse or no mouse. She lay down, shut her eyes, and slipped into the Fatewalker Realm.

Margali was nowhere to be seen.

Unfortunately, neither was a convenient rodent at this time of day. She'd have to risk being seen in one of her known forms.

She chose the snake. Not only was it well-camouflaged, it had the benefit of being well-equipped to seek out a mouse or rat. As she shifted into the sleek form, the rich aroma of rodents wafted to her tongue. She followed the smell out of Margali's room and through the curving alleyway outside. A gap in the stonework reeked of rat, and Kalish dove into it.

You must remember not to bite. Her lantan form came with the appetite of a snake. It would be a shame to accidentally kill the animal she wanted to inhabit.

When she arrived at the nest, the rat was frantic. She crowded it with the coils of her body, keeping her mouth clamped firmly shut. Before she could push her spirit into its body and take control, it bit her. Before her snake self could bite back, she shoved her way into its mind.

She felt the rat's momentary confusion when the lantan vanished, felt its lingering terror. She overrode all the rat's feelings and drove it out of the nest and firmly into the real world.

After the silence of the Fatewalker Realm, the activity of the real world was a shock. The alleyway was busy with people. Kalish poked the rat's nose out of the crack in between stones and sniffed the air. Dried meat, freshly dug root crops, and human urine—the storeroom where her friends were being held wasn't far away.

She was about to launch herself into the alley, to race toward the storeroom, when the rat's resistance brought her up short.

The rat knew another way into the storeroom. A way in darkness and safety. Kalish allowed it to lead her back to the nest and through an impossibly narrow crack that terrified Kalish—the fear of becoming stuck nearly made her take back control from the rodent.

But the rat was confident. It had done this countless times. That's why its nest was located where it was.

They popped out suddenly into the storeroom.

Now the rat shied away, fearful of the people in the room. Kalish forced the rat forward to the nearest person—Yinlan. Scooting along the wall, she came to his hands, tied behind his back, and began to gnaw at the leather bindings. He shook his hands and jerked forward. "Ah! Rat."

Don't give me away. Just let me get you free. She followed his hands and sunk her teeth into the bindings again.

"What the—"

"Shh!" Dayo warned from next to Yinlan. "Sit back," he whispered. "It's not a rat."

How Dayo knew, she had no idea. He'd always been in tune with her, though, and he must have expected this. No doubt he'd gone into the Fatewalker Realm and found Margali guarding Kalish there. He could have guessed her plan. And maybe the guard who had come to her had talked to him as well.

Yinlan relaxed, and Kalish got to work on the bindings. It didn't take long, and then she was on to Dayo's. The members of her delegation all sat with their backs against the wall, so it wasn't hard to stay out of sight while releasing everyone's hands. The ankles would be more difficult, but when she peeked around Umbel at the guard in the doorway, she was relieved to find him facing away from them. Apparently her friends didn't need constant watching like she did.

With one eye on the guard, she gnawed at Umbel's ankle bindings, focusing on the strands hidden below the elder's legs. With luck they would still appear well trussed until the time was right to break free.

She scampered to Benut and began gnawing. Benut shifted, drawing the guard's attention.

Kalish froze. *Spines!*

"We're still here," Dayo said, diverting the man's

gaze to his face. "Any excitement out there? It's getting pretty dull in here. Maybe you can step aside so we can at least have a view."

The guard snorted and turned his back again without a word. Kalish got back to work.

When all her friends' bindings were released, she scampered back to Dayo. If only she could talk to him. If only they could plan what would happen next. He brought his hand toward her, and she placed a paw on top.

Instantly, she found herself inside Dayo's body. *No, no, no!* The rat, released from her hold, darted away.

What the Fates? Dayo's thoughts intruded on her own, but mirrored hers exactly.

Somehow, her spirit had slipped from the rat into Dayo. His confusion was hers, and her panic fuelled his. Their consciousnesses, feelings and thoughts intertwined in a bewildering swirl.

How?
No!
Kalish?

With a monumental effort, she separated her spirit from his.

Dayo, listen.
You were in the rat.
Yes, I was. And now I'm in you.
What?
I can't stay here Dayo. I have to get back to my body.
Where are—
In Margali's room. A little storeroom off the side.
How—
I was going to give you a chance to escape, and then I'd transform and fly away, but I can't do that if I'm inside you. Her panic rose again, but Dayo had tamped his down.

It's okay. We'll get you. When we escape, we'll come to

Margali's room.

She's doing a fatecarving right now.

I know.

Kalish didn't need to voice her surprise—Dayo felt it, and she in turn felt his amusement.

The guard was bored. I chatted to him for a long time. About you, about the Fatekeepers, about Southcrag Clan. You know, you're lucky you found a rat—he devised a trap for rats. He turned his gaze to an unusually shaped clay vessel on the floor. *It's saved them a lot of crop losses. But no one knows he designed it—his wife got all the credit, because no one believed he could have done something clever.*

Kalish's spirit warmed with love and admiration for Dayo. He'd found them an ally.

And here I thought the great Fatewalker was going to save all her friends. I should have given you another day—you'd have been walking out of here with the blessing of the elders.

Hardly. But we'll get out. Hey, this is kind of cosy, with you in my head.

It's freaking me out. What if I lose my body!

You won't.

Let's get out of here.

That's the plan, as soon as—

There was a commotion outside.

Dayo and the others shared a glance. Inside Dayo's head, she understood this was a signal they'd been told to wait for.

I thought I told you to wait for me.

We planned to, but when opportunity presented itself …

Kalish huffed, thankful they hadn't waited on her, and pleased she had at least gotten them loose so they could take advantage of whatever this distraction was.

Feet pounded outside. Shouts, something about a raid. The guard at their door vanished. Instantly, all the Fatekeepers were on their feet.

The guard who had spoken to Kalish stepped into the doorway and gave a start. "You're loose? How?"

"Never mind," Umbel said. "Let's get out of here."

"No. We have to get Kalish first," said Dayo.

"Why? She can easily shift and escape once we're free," Benut said. "You said so yourself."

"Yeah, well, things have changed."

"What are you talking about?" Jenti asked.

"Long story. Now's not the time for explanations." He turned to the guard. "The Fatewalker?"

He nodded. "Follow me." The guard peeked out the doorway, then waved them all forward. The alleyway, a scene of frantic activity a few moments ago, was now deserted. They darted a few doorways down the alley to Margali's room, and drew up short when they encountered the two guards stationed inside.

Sorry. Forgot to tell you about these guys.

Dayo didn't respond as he dove at the closest guard's knees. The mens' surprise gave the Fatekeepers the advantage, in spite of the fact they had no weapons. The guard toppled, and Benut snatched his spear while Umbel twisted his arms behind his back.

Yinlan, Jenti and the Southcrag helping them took down the second man. Soon both guards were bound tightly with the same thongs her friends had been bound with.

My body. I think you'll need to touch it so I can go back into it.

Dayo picked himself off the floor and lurched into the storeroom where Kalish lay. He grabbed her hand, and the instant she felt the connection, Kalish rushed back.

She sat up in her own body, heart racing. "Go, go, go!"

The others fled. Kalish transformed into her falcon form and shot off behind them through the doorway.

She didn't follow them once she had clear skies overhead, but she kept a close eye on them as she powered up above the terrace.

The access points to the terrace bristled with spears in anticipation of the raid which, she presumed, would never come. How were the others going to leave with the entire population of the terrace armed and manning the entrances?

But they weren't headed for the entrances. They were sprinting toward the fatechamber. Why? She circled above, watching with her heart in her throat as the Southcrags at the entrances began to disperse in the absence of enemies.

The fatechamber sat near the edge of the cliff on which the terrace perched. A channel wound around the fatechamber, carrying water that Kalish presumed came from the spring that fed the elders' roof-vine, and spilled over the edge of the cliff through a deep notch.

The Fatekeepers sprinted straight for the notch. They weren't going to try to climb down there were they? Even from this height, Kalish could see the green slime that would make the rocks impossible to grip and send her friends tumbling to their deaths far below.

Then she spotted the rope. Secured just below the lip of the notch, it trailed down the waterfall to within two body lengths of the valley below. A little escape ladder. The rope wasn't quite as green as the rocks—it had been there a while, but was clearly maintained. An escape route for the fatecarver in case of a raid? Most likely.

The Southcrag guard reached the notch and waved Yinlan down, then Benut right after. He halted

Umbel, and Kalish realised he was waiting for Yinlan and Benut to reach the bottom, lest the rope snap.

People were returning to their interrupted tasks around the terrace. *Hurry!* Kalish silently urged her friends. It wouldn't be long before someone noticed the odd goings-on at the edge of the cliff.

Umbel and Jenti descended, with Dayo and the Southcrag watching from above. The Southcrag glanced up, and then waved Dayo away from the notch. The men pressed their backs against the fatechamber as the courtyard around the chamber began to fill with people going about their business.

There was no way for Dayo to descend without being seen now.

When Margali emerged from the fatechamber— thankfully on the opposite side from where Dayo and the Southcrag guard stood—Kalish knew she had to create a diversion.

With a scream, she folded her wings and plummeted toward Margali.

She noted the moment when Margali registered her presence. Her falcon eyes caught the word *Fatewalker* on her lips, and a look of anger on her face. If she were in human form, Kalish would have smiled.

Margali shouted for guards, and soon all eyes were on Kalish. She pulled out of her dive, wary of the spears and atlatls still on hand, and swooped over Margali's head. She looped around for another swipe, flying high enough to peek over the fatechamber to the notch.

Dayo dropped into the notch, and the Southcrag guard followed. *Thank the Fates.* Kalish dove again. The longer everyone focused on her, the further her friends would be from the terrace before their disappearance was noticed. She would taunt them for as long as she could.

CHAPTER 22

With trade established directly between the Treekeeper villages, the interaction among villages grew. Travel increased, and pathways between villages that had been seldom used for generations grew well-trodden over the course of only a few weeks.

Norili met several more times with the Speakers, and they assured her the goods she demanded were on their way down the rivers to Council Island. Meanwhile, said goods were travelling overland to the villages where they were needed. How long could they continue to fool Norili? With luck, Norili's people on Council Island would hide from her the fact that goods weren't arriving. By now they would have learned that Norili punished the messenger who brought bad news. Hana hoped Norili would stay away from Council Island for a long time.

As trade opened up, Hana's services were in demand. Villages wanted to become more self-sufficient or increase the variety of the goods they produced. Hana's skill in the old ways of hunting, fishing, weaving and other tasks meant she was spending more and more time in the other villages teaching the skills she'd needed to learn long ago as an outcast with her husband.

Today she was in Lower Falls teaching basketry. Lower Falls had a wealth of good fibre plants available, but no knowledge of how to use those fibres.

Nearly the entire village turned out for the lesson, and Hana sat on a stump surrounded by attentive students as she demonstrated how to begin forming the flat bottom of a basket. Even the children joined in, sitting at her feet and mimicking her motions on their own small baskets.

The atmosphere was that of a celebration. The village had cooked a communal meal at midday, and there was as much chatter as there was weaving going on. It pleased Hana to see people working together, eating together, helping each other. She hadn't realised how withdrawn they'd all become under the old council, under Norili. She imagined a future in which each village was like the intersection of the strands of a fishing net, with paths and personal connections drawing them together, providing for them all. No one would be hungry. No one would be alone. No one would be ostracised. Every community would look like Lower Falls did today. Her mind wandered on the waves of conversations around her.

None of them registered the attack until it was under way.

Three darts, launched simultaneously, found three marks. One woman screamed. A man slumped forward over his basket, and another cursed. "Run!" someone yelled.

Parents snatched up children and baskets tumbled to the ground as people leapt to their feet. The ululating cry of a Fatecarver raiding party echoed through the forest.

Onola, the Speaker of Lower Falls, grabbed Hana

by the wrist. "Come."

With a whoosh, one of the houses went up in flames. *Not again.* The scene was a replay of the attack on Upper Falls by the former council. Unfortunately, this time the attackers were Fatecarvers, who weren't stopping with the destruction of houses. They were targeting people, too.

Except the people vanished more rapidly than even Hana could have imagined. Before long, she felt as though Onola and she were the only two villagers fleeing the attack. After a short dash, Onola pulled Hana behind the smooth bole of a large nalati tree. "Up."

A rope ladder hung from far up the tree. Two more villagers arrived. Hana didn't hesitate. She leapt onto the ladder and climbed. Glancing down, she watched a man race by with two Fatecarvers at his heels. He didn't stop to climb the tree, and the Fatecarvers didn't look up. Hana kept climbing.

Far up in the branches, she stepped onto a platform of woven sticks. Radiating from the platform were rope walkways that swayed as people padded along them.

Hana turned to Onola. "You've created a refuge?"

The Speaker smiled. "We knew we would be one of the first villages targeted if Norili attacked, because we're so close to Council Island."

"But this! This is amazing!"

"Each of us has a specific tree we're meant to escape up. Once we're all up, we'll raise the ladder. The kids have been having great fun practising."

Hana frowned. "You know, their darts can probably reach us here."

"Only if they think to look up." Onola pressed a finger to her lips and pointed at the ground. A pair of

Fatecarvers stalked through the undergrowth, their heads swivelling left and right as they went. "To them it will seem as though we simply vanished into the forest."

Hana looked out across the canopy. Through the leaves she made out other platforms, more people among the branches. Teenagers tightroped between trees. "Where are they going?"

"They're the runners. They'll make sure we're all accounted for, and try to locate, from above, anyone we're missing. It was one of those kids who came up with the idea for the treetop refuge. The rest of us thought it was crazy until the kids built the first platform."

"They look like they've been doing this their whole lives," Hana commented in awe.

"I think they have." Onola's tone was wry. "The little squirrels."

Lower Falls lost only one resident in the attack. The man hit in the neck in the first volley of darts was dead before his body hit the ground. Five other people were struck by darts; none were seriously injured.

The villagers' houses didn't fare as well, and for a while Hana was worried they'd all be burnt out of the treetops as flames from the houses licked upward. But winter is a wet season in Treekeeper lands, and the flames couldn't take hold among the tree branches.

By nightfall it was safe to return to the ground. The Fatecarvers had given up looking for the villagers—they must have known they were outmatched in the Treekeepers' own lands. The villagers were eager to return to their houses before the trees came alive for their nightly depredations. Those who'd lost their homes crowded in with those who hadn't. Onola begged Hana to stay the night with her family, but Hana was impatient to return to Upper Falls. She didn't know where the Fatecarvers had gone after attacking Lower Falls, but she felt the need to see Boluso and her children. Thank Iskra she and Boluso had convinced the village not to return to the old site yet.

"I'll travel through the night, and get home before morning," she told Onola.

"But the trees—"

"Will not harm me." She smiled. "Trust me. The village of Upper Falls has been largely nocturnal for months. The trees have never once harmed us."

"Even so, you shouldn't go alone."

If only she knew how many years Hana had done everything alone. Well, Boluso had been with her when he could, but his missing toes hampered him. "I'm quite comfortable travelling alone. Better chance of slipping past those Fatecarvers in the dark if it's just me."

Onola shook her head. "These are strange times. Villages in the trees, people out and about at night … It is not the way."

"No. But *the way* has never been the *only* way."

Padding silently through the dark forest, Hana kept her senses alert and her spear handy. Ordinarily, forest cats would be her main concern, but tonight they were only one of the things she worried about. Where had the Fatecarvers gone? Back to Council Island? On to the village of Flatwater, not far upriver? Would they camp or travel at night? Did they have a goal other than intimidation? Were Boluso and the children safe?

For the sake of speed, she followed the well-worn path along the river. At this pace, she would be home well before dawn. She might even catch up to the Fatecarvers and find out what they were up to.

Twenty warriors unaccustomed to the forest aren't quiet. Hana heard them, rustling around in the undergrowth trying to find a place to camp for the night, in plenty of time to quit the path and pick her way in a wide arc around them without them discovering her presence. Under cover of a dense patch of ferns, she crept close, listening carefully.

"Wet. Everything is so wet." The irritation in the man's voice was almost comical. "We'll drown standing up."

"We could keep moving," suggested another voice.

"And end up lost in this jungle? Bad enough trying to find our way during the day. I'm not stumbling around here in the dark."

A third man spoke up. "Then shut up and go to sleep."

As Hana snuck away, she heard a whisper of cloth running over bark. Of course the Fatecarvers would have set a guard. But had he spotted her, or was it simply bad luck he was close? She was thankful for the cover of the ferns—if you knew how to move through them, you could creep along silently and unseen underneath the fronds. Her spear was a hindrance, but she clung to it—other than a small knife, it was her only weapon.

If you didn't know how to move through the ferns, the fronds would hiss and rattle as you waded through. And wade through is exactly what the Fatecarver did. Clearly, he knew she was in here.

She zigzagged through the dark tunnel of fern fronds, making no ripples and no sound. He might know she was among the ferns, but he couldn't know where. Meanwhile, she had a good fix on his location as he crashed around.

The edge of the patch of ferns was a sharp line where the land rose slightly. Staying low, she darted toward a large tree and slipped behind the trunk.

The hiss of the Fatecarver walking through the ferns turned to a crashing as he began to run. He'd seen her.

Avoiding the paths, Hana chose the roughest, most vine-entangled route she could find through the forest. A lifetime of running through the undergrowth, and months of nocturnal living allowed her to move with speed, deftly leaping over fallen logs, squeezing between loops of trailing vines, and avoiding the many treacherous, nearly invisible holes formed by the uneven buildup of decaying plant material on the forest floor.

To his credit, the Fatecarver stayed on his feet. But he couldn't match Hana's speed. After putting significant distance between them, she slowed her steps, switched directions, and silently slipped away.

When she was certain he'd lost her, she angled back toward the river path. Once there, she broke into a jog.

She reached Flatwater and took a moment to catch her breath before mounting the steps to the Speaker's house. She hated to do this—waking her in the middle of the night would terrify her—but the people of Flatwater needed to know what was coming. She knocked on the door. "Sarafee, it's Hana." She knocked again. "Sarafee, I need to talk to you now."

Sarafee opened the door. "Hana, what are you doing out at night? Come in, quickly, before the trees get you."

Hana didn't try to correct her. She stepped inside, and Sarafee shut the door behind her.

"I'm sorry to come to you like this," Hana whispered, hoping she wouldn't wake Sarafee's children or husband. "But Norili's people have attacked Lower Falls, and they're moving this way."

"So, she knows we haven't sent anything to

Council Island?"

"She must know we're up to something. No doubt this is her way of convincing us to do as she demands. Listen, the Fatecarvers she's sent know how to fight—it's part of their culture. We can't compete when it comes to a flat-out confrontation. You need to take the villagers and flee."

"At night?"

"Yes. They're not far away—they could be attacking by the time you sing the trees to sleep in the morning."

"But the trees—"

"Will do you less harm than Norili's warriors. You need to leave."

"We know how to use a spear." Some of the young men and women from Upper Falls, trained by Kalish's people to protect themselves, had been teaching other villages the same skills.

"It's not enough. You've never seen Fatecarvers fight. You can't stand against them. I'm telling you, you must leave."

"What happened at Lower Falls?"

Hana described the attack and the clever way the villagers had protected themselves.

"But, if there are only twenty of them—"

"The Fatecarvers learn to fight before they learn to walk. They have magical fire that can set a house ablaze in the blink of an eye. Sarafee, please, wake everyone and leave before they arrive. Maybe if they find no one here, they won't even burn any houses. They might move on without doing any harm. But if you're here ..."

"If we're here, we can defend our homes. What if they find us gone and burn all the houses?"

"Houses can be rebuilt. If they find you here, they'll kill you. Think of your children."

Sarafee was silent for a moment. "I'll wake everyone. We'll discuss it. I can't make this decision on my own."

Hana hurried home to Upper Falls, hoping the people of Flatwater would make the right decision, and wondering how long it would be before other villages were attacked.

CHAPTER 23

The escape from Southcrag took more than a five-day. Knowing the Southcrags were under Norili's influence, the Fatekeepers couldn't allow the pursuing Southcrags to know where they were currently hiding out. So the route they took was erratic. Kalish might have made it away alone in her falcon form, but she'd have to transform back and rest several times on the way home, and the risk of capture was too great.

On the third day, with a band of Southcrag warriors resolutely on their tail, Kalish finally contacted the Fatekeepers in the Fatewalker Realm and arranged for an air rescue.

Seven gliders, equipped for tandem flight, spent two days flying a roundabout course in order to obscure their origin if they were spotted.

Late on the second day, Kalish's group abandoned the relative safety of the brush-covered lowlands and scaled a rise to a grass-covered, windswept plain. If the gliders didn't arrive shortly, they'd have a mad scramble to elude the Southcrags—standing in the open, they were announcing their location.

The sun sank behind the mountains, and the already chilly wind grew even colder. Kalish resisted the urge to transform and scout out the locations of both the Southcrags and the Fatekeeper gliders. Not yet. Only if the gliders were late.

The light began to fade. Where were the gliders? When she'd spoken to them in the Fatewalker Realm this morning, they had been within easy flight of this hill.

"I'm going up," she said. Her companions nodded, their nervousness beginning to show.

"Keep it short," Dayo warned. "You've transformed a lot today."

"I will. Just long enough to see where the Southcrags are."

It took almost no time to spot the Southcrags. They weren't even trying to conceal themselves as they raced toward Kalish's group. They didn't need to rely on surprise to overwhelm the Fatekeepers—their numbers would be enough, once they caught up.

And they would catch up soon. She and her friends needed to move now. As she wheeled back toward the hill, seven gliders suddenly burst into view from the valley below. She'd been watching for them in the sky, but they'd come up the river valley, no doubt taking advantage of the concealment and funnelled winds it provided.

She dropped back to the hill as the gliders crested the slope and came to a running stop on the top. "Hurry! The Southcrags are almost here."

They each ran to a glider and strapped themselves in as the pilots who'd brought them tried to rub warmth back into their hands. One glider launched, and then a second. The third took off as a wild cry erupted over the hill. The Southcrags had arrived.

"Go, go, go!" Dayo urged their Southcrag helper, Garen, and his glider partner forward.

"I'm not secured yet," he griped. "I don't know

how." His partner yanked on the ropes, and then they ran down the slope.

A dart whizzed between Kalish and Dayo. They each nodded to their glider partner and took off running. More darts followed and missed. They lifted from the ground and soared away. Kalish swore, and then turned her head toward her fellow pilot.

"Thanks for coming for us, Pentel."

"Not a problem. Gave us something to do."

Kalish frowned. "People are getting restless, aren't they?"

"Only some—the young men, the ones who were warriors before. They don't know anything but fighting. But you know those men—they're restless every winter. They'll be fine when spring comes."

Maybe, or maybe they'd simply realise that winter hadn't been holding up their progress in defeating Norili.

Discouraged by her visit to Caverna and Southcrag's prime terraces, Kalish was unenthusiastic about visiting either clan's outlying terraces.

"How else are we going to change their minds except by visiting them and talking to them?" Dayo reasoned. "It was always going to be this way—the women in power were never going to simply give up their power. The people are going to have to demand it. And they will, once they understand what you are offering."

"What *we* are offering," she reminded him. "It's the Fatekeepers together who are creating a new society. I'm not doing it alone."

"No, but you're who the Fatekeepers follow. You're our connection to the Fates."

A few days later, in one of Caverna's outlying terraces, Kalish had to admit Dayo was right.

Gossip had naturally bounded from terrace to terrace after Kalish's blessing of Wex's child. By the time she arrived at Lightspring Terrace, the people were ready for her, desperate to hear what she had to say.

Dayo spoke to them passionately about gender equality, how women should have opportunities to cook and care for children just as men should be allowed to engage in artistic pursuits like pottery and have a say in the decisions that affected the entire terrace. His eyes were shining when he turned to Kalish and said, "Fatewalker Kalish has always treated me as an equal, and I believe all men deserve that respect."

The people hardly needed Kalish's encouragement. They eagerly slipped into the Fatewalker Realm with her and stared in wonder as she transformed into falcon and snake. She encouraged them to explore the Fatewalker Realm, to use it as a way to meet and connect with people from other terraces, other clans. She explained how the Fatekeepers used the Fatewalker Realm to maintain relationships with fellow Fatekeepers from the Treekeeper peoples, painting a picture of a future in which all people lived in peace and friendship.

"And the more people who spend time in the Fatewalker Realm, the stronger the Fates grow," she said. "If you listen hard enough, you can hear Iskra—the Fates combined as one." Except they couldn't. Not now. Every time she entered the Fatewalker Realm, it seemed to have faded more. People who had never been there didn't seem to notice, but there were fewer birds, fewer insects calling. The colours were less vibrant. She felt the great emptiness growing larger all the time. Pushing the sensation away, she focused on the people.

After, they wanted her blessing—on their children, their crops, their homes. Young women lined up to have Kalish reinterpret their storyscars. "We want to hear our futures directly from the Fates," explained one of them. Girls begged for their own storyscars to be carved by the great Fatewalker Kalish.

She promised to visit them in the Fatewalker Realm and encouraged them to spread the word of the Fatekeepers' new society. Many of them took the Fatekeeper pledge, and she and her delegation left weighed down with gifts of food, pottery and beads.

The same scene was replayed at three other terraces within Caverna Clan over the next moon cycle, and by the time spring had arrived, rumour had it that Caverna's elders might be ready to discuss Caverna joining the Fatekeepers.

Finally, they were gaining some traction.

Kalish's good news about Caverna Clan died on her lips when the Treekeeper contingent arrived at the next Fatekeeper advisory meeting. All their faces were grim, and Sendalee's face held a haunted look.

"Norili's people have attacked every village that has refused to send goods to Council Island," Hana explained. "They've burned houses and killed anyone they could."

"In Flatwater, the people fought back. They" — Sendalee's voice hitched— "They were slaughtered."

Kalish's heart sank. She knew what Hana would say next.

"We've lost about half of our Speakers. They're alive, but they're sending goods to Council Island to protect their people. Some won't speak to us any more, for fear they may be targeted again."

"I'm sorry," Kalish said. Would she ever stop apologising for her mother? "I understand if you need to—"

"We're planning an attack on Council Island."

"What?"

"As soon as we know Norili is back, physically, on the island."

"It won't be easy like it was last time," Kofri warned. "You'll be up against Fatecarvers."

"We know that," Boluso said. "That's why we need to bring your Fatecarvers over again, like we did before."

"I'll come," Yinlan said, his arm around Sendalee.

"Fino and I will, too," Tili said with a nod to her husband.

"And if we pull all our fighters over the mountains, we leave our elders and children without protection," Kalish argued.

"*We* are without protection right now," Sendalee said, anger lacing her voice.

"I know," Kalish said. "We simply don't have enough people—enough fighters. We're outnumbered." All their gains in Caverna Clan meant little—Caverna was the smallest of the clans, and the most protected by their terraces. Convincing large numbers of them to cross the mountains to fight wasn't likely. Besides, spring had only just begun, and the weather in the mountains still made crossing them difficult.

"What is Norili providing her people that keeps them loyal?" Kofri asked, coming to the root of the problem.

Yinlan snorted. "Nothing, by the sounds of it. Half the Surefoots who have come to us are practically starving."

"She's providing stability. Giving them what they know," Wathi said.

"And she's frightening them with the spectre of change," Umbel added.

Kalish smiled. "The Unknown Fate. Everybody is afraid of her, even more than they are of Death."

"Exactly. But what if you frightened them more than Norili?" Kofri said.

Kalish frowned at her.

"Kalish, you stay up at night in the Fatewalker Realm searching for Iskra. The Fatewalker Realm is dying, in spite of all the people you're bringing into it. Did you notice the winter rains? Of course not, because they didn't happen. The rivers didn't flood, replenishing the fields. The mountains hardly collected any snow."

"Do you think the loss of Iskra affected the rains?" Jenti asked.

"Maybe it did, maybe it didn't. The point is, if people believe it did, they'll be terrified. If they know Iskra is gone, they'll look for another god." Kofri glanced at Kalish.

"No."

"And if that god requires them to change their behaviour in order to preserve their world," Kofri continued, "they might do it."

"I won't."

"And if that god denounces Norili as a pretender, and can show unequivocally that she has the power to preserve the Fatewalker Realm and the world, and that Norili will drive the earth to destruction—"

Kalish stood. "But I *don't* have the power to preserve the Fatewalker Realm. You know that. It's why I spend every night there searching for Iskra. Because *they* are the god, not me."

"And you think your mother can do it?" Kofri stood too, glaring at Kalish.

"No, but—"

"If you don't play your mother's game, you've already lost."

"If the people know the Fates, Nalatassa, Iskra are gone, they'll panic." She had told no one beyond her advisors.

Kofri smiled. "Exactly, and they'll cling to the most powerful leader they can find to save them."

It always came to this, didn't it? Spines! Kalish's chest hurt.

You must become.

Iskra had never explained what she was supposed to become. Only that she must. Is this what they meant? She had to pretend to be a god?

A slow smile spread across Dayo's face. "That thing you did with me—where you got inside of me—do you think you could do that with other people?"

The bottom dropped out of Kalish's stomach. *No.* She didn't ever want to do that.

CHAPTER 24

Kalish groaned and dropped her head into her hands. "Why did I agree to this? I hate it."

"It's not exactly fun for me either," Dayo said, looking a little pale. He shuddered. "Do you know how weird it is to see my hands move without my doing it? Or to hear you speak out of my mouth?"

"You've got to try to resist it this time. Those Surefoot elders are going to fight me, not simply let me inside and hand over control of their bodies to me."

"How am I supposed to fight you inside my mind?"

"Don't look at me—I have no idea. Just do it." Kalish took a deep breath and prepared herself for another invasion into Dayo's body. She refused to practise with anyone else, even though Kofri and Umbel had both offered themselves as subjects. "Ready?"

Dayo nodded.

Without giving either of them time to back out, Kalish grasped Dayo's hand and shoved her spirit through the connection.

Ugh. Kalish, that hurts.

You think it's comfortable for me? Keep fighting. She felt the pressure of his resistance increase, and she pushed against him. His mind was like a cliff without a handhold. How was she supposed to get through that? The harder she pushed, the more pain she felt—like something squeezing her head. Is that what Dayo felt? If he could feel her pain too, would he relent and let her in? She reached for her own pain and shoved it at him along with her spirit. He crumbled instantly.

Kalish swooped into his body. *Cross your eyes, stick out your tongue, and say I am a potato.*

Dayo did as she commanded, and then Kalish fled from his body.

"I am a potato? What the Fates?" Dayo met her eyes, and then burst out laughing, even as he rubbed his head.

Kalish snorted a laugh. "I don't know. It was ridiculous. This whole thing is ridiculous. I just ..." She just what? She didn't want to do this. She didn't want to invade anyone, even someone willing to be invaded. Her laughter turned to sobs.

Dayo gathered her into his arms. "Shh. It's okay."

"No. It's not okay. I don't want to do this. I don't even want to know I *can* do this to people."

He rocked her gently as he spoke. "You only have to do it once, then never again. And while I can definitively say it's not fun for the person who's invaded, it's not doing me any harm. What you're going to do to the elders will embarrass them. It might even frighten them. But that's the point. Keep the bigger picture in mind—you're saving our people."

"But I'm not even doing that if I can't find Iskra."

"Doing this could tip the balance to our favour against Norili. Once we've dealt with her, then you'll have time to find Iskra. Take one step at a time, Kalish."

Kalish nodded against Dayo's chest. She wasn't happy about the plan her advisors had convinced her to undertake, but she'd go through with it, mostly because she had no better ideas.

Entering Surefoot's prime terrace had become routine for Kalish. Land by the granaries as a falcon, slip into a rat, and scamper around wherever she wanted to go, completely undetected. In fact, she'd found the same rat several times now, as though it was waiting for her. It was eager to get going every time she pushed her way into its consciousness. Funny how she didn't mind entering the rat, but entering another person made her feel horrible. Maybe it was because the rat liked it. Today she counted on its willingness to be commanded in order to get back to the Fatewalker Realm and then back to her body after she did what she needed to do.

Because today's mission wasn't routine. Once inside the rat, she scurried straight for the elders' compound, first along the rooftops, and then through back alleys, finally squeezing through a crack into a circular chamber where she knew the elders would be hearing and adjudicating complaints and conflicts the people brought to them. It was the biggest audience the elders entertained, so it was the best time for Kalish's trick.

The rat picked up on her nerves and pushed back against her wishes when they entered the room. She took a moment to calm herself and the rat, reassuring the rodent that there was a tasty treat for him if he stayed exactly where she told him to stay until she returned.

Then she edged him toward the nearest elder, sitting cross-legged on a thick cushion of furs. Kalish honed in on the elder's foot, bare and calloused with age. She reached out a paw, gave the rat one last order, and then touched the elder.

The woman flinched as Kalish shoved her way into her mind. Then she pushed back against Kalish's spirit, her eyes darting around the room as she wondered if anyone had noticed something was wrong with her.

Show no weakness, the woman thought.

It was a good place to start. Kalish began to speak to the elder, though it was without words.

You need not fear weakness, for I am Fatewalker Kalish, and I bring you strength. Hear my warning. Norili has poisoned the Fatewalker Realm and driven the Fates out of it. The Fatewalker Realm dies as you sit here. It will drag the entire world with it, sowing drought, famine, and war until suffering causes our people to cry out for death. Norili wishes this for you all, because it will bring her power, however fleeting.

But I, Fatewalker Kalish, chosen of the Fates, offer another path. A path on which all may soar as I do, all may walk among the Fates and listen to their wisdom. For I will return the Fates to my people, restore the glory of the Fatewalker Realm. Listen when I speak.

Kalish fought the elder's resistance, forcing her to reach out and touch the woman next to her. Thank the Fates she'd practised fighting to control human spirits with Dayo—they put up a great deal more resistance than animals did.

When the first elder's fingertips met the second's bare shin, Kalish streaked across the connection and gave her speech to the second. Then the third, and so on down the row. At no point did any of the women give any indication something strange was happening to them. Every one of them was terrified of showing weakness. Kalish recognised it as the price of power, the price of leadership. She understood the fear. She lived it daily.

As she spoke to each elder, the daily business of the council went on undisturbed. Only when she reached the final woman did Kalish make herself known to the gathered people.

She forced the final elder to stand, gaining the attention of the room. The woman was old, but far from feeble. Kalish strained against her will, forcing her to speak the words that Kalish fed to her.

"All gathered here. Listen! We, the elder council of Surefoot Clan, have been visited by the great Fatewalker Kalish. She has spoken to each of us and warned us of a great peril."

She kept her speech short—this much coercion was exhausting—but she told the people what she'd told all the elders—they must abandon Norili and follow Kalish if they didn't want to see the end of the world.

When the speech was over, she forced the elder to sit, tear a piece of bread off the stack of flatbreads that had been delivered in preparation for the midday meal, and scan the room for the rat. There he was, waiting as Kalish had asked. She forced the elder to lower the bread on the palm of her open hand.

Come on rat. Don't leave me stuck here.

The room seemed frozen, everyone watching the elder, probably wondering what the Fates she was doing.

The rat hesitated, nose twitching, whiskers quivering. Then he dashed out from the shadows and snatched up the bread.

The instant his feet touched the elder's hand, Kalish sprang out of her body and into his. The elder sucked in a surprised breath, but Kalish didn't wait around for the aftermath of what she'd done. The rat was in full agreement with a hasty retreat, and she dove into a crack in the wall and retraced her steps to the granary. There, she sent the rat a feeling of gratitude and then shifted back to a falcon to head home.

Returning to her body, the first thing Kalish did was to roll to her hands and knees and vomit. She was covered in sweat, and her vision swam. Her limbs shook. It was worse than when she spent too long in the real world in her alternate forms.

Dayo was at her side. He said nothing, waiting patiently for Kalish to recover and tell him how things had gone.

She sat back on her haunches, breathing as though she'd just scaled a cliff. "Water?"

Dayo sprang up to fetch it.

She took a swig, then looked at Dayo. "That was horrible."

He grimaced. "Didn't it work? We practised—"

"No, it worked. Perfectly. That's why it was horrible." She shuddered at the memory of the elders pushing back in a panic against her intrusion. The intimacy of being inside a stranger's body was far more disturbing than being inside Dayo's body.

Benut stepped into the room carrying several flatbreads. "Dayo, I—oh, she's back." She frowned. "Are you okay, Kalish?"

Kalish rubbed her face. "I will be."

"How did it go?" She sat on the floor, handed Dayo a bread, and offered one to Kalish.

Kalish refused the bread, but took another sip of water. "I did it, and a lot of people saw it. Now we wait and see if it does any good."

"How long before Norili hears of it?" Benut asked. Benut wasn't one of Kalish's advisors, but since she usually helped Dayo guard Kalish when she was in the Fatewalker Realm, she knew what Kalish had planned to do today.

"She probably already knows. When I was inside the elders, I could sense their worry that Norili would stop in and see them at a moment of weakness. She was at the terrace today." Her stomach flipped as she realised that the woman she spoke through—the only one of the elders who couldn't deny she'd been possessed—would probably not live until tomorrow. Norili would eliminate anyone she thought was a liability, and an elder who could be possessed by Kalish was definitely a threat.

"The more important question," Dayo said, "is how long until the Surefoots start coming over to our side?"

Benut shook her head. "I hate to tell you, but while I was getting some food, a runner came in—one of the scouts—apparently Zev and his band have attacked another Surefoot terrace."

Kalish swore. "And the Fatekeepers will be blamed for it, no doubt." Norili would see to that.

Within days, Norili had begun her backlash against Kalish's stunt with the elders of Surefoot Clan.

Fatekeepers within Surefoot and Caverna Clans began reporting visits from the Fates.

"Death came to me while I was in the Fatewalker Realm," recalled a young woman from Caverna. "She told me my presence there was destroying the Fatewalker Realm—that because I was not sacred enough, not performing the right rituals, I was offending the Fates and driving them away. When I told her Fatewalker Kalish invited me to the Fatewalker Realm and showed me how to enter, Death said that the Fatewalker was nothing but a traitorous Flintcrag who had betrayed her clan to its destruction, and that she was plotting to do the same to all the Fatecarvers."

Kalish had no doubt that 'Death' was Norili, impersonating Death. How many other people had she spoken to in the guise of a Fate? How many people would believe her?

Kalish began spending even more time in the Fatewalker Realm, meeting with her supporters in Caverna, Surefoot, and among the Treekeepers. No new Surefoots came to her, seeking to join the Fatekeepers. Her spies in Surefoot's prime terrace confirmed the fate of the elder through whom Kalish had spoken. "Norili has promised death to anyone who speaks of the incident. And after what she did to the elder, most aren't willing to say anything."

Chapter 25

Kalish flew over the mountains in falcon form on her way to visit Hana and the people of Upper Falls. Before she even got close, she knew things were not right.

The sky was dark with heavy clouds. The sunsinger birds were silent.

It was never cloudy in the Fatewalker Realm.

Flitting through the trees toward the cave in which the people of Upper Falls still lived since the destruction of their village, fat drops of rain began splattering the leaves overhead.

She reached the cave, where Hana and many of the villagers awaited her, and transformed back into her human form.

"Hana, what's happening?" She hugged her friend.

"I was going to ask you the same."

"Is it raining in the real world?"

Hana laughed without humour. "It's pouring. Has been for days. The rivers are flooded, and a landslide has nearly cut off the other entrance to our cave."

Jando, one of the young men of Upper Falls, added, "It's a good thing we haven't moved back to the village—the water is knee-deep there."

Treekeepers built their houses on stilts. Kalish had never really considered why, but flooding must be a regular issue in these rain-soaked lands. "Does this happen often?"

"It is always wetter at this time of year," Hana explained, "and I've seen floods before, but this? This is different."

Especially if it was raining in the Fatewalker Realm too.

The people of Upper Falls were solidly behind Kalish—Fatekeepers who had helped in the overthrow of the Treekeeper Council and were there when Norili usurped power. They didn't need Kalish to display power or warn them from Norili's false promises. But they were weary—tired of living as fugitives and frightened of the uncertainty of the future.

Kalish held the same weariness and fear. With the weight of the Fatewalker cloak on her shoulders, she pushed her own fears aside to offer encouragement and assurance to the villagers.

"Hana says you're not sending warriors to attack Council Island. Why not?" asked Londra, who had participated in the raid on Council Island that eliminated the corrupt Treekeeper Council.

"We're outnumbered, when it comes to fighters—"

"We can fight," Jando said.

Kalish continued, ignoring the interruption. "And an attack on Norili's warriors would require us to kill. They won't concede defeat until they're dead."

"Surely they would surrender rather than die," Londra reasoned.

"Only if they thought they were going to lose—but we can't out-fight them."

"What are we supposed to do then?" Frustration

laced Londra's voice, and Kalish saw the same feeling in the frowns of the other people.

"There will be a time to take back Council Island, but only after Norili is gone." She wished she had specific plans to tell them. But she and her advisors were making it up as they went, trying to scrape together enough supporters to tip the balance away from Norili.

And none of it would matter if they didn't find Iskra.

After the meeting, Kalish flew to Council Island. The ancient nalati trees still lay where they'd fallen, but two had been stripped of bark, and great slabs had been cut off them. Five new catapults protected the island from assault, and a wooden palisade now surrounded the main council building. No one stirred in the Fatewalker Realm. No sign of Iskra remained here, and rain fell steadily from a dark sky.

She flew to several small nalati groves, hoping to catch a hint of Iskra. Each was silent. At the third, she was standing with her hands on the trunk of one of the trees when a withered nalati leaf fell on her head. It drifted to the ground, and she bent to pick it up. The leaf was limp and wrinkled. A glance upward revealed more dead and dying leaves on the lower branches of all the nalati trees in the grove.

Her heart sank. "Where are you, Iskra?"

"Raid!"

It felt like mere moments since Kalish had fallen asleep when the shout woke her, but instinct rolled her out of bed in an instant.

So Norili had found them. Kalish was thankful it had taken her this long. They were ready.

Of course, a night raid changed things. They

wouldn't send the gliders up in the dark.

Kalish shook Dayo. "Come on. Get up."

"I'm up, I'm up." He stumbled to his feet and grabbed his spear.

Kalish almost smiled. It had always been this way during raids when they were kids—Dayo groggy and unprepared, Kalish alert and shoving him out the door.

Today, they both waited for the rest of her guards. It chafed Kalish, knowing others in the terrace were gathering on the lower terrace, preparing the catapults, maybe even already dropping rocks on raiders scaling the cliff. But it was the plan, and she understood her role.

"Don't get caught. Or killed." Kofri's eyes had narrowed when she said it, as though she knew Kalish would insist on being out there fighting with everyone else. "You are the only one of us who matters."

It wasn't true. Kalish needed all the Fatekeepers. She especially needed her friends and advisors.

"Ready?" Yinlan poked his head through the doorway.

Kalish's pulse quickened. "Let's go." She and Dayo followed Yinlan to the entrance of the former elder compound, where they met up with Benut, Tili and Fino, the other members of Kalish's guard.

It might have made sense for Kalish to simply slip away as a falcon or snake, returning when the fight was over. But she would never have agreed to that. And her advisors hadn't asked her to do it unless it was absolutely necessary. They understood Kalish needed to be seen fighting alongside her people, fighting for them.

Her guard formed up around her, and they jogged toward the main terrace.

Over winter, the Fatekeepers had improved the defences of the terrace. A waist-high wall of rubble along the edge of the lower terrace provided cover for dart throwers, supplied rocks to be dropped on raiders scaling the cliff, and made the final ascent to the terrace particularly treacherous for the raiders, as the loose rocks provided no secure handholds. Two new catapults could be used to take out enemy catapults in the valley below. And the two 'rear entrances' to the terrace, along the cliff edge, had been blocked completely with stonework.

Additionally, they'd distributed valuable food and gliders among outlying terraces, so that one raid couldn't wipe out all their supplies, and glider reinforcements could supplement their defence.

They'd have to rely on local, ground-based defence tonight.

Rounding the corner onto the main courtyard, the clatter of darts hitting the rock sent them dashing for cover behind the remains of the fatechamber, where a large number of fighters gathered.

"Fatewalker." The murmured greeting followed Kalish as she joined her people.

"Remember, our object is to repel them, not kill them all," Kalish said. "We're in a good position. As long as we remain alert and focus on preventing them from entering the terrace, we can hold out as long as it takes."

Kofri's voice came from the darkness behind Kalish. "And if any of the raiders do make it to the terrace, remember to capture, not kill. Information is our ally."

Kalish frowned. "Aren't you supposed to be safe in the elders' compound?"

In the dark, Kalish could practically hear Kofri's feral grin. "And miss this?" She chuckled. "If the Fatewalker can fight, so can the elders."

Sounds of approval rippled through the gathered Fatekeepers. The presence of Kofri, Dayo, and everyone else around her warmed Kalish from head to toe. "May the Fates be with all of you."

"And also with you," they echoed. With a wild ululation, they burst from the shelter of the fatechamber and jumped onto the lower terrace.

Kalish and her guard ducked low and scrambled to the rubble wall along with the other Fatekeepers. Darts continued to rain onto the terrace, whizzing over the wall.

"Why are they doing that in the dark?" Yinlan asked. "Do they expect to hit anyone?"

"As many as they're hurling up here, they probably will hit someone, sooner or later," Tili responded.

"They're providing cover for the climbers," Dayo explained.

"Climbers!" The shout came from further along the wall.

"See?" Dayo chuckled.

A thrill of excitement surged through Kalish. Time for action.

She picked up a rock, testing its weight, and made to stand, only to be yanked back down by Dayo. "Don't you dare."

"What?"

"You stick your head above this wall, and you're likely to get a dart in the face."

"So is everyone else. What am I here for if not to fight?" she hissed.

"You're here to give the others encouragement. Let them fight for you," Dayo murmured loud enough for only her to hear.

"That wasn't the deal. The plan was I would fight unless I was about to be captured, then I'd flee. Norili doesn't want me dead."

"The enemy can't see who you are in the dark.

They're firing randomly. Don't let yourself get in the way of a dart."

"On the left!" someone shouted. That was Kalish's section of the wall. She jumped up, leaned over the wall and dropped a rock toward a dark form on the face of the cliff before Dayo could stop her.

"There are dozens of them," she said. No way was she going to sit here while enemies scaled the cliff below her.

Yinlan rose and dropped a rock. Fino and Tili made simultaneous drops. Dayo squeezed Kalish's wrist fiercely, then rose to drop his own missile.

The cliff face swarmed with climbers. Is this what it had been like when Surefoot destroyed the Flintcrag Clan? Anger shot through Kalish's chest as she bobbed up and down with the others, dropping rock after rock on the enemies.

No one reached the top, but it wasn't long before the stash of rocks behind the wall gave out. When that happened, they started hurling down rubble from the wall itself, and their cover slowly grew lower and lower. Pick up a stone, pop up, find a target, drop, bob down— Kalish repeated the moves over and over again until it was the only thing she registered.

The darts kept coming. Most flew over the wall harmlessly. Occasionally a fighter would cry out or grunt as a dart found a target. One pinged off the wall just below Kalish's hand.

Then a shout came up from the other end of the wall. A climber had reached the top.

"That's our cue. Let's go," Dayo said.

Kalish wanted to argue, but she'd agreed—if enemies reached the terrace, she would retreat with her guard to a safer location from which she could transform and escape if need be.

With her guards surrounding her, Kalish dashed toward the main terrace. As they passed the fatechamber, a large rock smashed the wall beside them with a boom, sending masonry and rocks bursting outward.

Kalish ducked, covering her head as she ran through the hail of rock. Spines! The enemy had brought catapults. And in the dark there was little chance the Fatekeepers could return fire and destroy them.

Her tight group raced down the alleyway toward the elders' compound, but turned away before they reached it, skirting the outside. A tight squeeze between two buildings brought them to a tiny, sheltered courtyard beside what used to be cliffside access to the terrace. Two massive slabs of rock protected the courtyard from attackers below, and the cliffside access had been walled off. The only way for a human to get into the courtyard was through the narrow alley, but Kalish could fly out over the rocks if she had to.

She pushed her way into the courtyard, breathing hard, her guards on her heels. It was even darker back here than out on the lower terrace, and the sound of the battle was muted, as if nothing untoward was happening at all.

Kalish felt trapped. Kofri, Umbel, Wathi, Jenti ... practically everyone she loved was out there fighting, and she wasn't there with them. All of her guards would be feeling the same—they all had parents or siblings fighting.

"If you all want to go back out there, go," she said. "From here, the only thing I can do is transform and get away if I have to."

"Our orders are to stay with you," Yinlan said.

"To protect you," Fino said.

"And make sure you don't do anything stupid," Tili added.

"Where's Dayo?" Benut asked.

Silence.

Kalish's heart was suddenly racing. "Dayo?" she called. Maybe he had slipped between the rocks to check on the newly constructed wall. But he didn't answer.

Panic gripped Kalish. The only reason Dayo wouldn't be with them was if—

She lunged toward the exit, only to be brought up short by Yinlan's bulk. "Kalish, you can't go."

"But Dayo's out there. He must be hurt." She struggled against his hold, but he was larger and stronger.

"If he's hurt, someone will be taking care of him."

"I need to know he's okay. It's dark. What if no one knows he's hurt?"

"Kalish. Yinlan is right," Tili said. "You need to stay here."

"I'll go look for him." Benut's voice shook a little.

Kalish wanted to scream. She should be the one to go to Dayo, not Benut, not anyone else.

And isn't that exactly what your mother would expect?

She sucked in a breath. "What if Norili has purposely captured him?"

"Then you definitely shouldn't go," Tili declared. "Stay here. Benut will find him and come back to tell you where he is."

Benut took off at a run, and Kalish shrugged Yinlan off her. "You can let go now."

CHAPTER 26

Kalish paced. Back and forth, drawn more and more strongly to the alleyway that led to wherever Dayo was. The light began to grow, and now she could see the shadowy figures of her guards, looking as tense as she was. Where was Benut? Surely she had found Dayo by now.

Tili and Fino moved to the exit, standing shoulder to shoulder, blocking Kalish from leaving.

"I have to go out there," Kalish begged.

"No." Tili could be stubborn.

"You know I can simply transform and fly out if you block the exit."

"But you won't do that, either."

And she was right. Kalish knew she needed to stay where she was, no matter what. But—

Footsteps hurried toward them, and Kalish recognised Kofri's shadowy form in the alleyway. The elder stepped into the courtyard. "It's over. They're gone."

"And Dayo?"

There was a pause. "I'm sorry Kalish."

"No!" She shoved past Kofri, pounding out to the main terrace, barely able to take a breath.

She burst into the main courtyard around the fatechamber. The courtyard was full of people. Some were tidying the mess of rubble from the fatechamber, others were being tended to by healers.

A knot of people on the lower terrace crowded around a figure on the ground. "No." Kalish's whisper wasn't loud enough for them to hear, but Wathi, kneeling over the prone figure, raised her head and turned toward Kalish. The look on her face told Kalish all she needed to know.

Her feet faltered, and she slowed to a walk. Speed didn't matter now. The longer it took to reach Dayo's body the longer she could pretend he would simply sit up and smile at her, apologise for leaving her side. He'd make a story out of it—he'd be spinning a tale by midday about his mishap, and when he smiled at his own clumsiness, his dimple would make her want to reach out and touch his cheek.

Wathi held her gaze, but out of the corner of her eye, Kalish registered the presence of Dayo's father, Jenti. Umbel was there, too, along with Jalen and Wend.

A tear rolled down Wathi's cheek, and when Kalish got within arm's reach, the woman who had been mother to both Dayo and her wrapped her in a hug. Jenti joined them a moment later, his arms encompassing both women.

No one spoke. Wathi sniffed, and Jenti heaved a shuddering sob that nearly broke Kalish. When they released one another, everyone took a step back, allowing Kalish to finally see Dayo.

They had already rolled him to his back, closed his eyes, and crossed his arms over his chest. He looked peaceful, if you didn't pay attention to the blood. She knelt down at his side and placed a hand on his chest, right where hers felt it was being squeezed.

"Dayo." They would never have the chance to proof, to marry. She would never fly tandem with him again.

Wathi laid a hand on her shoulder. "He's protected you since you were four. He wouldn't have asked for a different fate."

"I know. I know." Her voice broke and she laid her head on Dayo's chest and let her tears flow, silently, as she had when her father died.

Umbel stepped forward and dropped a dart next to Kalish. "Bladestone. Not that we doubted it was Norili's people."

Footsteps hurried toward them. "Fatewalker?"

Kalish swallowed against the tears. Fatewalker. She was Fatewalker. *Oh Iskra*, in this moment she didn't want to be Fatewalker. She wanted to throw herself on the ground beside Dayo and stay there forever.

But the Fatewalker cloak rested heavy on her shoulders.

I am Fatewalker Kalish, and I am surrounded by my people.

People whom she had yet to speak to. People who may be grieving like she was. People who needed her.

I am Fatewalker Kalish, and I am surrounded by my people.

She raised her head, kissed Dayo's still, cold lips, and got to her feet, pulling her cloak around her like armour.

When she turned, the young woman, Linc, bowed her head in respect. "Fatewalker Kalish. Benut is asking for you."

Benut. Yes, where had Benut gone? She cast a questioning glance toward Umbel.

The elder pressed her lips together. "We had to restrain her. I'm not certain now is the best time—"

"I'll speak to her." Kalish had already suspected Benut was in love with Dayo. It hadn't bothered her. Dayo was hers, and although he was always kind, and enjoyed Benut's company, she knew he had never felt any attraction to Benut. When Benut discovered Dayo was dead, perhaps she lost her senses. In any case, she sensed Benut had answers to questions perhaps Kalish hadn't even thought of.

Linc led Kalish, with the remainder of her guard in tow, into the back of the terrace. They passed a number of people having wounds bound or sewn up. They all greeted her with bowed heads and a reverent, "Fatewalker."

She let the title take over, pushing the part of her that was Kalish aside while she made it through the aftermath of the raid. She nodded back to everyone, greeting them by name, and making certain they saw the gratitude on her face for their willingness to fight for her.

They reached a small storeroom, and Linc waved her inside.

Benut's hands and feet were bound, and she lay on her side on the floor. Tears streaked trails in the dirt on her face, and her eyes were shut.

"Benut?"

The woman's eyes flew open, and she cried out. "Fatewalker Kalish! I'm so sorry!" Then she wailed, her face contorted into something ugly and misshapen. Kalish clamped down on her own emotions lest she break down like Benut.

Benut who had no right to mourn Dayo more loudly than Kalish herself did. Kalish allowed a spark of anger to override her grief. "Be quiet! Why have my advisors deemed it necessary to bind you?"

Linc stepped into the room, past Kalish, grabbed Benut by the shoulders and hauled her into a sitting position. Shaking the woman a little she growled, "Tell her. Tell her what you did, you snake."

Kalish winced at the word snake. How many times had she been called that in the same tone of voice?

But Linc's rough handling of Benut had the desired effect. She took a ragged breath and began a broken story.

"I … I … I loved Dayo."

No surprise. Kalish waited for more.

"He was always so … supportive and loving … He told great stories … And you practically ignored him. Always off in the Fatewalker Realm." She glared at Kalish for a moment.

She did not ignore Dayo. He had never complained about the amount of time she spent alone in the Fatewalker Realm.

"I started keeping him company while he was guarding you."

"Yes, I know that." Kalish was losing patience, and she didn't know how long she could hold it together if Benut was going to keep talking about how wonderful Dayo had been. "What did you do, Benut?"

"All I wanted was for Dayo to stop mooning after you, because you were never going to love him like he loved you—you were always leaving him to help *your people*."

"What. Did. You. Do."

"I … I told everyone you'd banished Zev and his band. I encouraged them to keep attacking Surefoots, telling him that was the only way we could beat Norili. Knowing that it would irritate you and Norili both." She laughed bitterly. "It's what he intended to do anyway."

"And?" Kalish was certain there was more.

"And when Zev's attacks didn't bring Norili after you, I told her where you were."

"You *what?*"

"The only way Dayo was going to look at me is if you were out of the picture. If your plans failed, maybe he'd see you weren't as great as he thought. And if Norili captured or killed you … well, then I'd have him to myself."

Flames erupted in Kalish's chest. She clenched her hands so hard they hurt. "You told Norili where we were hiding out so that you could seduce Dayo?"

Benut shrugged, her eyes on the floor.

"You *killed* Dayo."

Benut wailed, "I know!" She rolled back to her side, sobbing.

Kalish turned and stalked away, not certain where she was going. Her chest was tight, her stomach in knots. Her fists were clenched so tightly, her fingernails pressed painfully into her palms. She needed to get away from everyone. The Fatewalker armour was cracking.

Yinlan, Tili and Fino followed silently as Kalish brushed past Umbel, Kofri, Wathi, Jenti, Ino, Leithe … all people she loved. She couldn't bear even looking at them right now.

She returned to her room in the elders' compound and threw herself onto her sleeping platform. Yinlan, Tili and Fino whispered to one another, and then Tili sat down beside Kalish while Yinlan and Fino guarded the doorway.

At Tili's touch, Kalish lost her composure. Tears poured down her face, and she could barely breathe.

"I thought she was my friend," she gasped through her sobs.

Tili stroked her arm soothingly. "We all did."

Since childhood, when Kalish was in pain, she escaped to the Fatewalker Realm. And that's what she did now. It didn't matter that her advisors were busy dealing with the aftermath of the raid along with their own grief, that Benut was trussed up in a dark room wondering what punishment would be meted out to her, that Norili knew where they were. She needed the peace of the Fatewalker Realm.

She shrugged off her body with a sense of relief. The weight of the Fatewalker cloak vanished here.

Without conscious thought, her feet took her along the cliffside path past the proofing rooms to a tiny ledge where she and Dayo had met countless times when they were children. She settled herself on the ledge, back against the warm rock, knees pulled to her chest. Shutting her eyes, she waited for the Fatewalker Realm to soothe her spirit, as it had so many times in the past. Without the sounds of people in the terrace, she could tune into the swish of wind through tussocks, the buzz of grasshoppers, the snick of beetle wings in flight, and the chitter of rock skippers feeding among the bushes.

Today, the silence was absolute.

After a moment, her eyes flew open, unease coursing through her veins. Nothing stirred in the landscape, not even a leaf. She transformed into a falcon, swooping low over the valley, scanning for life with falcon-enhanced sight.

Not a single bird flitted through the brush, no ant or beetle scuttled along the ground. No lizards sunned themselves on the rocks. No fellow falcons soared overhead.

In silence, she returned to the ledge and transformed back into her human form, her unease growing. Was the rock cooler than usual? She squinted up at the sun—could it be less intense than before? She wrapped her arms around her legs and rested her forehead on her knees, as if she could protect herself that way.

It was scant comfort. Dayo was gone. Iskra was gone. What was she striving for, if the world was descending into chaos and she had no one to share life with anyway? Maybe she should let her mother have her power. It wouldn't last long. Drought would starve out the Fatecarvers, and floods would wash away the Treekeepers. Norili would be left alone in her cavernous fatechamber to rule over the rats.

If there were any rats left.

The scuff of a foot on the gritty cliff path brought Kalish's head up. She forgot to breathe, and her mouth fell open. For a moment, the entire world froze in place.

"Dayo." At her whisper, he rushed to her.

She stood, and they embraced, gripping fiercely, both crying.

"Dayo. You … you're dead."

He took a shuddering breath. "Yeah."

"And you came here, before."

He pulled back and brushed his fingers across her face. "I couldn't leave you alone. I promised I'd look after you, promised I'd be with you." A smile. "And since you spend at least half your time here, I figured I'd probably see you as much as before."

Kalish's heart plummeted. "I'm sorry I spent so much time here. I didn't mean to drive you away. I—"

"You didn't drive me away. You were—*are*—saving our people. You are a Fatewalker. Of course you would spend time in the Fatewalker Realm."

"Benut said—"

"What's Benut got to do with it?"

Dayo was here. He was still here. The knowledge allowed her to see the grim humour in what led to Dayo's death. She huffed a dry laugh. "Sit with me. It's quite a story."

CHAPTER 27

Kalish was calm when she returned to her body, though her heart still ached for the loss of Dayo in the real world. But his presence in the Fatewalker Realm lent new urgency to the search for Iskra. If the Fatewalker Realm died, Dayo would die, for good.

She and Dayo had debated whether they should tell everyone else his spirit lived on in the Fatewalker Realm. Kalish had never told anyone except Dayo that Grandmother Ma remained—she feared what might happen to the Fatewalker Realm if everyone chose immortality at the point of death. And if Norili ever heard of it? She shuddered at the thought.

But Dayo insisted his parents should know, and Kalish couldn't deny them that comfort. Dayo's friends would have to simply accept his death. But if they didn't have to support Kalish, Wathi and Jenti through it, they would manage.

Kalish pulled her Fatewalker cloak around her shoulders with new resolve. Tili, Yinlan and Fino still stood guard, and she embraced all three. "Go. Rest. The raid is over, and I'm okay. Take time to grieve."

Then she went to Wathi and Jenti, who cried as much over the news of Dayo's continued existence as they had over his death.

Kofri and Umbel intercepted her on her way to the main terrace. Kofri scrutinised her face. "Kalish. How are you?"

"I'm okay." She met the elder's gaze, hoping her eyes conveyed the truth. She was okay. Bruised and grieving, because having Dayo present only in the Fatewalker Realm wasn't the same as having him here, but okay nonetheless.

Kofri nodded. "Umbel and I have organised a group to reinforce the terrace's defences and repair the damage done. Breakfast has been rearranged as a funeral feast, and a sizeable group of women have volunteered to prepare it."

If Benut's betrayal hadn't stung so much, Kalish might have laughed. Women loved Dayo, and whenever he announced he would teach cooking, a crowd formed.

Umbel took up the briefing. "We've had Dayo's body taken directly to the burial grounds, since we have no functional fatechamber for the ceremony. We'll farewell him there. Glider crews are flying scouting trips, following the raiders as they retreat and keeping an eye out for the next raid."

Because there would be one. Kalish didn't doubt that.

"Which leaves only the fate of Benut to deal with," Kofri concluded. "We thought you would want to be involved in that decision."

"Thank you." Kalish was deeply grateful for these two elders. And for all the people who had stepped up to do what needed to be done while Kalish retreated to her own misery. *I am Fatewalker Kalish, and I am surrounded by my people.*

It had never felt more true.

She ran her fingers through her hair—it was limp,

needed more clay. She must look a mess. "You know what she did?"

"She hasn't kept it a secret. The whole terrace knows." Kofri's voice softened. "I don't think we could devise a harsher punishment for her actions than she has suffered today."

Kalish wasn't quite as ready to forgive Benut. "She threatened *all* Fatekeepers with her foolish scheme to win Dayo. She betrayed us all."

"Norili would have found us, regardless of Benut," Umbel observed.

True. In fact, they'd remained hidden far longer than Kalish expected when they first came to Flintcrag's prime terrace. Kalish fought her desire to shove Benut off a cliff. She knew the kind of draw Dayo could exert on a woman, without him even trying. She'd felt it herself. She also knew what it was like to be the woman Dayo ignored while he chased after another. Kalish had begun seeing Dayo as more than a big brother long before he viewed her as anything but a little sister.

Kalish huffed in frustration. "Well, what are we supposed to do with her? Can we trust her any more? I'm certainly not letting her act as my guard again."

"No, I don't think we can trust her until she proves the lesson she's learned today is lasting. But living with herself is the best punishment she could receive."

Anger still simmered, but Kalish unclenched her fists. "I don't want her at Dayo's funeral."

"I don't think anyone does," Umbel said. "And after?"

"I'll talk to her."

The entire terrace turned out for Dayo's funeral. Kalish wasn't alone shouting the death chant with tears tracking down her cheeks. As the final words echoed back to her from the valley below, five warriors lowered Dayo's body into the shallow hole that had been scraped in the rocky soil. A warrior's burial—Dayo would be pleased when she told him. As Fatewalker and as Dayo's unofficial, but de facto wife, Kalish laid the first five stones over his body—one for each of the Fates.

"Love, Life, War, Death, and the Unknown." Kalish spoke the ritual words as she placed the stones. "Death has taken what Love and Life gave to us all. Dayo walks beside the Unknown, where all of us will one day follow. May he leave a shining path for his people." Even knowing Dayo awaited her in the Fatewalker Realm, saying the words that finalised his death brought fresh tears to her eyes.

She stepped back. Everyone filed past the grave, each depositing a rock until the hole was full and a cairn rose high above the soil. No one spoke until the final stone was placed, the click of stone and sigh of the wind the only accompaniment to the trauma of burying Kalish's best friend, her lover and partner.

When the cairn was finished, Umbel raised her voice. "Dayo's work here is done, but ours continues. Our stomachs growl. Let us eat and remember the friend and warrior gone."

Kalish's stomach *did* growl. There had been no morning meal, because of the raid. Earlier, she would have refused food, her stomach roiling with emotion, but now she joined her people in celebration and commemoration. Wathi and Jenti—revived by a few words with Dayo in the Fatewalker Realm—regaled their friends with stories of Dayo's youth. And there were plenty of them—Dayo had a personality that made up for his small stature. Kalish smiled at her own memories of his bravado, his stubborn dreams.

In addition to the stories about Dayo, people recounted their version of the events of the morning. Gossip about Benut was rife. She was vilified as a traitor, a snake. Kalish listened as Linc related how Benut had first clung to Dayo's body, then attacked anyone who tried to tend to him. That's when a group of men had tackled her and trussed her up.

"She was completely out of her mind. We were worried that she would injure someone, or worse, kill herself," Linc said.

The more Kalish heard, the more she agreed with Kofri—the consequences of Benut's actions were the harshest punishment possible.

Before she left the funeral, Kalish spoke to each of her advisors. They would meet in the afternoon to discuss their next steps. The next meeting of the entire Fatekeeper advisory group, including the Treekeepers, was in three days. Kalish was thankful she had a few days before she would have to revisit and recount the events of this morning for others.

She spoke to Kofri last. "I'm going to release her. She can remain in the terrace, among the Fatekeepers if she wishes, but I will not have her near me, nor will I require anyone else to take her into their rooms. She will need to prove to us all that we can trust her."

Kofri nodded her approval, and Kalish descended to the terrace. People were trickling away from the funeral, but the lanes of the terrace were quiet as Kalish made her way to the storage room where Benut was being held.

She entered the room, determined to control her own emotions while still showing Benut exactly what she thought of her treachery.

Benut was asleep, and Kalish resisted the urge to kick her awake. Instead she drew out her knife and sliced the bonds that held Benut's wrists. With a start, Benut woke. Her eyes widened, and she let out a squeak. In the same position, Kalish would have been terrified—to wake to the sight of the person she'd betrayed brandishing a knife. With a small note of satisfaction, Kalish cut the bonds around Benut's ankles.

Benut scooted backward across the floor, away from Kalish, eyes wide, and pressed her back against the wall.

Kalish sheathed her knife to avoid the temptation of brandishing it at Benut. "You will not come near me, nor any of my advisors. All the Fatekeepers will be watching you. I never abandoned Dayo for *my people*. Dayo and I worked together on a shared vision for *our people*. Honour him by joining that shared vision."

Without waiting for a response from Benut, Kalish turned and left.

When Kalish entered the Fatewalker Realm next, she expected to find Dayo waiting for her. Instead, when she arrived at their usual meeting spot, she found Grandmother Ma.

"Where's Dayo?" she asked after hugging her grandmother.

She laughed. "He's off flying somewhere." Of course he'd spend his time winging around on the gliders he loved so much. Grandmother Ma's smile fell. "I'm sorry, Kalish."

"He told you?"

The old woman nodded and squeezed Kalish's hand. "But I'm glad you have him here."

Kalish had come here to tell Dayo about his funeral, but Grandmother Ma must be here for a reason. "Have you found Iskra?"

"No. But Tensa has found something of interest she wants you to see."

"What is it? Where?"

"There is a cave on the coast. Come. She's waiting for us there."

The journey to the coast would have taken a five-day in the real world. Here, Kalish and Grandmother Ma seemed to fly across the landscape. Buttes and mesas gave way to wide grassy plains. Kalish tried to imagine the great herds of goat-like creatures that once roamed the plains, back when her people lived here.

When she first caught sight of the ocean, she sucked in a breath. "Does it have an end?" The flat blue expanse spread out until it merged with the sky in a hazy line.

"If it does, I have not seen it," Grandmother Ma replied.

The coast was a tall cliff dropping into the sea. Water rushed and crashed rhythmically against the jumble of boulders at the cliff's foot. It reminded her of the shore of Council Island, but on a much larger scale.

"Down we go," Grandmother Ma declared.

"Into the water?" The idea of getting anywhere near those violent waves terrified Kalish, even in the Fatewalker Realm where the normal rules of survival seemed relaxed.

"No. Halfway down the cliff is the cave."

Climbing a cliff wasn't difficult for a Fatecarver—it was the only way to reach most of their dwellings, and children learned to climb before they learned to walk. The cliff along the coast, however, was slick with salty spray, and Kalish was thankful for her enhanced abilities in the Fatewalker Realm.

Grandmother Ma picked her way confidently down the rock face and swung herself into a cavern just a few body lengths from the top. Kalish followed, stepping onto the floor of the cave moments after Grandmother Ma.

"Kalish!" Tensa smiled in greeting.

Kalish's eyes adjusted to the dim light, and her mouth dropped open. "What have you found here?" The entire interior of the cave was covered in drawings. People, animals, plants, rocks, rivers—figures and images rioted across the walls.

"I think," Tensa said, "this is a description of the summoning of Iskra."

CHAPTER 28

"Are we doing the right thing?" Hana asked Boluso as they waited for the arrival of the village Speakers. Here in the Fatewalker Realm, on the banks of the still swollen river in Upper Falls, the sun shone again. Not strongly, but at least it wasn't raining, which was a relief. Its weak rays filtered through the leaves overhead and dappled the forest floor.

Boluso squeezed Hana's hand. "We are. If we didn't organise this, individual villages would rebel, and the cost in lives would be even higher."

Slowly, the Speakers trickled in, hiking or paddling the river to their meeting spot in the abandoned village centre. They all looked weary. It was time to act.

"The tragedies in many of our villages recently have convinced me we need to strike against Norili's people," Hana explained. "We need to take back Council Island."

"Didn't we already decide we couldn't do that? Few of us know how to fight," said Nara, Speaker of Fern Gully.

"Yes, but if we wait until Norili's people attack each of our villages, the outcome will be the same. Plus, I think the timing is right to strike soon."

"Really? With all the rain we've been having, you want us travelling?" Benha asked.

Hana nodded. "Norili's Fatecarvers aren't used to rain. Their side of the mountains is arid. They don't use boats, don't know how to swim, and hate being wet. After this downpour, their spirits will be low; they'll be frightened, because the water in Council Bay will be full of mud and debris. Add to that the fact that their supplies must be running low by this point, because very little has been sent to them recently."

Boluso spoke up. "And most importantly, Norili isn't there. We know she's on the other side of the mountains, so they are without a leader."

"But even travelling down the rivers right now is dangerous," Nara said.

Hana nodded. "I know. I'm only asking those who are willing to take the risk. I can't guarantee anyone's safety, and I expect some of us won't return. But I believe we have a chance of capturing Council Island without even fighting at the moment. If we come at Norili's people with overwhelming numbers and appear prepared to fight, they might simply hand the island back to us so they can leave and go home. At this point, they're hungry, wet and stuck on the island. Would you fight to stay there?"

"Well, I'm in, and I know High Reaches can send thirty to forty to join your force," Benha said. "And we now have two catapults to help us lay siege to the island, courtesy of Norili herself." She smiled. "We've been practising, and some of our young women have gotten quite accurate with their aim."

Nara nodded. "I bet I can convince another forty to join you."

"We'll send fifty," said the Speaker of Flat Bottom. "We don't have far to travel, and there's no farm work to do at this time of year—you'll get most of the village."

The offers of people came thick and fast, as more Speakers realised the majority of villages were behind the plan. In the end, it looked as though they might have nearly four hundred people willing to attack the island. More than enough to terrify Norili's people.

"So, when do we attack?" Benha asked.

Hana turned to the Speaker of Lost River, the most distant village from Council Island. "How long will it take your people to arrive?"

"Six days, if we travel day and night, paddling in shifts."

"Are you willing to do that?" Hana asked.

"To reclaim Treekeeper lands from that tyrant? Absolutely."

"Then we attack in six days."

They spent some time hashing out details, planning how to use the catapults most effectively, how to make their people seem even more numerous and dangerous than they were. Intimidation was their main weapon—no one really wanted to fight, even if they did outnumber the enemy.

When the meeting was over, Hana was filled with nervous energy. She and Boluso returned to their bodies and called the village of Upper Falls together to decide who would go, and what needed to be done in preparation.

"I know this is dangerous, but it feels so good to be *doing* something," Sendalee commented as she stitched a new waterproof bag to carry food for the journey.

"It does. Let's hope it works," Hana replied.

"Are you going to tell Kalish what we're doing?"

Kalish would counsel them not to attack. But she couldn't do everything alone. The Treekeepers needed to take back what Norili had stolen from them, just as Kalish's Fatecarvers were trying to do. If they attacked Norili on both fronts at once, maybe they would all have better luck.

Hana sighed. "Let's tell her once we're already on our way. That way she can't talk us out of it."

Chapter 29

Together the three women studied the drawings. Some were dark and bold with charcoal, others were partly rubbed off, and others were carved into the rock itself.

"They've been done at different times," Grandmother Ma said.

"And each set of drawings, from each time period, depicts a version of the same thing," Tensa added. "The same sequence of events."

Five figures, each slightly different from the others, converged on a lone nalati tree. Each figure carried something—a leafy plant, a knife, a dead rabbit, a clay pot—the items were strange and not consistent among the different depictions.

"Are they bringing offerings?" Grandmother Ma wondered.

The figures were depicted presenting their offerings to the nalati tree.

Kalish leaned close, peering intently at the clearest of the drawings. "Is that the symbol for Life?" The charcoal of the tree trunk had been scratched away to reveal the grey rock beneath.

"On this one, the tree is surrounded by the symbols of the Fates," Tensa said, running a finger over a set of drawings carved into the rock.

Kalish glanced at the picture Tensa referred to and sucked in a breath. "That's not a tree—it's Iskra."

"No, it's clearly the same tree depicted here." Tensa pointed to another carving.

"Step back," Kalish said. "Can you see it?"

Tensa stepped back. "A face."

The face of Iskra. Kalish couldn't have described Iskra in words—she'd never actually seen the god—but she knew them. The nalati tree—nothing but a tree in the previous carving—had been transformed. The symbols of the Fates circled its trunk like a cloak. Within the bark patterns carved on the trunk were eyes that projected the aura of age and wisdom. Branches and leaves were a shock of hair standing on end, just like a Fatecarver woman's clay-spiked locks.

"These people have somehow called Iskra into the tree," Grandmother Ma said.

"Five people, five Fates," Tensa said, excitement in her tone. "Are their offerings related to the Fates?"

"Here is someone with an atlatl—the place where they offer it becomes the symbol for War," Grandmother Ma said.

"This plant becomes Life," Tensa said.

"I can't tell what all the offerings are supposed to be," Kalish said. "What's this thing?" She pointed to a squiggly line draped limply over one of the people's hands. "It is placed on the tree where the symbol for Love shows up."

The three women scrutinised the drawing in silence for a moment. Then Grandmother Ma laughed. "The figure is a woman—see the hair—she's carrying a man's braid. Her husband's or lover's hair."

The offerings in each drawing differed, but in each one, there was an offering representing each of the five Fates. The same offering could represent a different Fate in different drawings. For example in one charcoal drawing, a clay pot represented the Unknown. A similar pot in another represented Love.

"The item hidden in the pot, or the food prepared for a loved one," Grandmother Ma murmured.

"The way I interpret this," Tensa concluded, "is that five people each bring an offering that represents one of the Fates—the details of the offering aren't critical, but the intent is. They present their offerings to the nalati tree. If the tree accepts their offerings, Iskra enters the tree."

Wouldn't Iskra have to be present *somewhere* to be called to a nalati tree? Kalish had searched everywhere for Iskra and found not a trace of them. She frowned at the images. Tensa's interpretation was logical, but it didn't *feel* right. Something about the images bothered her.

When she recognised what it was, she asked, "Why aren't the people shown with Iskra?"

In all the depictions of the scene, Iskra was drawn alone. Not one showed the people kneeling in front of the god or otherwise worshipping them. They were simply gone.

What happened to the five people who called Iskra?

You must become.

Kalish shivered at the memory of Iskra's words. She looked back at the scenes in which the people were giving their offerings to the trees. In some, the offerings disappeared. In others, it looked as though the people's arms had sunk right into the trunk of the tree.

More of Iskra's words came to her.

You will not do it alone, but you are the key. When I am gone, you must find them. Choose wisely, my little falcon.

"Find who?" she'd asked.

250

Death, Love, War and the Unknown.

Four of the five Fates. And Life?

That is you, my falcon.

She swallowed hard as realisation dawned.

"They're not calling the Fates. They're *becoming* them." She related Iskra's words to Grandmother Ma and Tensa. "Iskra knew. Because they had once been five people."

If she was Life, who were the other four Fates? Who would she choose to become a god? She nearly laughed out loud—she would definitely not choose herself.

If she became a god, would she die in the real world? Her gut said that she would have to be dead in the real world in order to become a god.

You will have to hurry, Iskra had said. But what did that mean for her efforts to oust Norili, change Fatecarver culture, and unite the Fatecarvers and Treekeepers?

Grandmother Ma and Tensa were both watching her, and Kalish was certain her thoughts and questions, her growing distress, showed on her face.

Grandmother Ma nodded briskly. "So we know basically what needs to happen. But where? Will any nalati tree do, or is there a special tree?"

They turned back to the drawings to seek the answer. Each one included different details. In one, the tree was shown growing out of bare rock. In another, sparse grass sprouted at its base.

"This one shows a mountain behind the tree," Tensa said, tracing the shape of the mountain with her finger.

"There's a mountain here, too," Grandmother Ma said from the other side of the cave.

"Are they the same?" Kalish asked.

They were. A tall narrow spire flanked by a shorter flat-topped peak on the left, and a spine of jagged teeth undulating downward on the right. "Well, it's in the mountains, and the tree isn't within a grove of trees." Kalish sighed. "As a falcon, I might be able to find the place."

Tensa placed a hand on Kalish's shoulder. "You'll find it. Iskra had confidence in you."

"They had confidence I could become a god— I'm not sure I can make it through the advisory meeting this afternoon." She rubbed her temples. "And I'm supposed to become Life?"

"You will not do it alone. If you are Life, then I am Death," Grandmother Ma said. "My offering will be the drought-parched leaves of the gingilato." A woody herb that died every summer, regrowing at the start of winter rains.

"And I am the Unknown," Tensa said. "My offering will be a sugarspike pouch tied shut."

They were offering to—die wasn't the right word—to cease existing? What was it like to become a god? Kalish almost told them they didn't have to do it, but Iskra said she had to choose, and she would have chosen Grandmother Ma and Tensa. She nodded. "I will bring ..." It would have to be a live thing. Something that she could easily carry. "I will bring a live rat." She had a particular rat in mind who she thought would enjoy the adventure.

"Now we simply need Love, War, and a location," Tensa declared. As if it were that easy.

"You know who Love needs to be." Grandmother Ma pinned Kalish with her gaze.

Kalish swallowed. Yes. She knew. But would he agree to it?

CHAPTER 30

"Kalish! Kalish!"

The insistent voice and accompanying shaking yanked Kalish from the Fatewalker Realm and back into her body.

"Thank the Fates you're back." Tili's worried face peered down at Kalish.

Kalish groaned. "Don't tell me it's another raid."

Tili grimaced.

"Spines! Another?" Kalish sat up. "Are they here yet?"

"No, but Kalish, there are *hundreds* of them. And—"

"Do they have gliders? Incendiaries?" What could make Tili pause like that?

"Norili's with them."

"Spines! Gather the advisors—we need to make a plan."

"Everyone's here, waiting for you."

In the elder courtyard sat Wathi, Jenti, Kofri, Wend, Umbel, Fino and Yinlan. Tili sat down next to Fino. A pang shot through Kalish's chest at the absence of Dayo. Although she'd just been speaking to him in the Fatewalker Realm—where he'd agreed to become

Love—she wanted him here.

"Tell me what we know," she said as she joined the group.

"The band that struck us last night retreated to an outlying Surefoot terrace, where they were met by several hundred others from Surefoot's prime terrace," Wend explained. "Two of the scouts who intercepted them were former Flintcrags. They recognised Norili."

"They weren't trying to hide their presence, or Norili," Umbel added. "She clearly wants you to know she's coming."

"Do they have gliders?" This early in the spring, and without the winter rains, there was little to burn in the valley, but they could drop incendiaries, or simply rocks, on the terrace.

"We haven't seen any, but it doesn't mean they're not going to use them," Wend said.

The faces around the circle were grim. They couldn't win against hundreds of raiders. Even if they didn't have gliders.

"Can we evacuate before they get here?"

Umbel nodded. "I've already sent the children and those unable to fight to the glider launch—a crew of pilots will carry them to a relatively safe place and return for more."

"Do we need to evacuate everyone? What's the point of anyone staying here if they'll only be killed? We can't leave our most vulnerable people to fend for themselves outside of a terrace," Tili argued.

"We can't simply keep running away," Yinlan said. "We chose to take back Flintcrag Prime Terrace because it was defensible. Let's defend it."

"Let's send a glider to Caverna—they're close by and might come to our aid," Kofri suggested.

"What if we sent a whole lot of gliders to

Caverna and brought back fighters by glider?" Jenti said. "They'd get here faster."

Kalish smiled. "And it would be impressive."

Kofri nodded. "It would. A little intimidation could go a long way."

"So, we stay and fight?" Yinlan asked.

"Those who can," Umbel said. "Let's continue to try to get our vulnerable people away, though."

Kalish nodded. "Agreed. Kofri, can you organise a group of glider pilots to go to Caverna? Yinlan, can you get all our fighters ready, and have some people reopen one of the side exits to the terrace—in case the rest need to evacuate."

"What are we going to do about you?" Wathi asked. "You know Norili is here for you."

Kalish nodded. "I'm going to go out and meet her."

Her statement caused an uproar among her advisors—she was the most important person to protect; it didn't matter if others died as long as Kalish survived. They didn't know what she had learned earlier—in order to save the world, Kalish *needed* to die.

She wasn't going to tell them that. Who knew? Maybe she'd find a way to do it differently. Either way, her friends and advisors didn't need the weight of that knowledge.

"Look. My mother won't kill me." Of that, she was certain. "And the longer I talk with her, the longer everyone has time to prepare."

"What if she captures you?" Tili asked.

Kalish laughed. "Let her try. You know what they say about catching a lantan—*she who catches the lantan knows its bite.*"

"But if you're safely in the terrace—" Fino began.

"Then I could be killed by an incendiary, or a rock, or a stray dart. Norili wants me alive. If the Surefoots don't know where I am, they could easily kill me by accident. I'm actually safest confronting Norili."

Her advisors were silent for a moment before Kalish added, "And if she thinks she has me, she may not even attack the terrace."

"Well, you'll go with a guard," Wathi said.

Kalish shook her head. "I won't. Any guard who goes with me will die."

Emotions warred on her advisors' faces. They wanted to protect her, but they couldn't. She was the one with the power. She was the Fatewalker. She was the one who would protect them all.

She hoped.

"Will you kill Norili?" Kofri, asking the difficult question.

Would Kalish kill her mother? It wasn't the first time she'd faced the question, wasn't the first time she had the opportunity. Sometimes she regretted not killing her, but with power-hungry women like Margali and Sintala waiting for Norili to falter, waiting to step into her place, she wasn't certain it would have made a difference.

Would she kill her mother? "Only if I have to."

The sun had just passed its zenith when Norili's forces came into view. Only those able to fight remained in the terrace, and the bulk of their glider force was away, hopefully to bring back Caverna fighters before it was too late.

Kalish stood on the lower terrace, flanked by her advisors, watching the dust cloud from hundreds of feet billow up the valley. Tension was high, and all the Fatekeeper fighters were silent, gripping their weapons.

It was time for her to go, before Norili's people drew any closer. After Dayo's loss, she feared for all her friends and advisors. She was less worried for herself, in spite of her plan to face Norili alone. But it was possible she would never see her friends alive again.

"I'm going." She turned to Tili and gave her a hug. "Stay safe. Flee if you must."

Then she hugged each of her other advisors, begging them not to foolishly hold the terrace until death, but to escape, reminding them that the children, injured, and elderly who had already fled would need them.

"May the Fates be with you," Kofri said as Kalish finally stepped back from them all.

"And also with you." Kalish transformed into a falcon and dove off the terrace, swooping low before soaring up into the clear sky. A cheer rose from the terrace, ending in a wild ululation—a challenge to Norili's approaching forces.

Kalish sped toward the Surefoots. With falcon eyesight, she spotted Norili at the head of the column, striding like the Fate, War, herself.

When she reached the Surefoots, Kalish wheeled overhead, her falcon cry drawing their attention. Norili raised a hand, and the Surefoots shuffled to a halt, their dust cloud separating and wafting away in the stillness.

Two warriors flanking Norili raised their atlatls, but at a flick of her hand, they lowered them again.

In a swirl of feathers, Kalish swooped around the staring Surefoots, and then landed ten paces in front of Norili and transformed back into her human form.

"Mother. Nice of you to visit." She didn't smile.

"Kalish. If you're done with your little stunts—"

Kalish laughed. "Don't you wish you could do the same? I can see it in your eyes—you lust for power of every kind. But all your power is borrowed." She waved at the assembled warriors. "You know you can't match me, so you drag half the Surefoots here to lend you their power, provide you the power you lack on your own. Meanwhile, I'm prepared to face you alone. Because I don't need to steal power by forcing others to fight my battles for me. I don't need to gain my power by bullying and threatening, by starving people until they'll take any scraps I throw their way." She made certain her voice was loud enough to carry. "You've brought these people—*our* people—here to fight and die. For what? So you can gloat? What do they get out of it? Maybe you steal a little less food from them? Allow them to maintain the terrace they live in rather than slave away to build you a fortress of a fatechamber?" She laughed. "You abuse your people so they'll thank you when you stop."

Norili scowled. "My people follow me willingly."

"Do they? Or do they follow you in fear and desperation. Do these men really enjoy how you treat them as ignorant slaves, or would they actually rather live in a society where they're valued for something other than their ability to thrust a spear?"

The man to Norili's left pressed his lips together, clearly fighting a smile at the double entendre.

"I am not here to fight with you, Kalish."

"Well, you have a strange way of showing that."

"I am here to make a deal with you."

Kalish laughed. "And what sort of deal do you think you can strike with me?"

"Join us. Join the Surefoots before we destroy you." She waved a hand to indicate the massive force behind her. "You can't defend that terrace against my forces. You know we will crush you. Would you leave your friends, your people, to that fate? Would you allow Dayo to die because you refused to acknowledge when you were beaten?"

"Dayo is dead, thanks to you."

Norili's eyes registered her momentary shock, but she recovered quickly. "So you already know how futile any effort to oppose me is."

"The Fatekeepers know it is better to live, however briefly, in a just and equitable society, valued and loved for who we are than to suffer for a moment under the sort of oppression you subject your people to."

Norili scoffed. "Love. Value. I've brought bladestone to my people, I've opened up the riches of the Treekeeper lands to them."

"Oh? How much bladestone have *you* carried on your back over the mountains? How many of those Treekeeper riches has the average Surefoot seen?"

Uneasy shuffling among the Surefoots told Kalish that at least some of her comments resonated. Good. Because while her words were directed at Norili, they were meant for the amassed Surefoots.

"And how much bladestone do your Fatekeepers have? Do they have access to Treekeeper lands?"

Kalish smiled. "My Fatekeepers *are* Treekeepers. We are from both sides of the mountain, and we trade goods, share ideas, and build relationships among one another. You think that if you wipe out everyone at this terrace you'll stop us? Not even close. There will be no deal, Norili. And if you think your display of stolen power is so good, wait until you see the display the Fatekeepers will put on for you once you've threatened us."

Norili lowered her voice. "Kalish. Think what we could do together. We could control everything. All peoples at our fingertips, doing our bidding. You don't want fighting? Fine. Once we're united, there will be no need. With your status as Fatewalker, you could have every luxury, not be living like this in a half-destroyed terrace, without even a functional fatechamber."

Kalish shook her head. Her heart was heavy—how could her mother think this way? What was wrong with her? "You don't get it, do you? I don't *want* power. I don't want people fawning over me, doing my bidding whenever I snap my fingers." *I just want to belong.* She didn't voice it, for fear it would bring tears to her eyes. "You know, I always thought I was a disappointment to you. But the truth is, you've always been a disappointment to *me*." She raised her voice again, so all could hear. "Norili, the Fatekeepers will never agree to join you. Your actions have crippled the Fatewalker Realm, and the chaos you have sown there bleeds into the real world in the form of the drought that threatens us all. Your path leads to the destruction of all people, including yourself. We will not follow that path. We welcome any of your people to join us. I can't promise luxury, but I can promise that everyone will be valued as equals." Then she turned to the warriors next to Norili, and said, "May the Fates be with you."

Norili scowled as the warriors responded, "And also with you." Kalish would have laughed, but she was already transforming, launching into the air to make a circuit around Norili's warriors before winging back to the terrace.

CHAPTER 31

Kalish's advisors' tense shoulders relaxed as she landed on the lower terrace and transformed back into her human form.

"Well?" Tili asked.

"She wanted us to join them. Promised me a life of luxury if only I'd turn you all over to her."

"So, we start hauling bladestone for her tomorrow?" Umbel asked dryly.

Kalish smiled. "I invited her people to join us. Not her, of course."

"Do you think they will?" Fino asked.

"If they don't, we won't stand a chance." She raised her voice, addressing the Fatekeepers arrayed around the terrace. "Norili comes with a force we cannot stand long against. Any of you who wish to flee, now is the time to do it. Go to the rest of our people, and find safety. There is no dishonour in recognising your opponent's strength and acting wisely."

Nobody moved, and Kalish continued. "It is possible that Norili's warriors are weary of the abuse she heaps upon them. I have invited them to join us if they wish. Do not be quick to kill warriors who gain the terrace. We will take no prisoners, and kill only when we must."

"And if we are overrun?" a voice called from the back of the crowd.

"This conflict will not be won by force. Your lives are more valuable than control of this terrace. If we are overrun, we flee."

The time for talk was over. Dust billowed as Norili's force advanced, and soon the first darts whizzed over the wall.

The catapults of the terrace were loaded with clusters of small rocks, and the first creak and swoosh was followed by a patter of rocks among the attackers. Within range of the catapults, the attackers rushed the base of the cliff. Kalish crouched below the wall, rising just enough to fire darts at the attackers before popping back down. Once some of the attackers had reached the cliff, she switched to rocks, allowing the Fatekeepers behind her to continue launching darts over her head.

Rock in hand, Kalish rose to lean over the wall. What she saw froze her in mid-movement.

At least thirty Surefoots had reached the cliff in the first wave. But only four had begun to scale it. The remainder had turned their spears back on the Surefoots, forming a bristling line across which any others would have to advance before accessing the cliff. The four climbers were easily picked off by rocks from the Fatekeepers above. Kalish dropped back behind the wall, without having released her rock, grinning.

Other Fatekeepers, having seen the Surefoot turncoats, cheered them on. Another wave of attackers reached the cliff. Some engaged the turncoats in fighting, others joined them against their own. In the confusion below, more Surefoots began scaling the cliff. Soon there was work for everyone, dropping rocks on the attackers. The melee at the bottom of the cliff grew.

Kalish was busy dropping rocks, but she kept her eye on Norili. She wished for falcon eyesight to see the scowl she knew must be on her mother's face at the turn of events.

When Norili slipped away from her people with two guards in tow, Kalish turned to Tili, next to her. "I'm going after Norili."

Tili gripped her arm. "Be safe."

"You too."

Kalish worked her way to the side of the terrace, and then quietly transformed into her falcon form. What was Norili up to? She wasn't running away. She and her guards skirted the mass of warriors and slipped behind a series of boulders. Trying to be stealthy? Kalish could play that game too. She dropped from the terrace, skimming the cliff until she was nearly at the ground, then flicking her wings open to glide noiselessly just above the tussocks. When Norili and her guards emerged from behind the boulders, she folded her wings and vanished behind a bush.

She flitted along behind them, staying low to the ground and remaining concealed behind tussocks and shrubs as much as possible.

When Norili angled back toward the butte, Kalish knew exactly where she was headed—the glider launch. Maybe she meant to destroy their gliders. Maybe she planned to steal one and vanish. Either way, she was out of luck. Kalish angled away from her, circling around until she was hidden by the butte, and then soaring up to the top to await her mother.

She transformed at the top and alerted the crew guarding the gliders what was happening. "She's only got two guards with her, so the four of us should be able to handle it."

Her palms grew sweaty as she awaited another

confrontation with her mother.

I always thought I was a disappointment to you. But the truth is, you've always been a disappointment to me.

The words she'd blurted out were true. She'd never realised it until they came tumbling out of her mouth, but now that she understood, it gave her strength. Kalish had never been the problem—Norili was.

I am Fatewalker Kalish, and I am surrounded by my people.

She squared her shoulders, gripped her spear and prepared to meet her mother.

A guard was first up the slope. Kalish braced to meet his spear, but one of the Fatekeepers stepped in front of her to engage him. He parried one thrust, and then dropped his spear, kneeling and saying, "Fatewalker."

Kalish would have smiled at him and welcomed him, but her mother appeared at that moment, growled in frustration and charged at Kalish, murder in her eyes.

"You!" she screamed, thrusting a spear at Kalish's gut.

Kalish knocked the spear away. "Don't blame me if your people hate you, Mother."

The second guard appeared, and then a host of Surefoot warriors poured over the edge of the butte. Spines! Where had they come from? In an instant, the three Fatekeepers and Kalish were vastly outnumbered.

"She's mine! The Fatewalker is mine!" Norili waved her warriors away, and then lunged at Kalish again. "I offered you everything, and you refused it."

Kalish laughed, swatting away her mother's spear again. "You offered me nothing of value."

"I offered you power!" Another lunge.

Kalish sidestepped it. "You offered me slaves, weapons, cushions for my butt. As I said, nothing of value."

"Power is everything, Kalish. When will you learn that? You say you don't want power, yet you flit around brandishing yours like a double-tipped spear." Three quick spear thrusts had Kalish dancing backwards. Nearby, one of the Fatekeepers with her went down. Spines!

Kalish thrust her spear back at her mother. "I use my power to protect my people. I never asked for it, and it's brought me nothing but pain from the moment you carved my fate onto my face and turned me into an outcast." She was done justifying herself to her mother.

A shout to her right, and suddenly it seemed there were crowds of people on top of the butte. Fatekeepers and Surefoots engaged with spear, knife, and fists. It was almost impossible to tell who was fighting whom.

Her mother's spear grazed her leg, its bladestone tip slicing a long trail across her thigh. *Focus.* This had gone on long enough. With a growl, she launched herself at Norili, thrusting high, then low, then aiming for her gut as she allowed years of anger to well in her chest. Norili parried and dodged every blow, sidestepping the last, and angling her own blow from the side.

Kalish arched her back as the tip of Norili's spear tore into the Fatewalker cloak. The barb caught in the fabric, and Kalish's next step slammed her hip against the spear's shaft, knocking it out of Norili's hand, surprising both of them.

But Norili was a consummate fighter. Taking advantage of Kalish's clumsiness with a spear caught in her cloak, she lunged, giving Kalish a two-handed shove that sent her tumbling backwards.

Kalish's spine hit the spear hard, sending a jolt of pain all along her back. She ignored it, yanking off her cloak and rolling out of the fall.

Her movements weren't quick enough, and before Kalish had a chance to get to her feet, Norili had planted her foot in the centre of her chest and pressed Kalish's own spear to the base of her neck. Norili's eyes were wild, as though something in her had snapped.

From this perspective, Kalish once again had a vision of her mother as War.

All they needed was War.

"Kalish!" The voice carried above the sound of the melee.

Zev? What was he doing here? And whose side was he on?

Zev barrelled into Norili, knocking her away and placing himself between Kalish and her mother.

Norili rolled to her feet and growled at Zev, "Let me at her." With a snarl, she charged at him. They met in a clacking of spears that had them both shuffling toward the cliff edge.

No. This was Kalish's fight, and she knew what she needed to do. She scrambled to her feet. "Mother! Stop!"

She had never used that tone of command on Norili, and her mother hesitated. Zev lunged.

"No Zev!"

He stopped mid-blow and stepped back.

"Mother. We don't need to do this. We don't need to fight. There's a way for you and me to work together."

"I offered you that before, and you refused. Now that you see I have superior power, you want to compromise. Is that it?"

Kalish stepped forward. "Look around us. Do you see your people winning?" More and more of Norili's people had reached the top of the butte, but it was unclear how many of them were actually fighting against the Fatekeepers. Norili's eyes darted around. She was cornered, and she finally knew it. Kalish took another step forward. "Mother. Put down your spear."

Quicker than a lantan, Norili struck. The spear sank into Kalish's stomach, setting her body on fire with pain. She'd seen wounds like that before, but only on dead warriors.

Well, if that was what Norili wanted, that's what she'd get. Kalish stumbled forward and gripped Norili by the shoulders, knocking them both off balance.

Zev screamed her name as Kalish and Norili tipped off the edge of the cliff together.

This side of the butte was not quite vertical. The first lurching drop broke several of Kalish's ribs. She barely noticed.

"The Fatewalker Realm!" Kalish gripped her mother tightly. "Enter the Fatewalker Realm now!"

Norili struggled against Kalish, her eyes wide with fear as they tumbled and spun down the cliff. They hit a rock square on, knocking Kalish's breath out of her. Her leg smashed against another rock, and she knew it was broken. When they went into free fall, with Norili still fighting her, Kalish mentally latched onto her mother and yanked her into the Fatewalker Realm.

Their bodies bounced when they hit the bottom. The echo of the blow shuddered through Kalish as she picked herself up in the Fatewalker Realm. *I'm sorry you had to watch that, Zev.*

CHAPTER 32

"I'm dead?" Norili's voice shook, and she lay where her body had fallen.

Kalish stretched, wincing a little at the memory of pain. "Yes. I am too. Lucky for both of us I had the sense to drag us into the Fatewalker Realm."

"But I'm dead."

"Your body is. Your spirit—as far as I know it could exist forever here. I mean, Tensa's still hanging around."

"Tensa? Fatewalker Tensa? She's a tale told to children."

"No, she's not. She's real, and you're going to meet her soon. I have a job for you. Get up."

Norili's bewilderment was dissipating, and at Kalish's barked order, she frowned. "You can't order me around, girl."

Kalish laughed. Who knew that killing her own mother could be so liberating? "Mother, I am a Fatewalker. This is my home, the seat of my power. I can order you to do anything here."

"I am still your mother."

"You have never been a mother to me." Kalish was out of patience. She felt power surge through her, as though in shrugging off her body, she'd freed her spirit. Maybe it was time to brandish that power. She flicked into her falcon form, then the lantan. Her mother sucked in a breath, and Kalish slithered around her, tasting her unease.

But that wasn't all she could do.

Do not be afraid to reach for power—you have much unrealised potential still within you.

She hadn't believed Iskra's words, but now she felt the potential thrumming through her. Shifting back to her human form, she flashed her mother a feral smile, then became a goat, a beetle, a lizard, a mountain cat— she flickered from form to form faster and faster until she was dizzy.

Returning to her human form, she glared at her mother, who had gone pale and quiet.

Norili swallowed. "Where are we going?"

"First, we're going to collect Dayo."

"I thought you said Dayo was dead."

"So are you." Kalish began walking. Had this been a mistake? There hadn't been time to think it through, and now that she was here, the implication of what she'd done trickled in.

She was dead. What would her people do now? How were her friends going to react? To lose Dayo and her on the same day? Would Wathi and Jenti tell everyone about how Dayo's spirit lived in the Fatewalker Realm? Should she attend the next advisors' meeting in the Fatewalker Realm? Would there even be another, if she wasn't around? It chafed her to not know how things were going in the battle. Would Caverna Clan show up in time to help? Would they agree to come at all? What would the Surefoots do when they realised Norili was dead?

Who would step in to fill the power gap now?

And what if her mother continued to try to cling to power from the Fatewalker Realm?

Spines! It *had* been a mistake. And she couldn't undo it.

She and Norili cut through a cluster of tussocks that crunched and crackled underfoot. Kalish stopped— tussocks shouldn't crackle in springtime. She crouched to examine the brown, dead plant. Leaves crumbled in her hand. Glancing up, she saw that all the tussocks were the same.

The Fatewalker Realm was dying. The real world would follow. And if that happened, nothing about the battle or the struggles for political power would matter in the least. Kalish stood and brushed the fragments of tussock off her hands.

She'd made the right decision.

They found Dayo at the base of the cliff below the terrace, gazing up. He turned to them, and the momentary smile turned to a frown. "What is going on?" Unease laced his voice. "Why are you two together?"

Kalish would have been worried and confused, too. "It's okay Dayo." How to say it? "Norili's dead. We're both dead."

His eyes widened and filled with tears. "Oh, Kalish." He closed the distance between them and embraced her.

"It had to happen," she whispered in his ear. "In order to become Iskra, I had to die in the real world."

He gripped her harder for a moment, and then pulled away. "Why is *she* here? She should have stayed in the real world to die."

"No. We need her. We need War."

Dayo's eyes widened. "You want to make her—"

he stopped. "Have you told her yet?"

"Told me what? I don't like being kept in the dark. I am the Exalted Norili. I demand to know what is happening. I will not be dragged all over the place. My people—"

"Your people are not here," Kalish said. "You have no more influence over them, and they no longer lend you power."

"You can at least explain to me what is going on. You owe me that much."

"I don't owe you anything, Mother." Was she really going to turn this woman into a god? "But I will explain what is happening, because I think you won't actually mind once you know why I've brought you here."

"Why you murdered your own mother?"

Kalish rolled her eyes. "You killed me first. Just listen." She explained how Norili's destruction of the nalati grove killed what remained of an already-weakened Iskra. The loss of Iskra was destroying the Fatewalker Realm, which in turn would bring about the loss of the real world. "So even if I hadn't killed you, you and all your people and power would have vanished into nothing. You were going to fail, one way or another."

"Nonsense! My—"

"Shut up and listen."

Behind Norili, Dayo shook with suppressed laughter. No doubt he was enjoying this change of roles. He'd heard Norili bark, "Shut up and listen!" to Kalish countless times as a child.

Kalish went on. "The only way to preserve the Fatewalker Realm and the real world is to create a new god, a new Iskra."

"You can't *make* a god." Norili snapped her mouth shut at Kalish's glare. Dayo continued to shake with laughter.

"We can, and we must. You will join me, Dayo, Grandmother Ma and Tensa to create a new god."

Norili frowned, and Kalish could see the questions forming on her lips. She preempted them. "Yes, Grandmother Ma is here too. She is with Tensa right now, and we're going to meet them as soon as I've finished explaining. The five of us will become the five Fates, Iskra, Nalatassa. Together, we will become a god."

Norili snorted. "That's ridiculous."

"It's been done before."

"No it hasn't."

Kalish took a deep breath, trying to dredge up the patience to deal with her mother. It *was* a lot to throw at her all at once.

Dayo finally got control of his laughter and spoke up. "Kalish, I think you've made the right choice for War. What do you say we walk while you explain the rest? Tensa and Grandmother Ma aren't far."

Dayo held her hand as they walked. Eventually, Norili's protests subsided as Kalish explained how she, Grandmother Ma and Tensa had deciphered the cave drawings and connected them to what Iskra had told Kalish.

It was impossible to feel weary in the Fatewalker Realm, but in the respite from fighting with her mother, Kalish registered the sadness that weighed on her. Everything she'd wanted, everything she'd worked so hard to create in the real world were out of her grasp now. She would never have a home, a normal life, a marriage to Dayo.

What was it like to become a god? Would she recognise herself? How did five people become one being? Would it feel the same as when she'd entered the bodies of the Surefoot elders? She hoped not. That had been horrific. But sharing a consciousness with Norili wouldn't be fun.

Dayo must have felt the tension in her hand. He gave it a squeeze. It was a good reminder—she'd be sharing a consciousness with Dayo, too. That wouldn't be bad at all.

They met up with Tensa and Grandmother Ma. Norili regained some of her combativeness—she and Grandmother Ma had never gotten along. Tensa, observing the barbed exchange between the two, raised her eyebrows in Kalish's direction, as if to say, "*Really? You chose* her?" Kalish shrugged. Norili was War. For her, everything was a combat.

She interrupted Norili's sparring with Grandmother Ma. "Let's get to work. We need to find the location, and we each need to gather our offerings."

Grandmother Ma held up a dead gingilato plant. "I have my offering."

"I have mine, too," Tensa said, patting a pouch at her side.

"What will you offer, Mother?" Kalish asked.

"Your knife or atlatl would be appropriate choices," Tensa suggested.

"I'm not going to give away my knife or atlatl. I might need them."

Kalish shook her head. "You won't need them. I don't think any of us will need anything after we do this."

Norili grunted. "My knife, then."

Dayo rummaged in his pouch and pulled out a misshapen clay bead. The red and black design painted on it was nearly worn away. "This is my offering."

"You kept that?" It was the first gift Kalish had ever given Dayo. She'd been all of five years old, and she worshipped Dayo as big brother and protector. She'd been so proud of that bead—one of her first.

Dayo held her gaze. "Of course I kept it. It was

my lucky bead."

Oh, spines. She was going to cry. *Focus.* She blinked back the tears. "I need to collect my rat at Surefoot Prime Terrace, and then I suppose we have a long search ahead." In her falcon form, she could cover ground quickly, but there was still a lot of mountain to search to find a single tree.

"Go get your rat," Grandmother Ma said. "And meet us at the top of the Surefoot River. We'll start our search there."

"I'll go with Kalish," Dayo said.

Grandmother Ma smiled, and Kalish had the feeling that had been her plan when she suggested they take different routes to the mountains.

Dayo slipped an arm around Kalish's waist. "Want to fly?"

Her heart lifted. "Absolutely!"

Grandmother Ma chuckled. "See you kids later."

Flying tandem with Dayo. Kalish tried not to think about the fact it was the last time she would ever do it. Their shoulders bumped together as they ran to take off, and they both laughed aloud when their feet left the ground.

Fear, pain, and uncertainty were all swept away in the joy of flight. They circled high into the sky on a thermal, until Kalish felt like the whole world was visible, laid out below them. Then they eased into a long glide toward Surefoot Prime Terrace.

They spoke little. Kalish didn't want to voice her sadness over what they'd both lost. She wanted to enjoy this time, remember it, if gods remembered joy and love.

Kalish's rat was waiting for her. He hesitated at first, until Kalish waved Dayo away, and then came to her outstretched hand. She lifted him gently, nudging her way into his mind to reassure him as she slipped him into a small pouch. *We're going on another adventure, my friend.* The rat quivered with excitement.

As she and Dayo glided upriver toward the mountains, Kalish scanned the clouds boiling up from the Treekeeper side—clouds that shouldn't be there in the Fatewalker Realm. They passed under the tattered edges of the clouds, and Kalish shivered. Mountains that should be bathed in sunlight loomed dark and foreboding ahead. The peaks, usually sparkling with snow, were shrouded in cloaks of mist.

Kalish and Dayo began a spiralling descent to the spring where the Surefoot River began its journey. As they circled, she viewed the dry, flat-topped buttes and mesas of her home for the last time. Turning back toward the mountains, her eye was drawn to a spot of sunlight, lancing down from a break in the clouds. It struck a tall spire of rock that fell in a jagged-toothed ridge to the right. A flat-topped peak to the left swirled in and out of view.

"There it is!" Kalish pointed. "The place we need to go!"

Chapter 33

The nalati tree sprouted improbably from a jumble of boulders and crushed rock. Storm-damaged branches formed a sparse canopy atop a gnarled and stunted trunk.

"*This* is the place?" Norili scoffed.

"It is." Kalish was sure of it.

"Well, let's do this." Dayo's confident words were at odds with the reluctance in his voice. "What do we need to do? What did the drawings show?"

The drawings. "Wait. We need witnesses."

"Witnesses?" Dayo asked.

Tensa nodded. "You're right. Witnesses to draw our story on the cave walls. How else will the next Iskra know how it's done?"

"How else will the people understand the power of what we've done?" Norili agreed.

Of course, Norili would view it that way. Kalish tried not to be annoyed.

"Aren't there already drawings in the cave?" Dayo asked.

Grandmother Ma spoke up. "Yes, but drawings fade. Who knows how long it will be before Iskra needs to be remade? Kalish is right. We need witnesses."

"The advisors?" Dayo asked.

Kalish nodded. "There was supposed to be a meeting this evening. I don't know if it will still happen, given ..." She glared at Norili.

Norili snorted. "I'm sorry my attack disturbed your *meeting*."

"I'll go," Kalish said. If the Fatekeepers had prevailed against the Surefoots, they would keep their meeting—they would need to tell Hana and the other Treekeepers what had happened.

Kalish transformed into a falcon and flew north, toward Market Rock, where the advisors held their meetings.

Even from a distance, Kalish could see the grief on the faces of her friends. It squeezed her chest, and she cried out as she circled down to Market Rock.

Tili glanced up first, and her eyes went wide. By the time Kalish touched the ground and transformed into her human form, Tili's wasn't the only mouth hanging open.

"Kalish?" Tili whispered. "But ..."

Kalish nodded. "I'm dead. Yes." She took a deep breath. When she said it bluntly like that, the reality of the situation was terrifying.

Yinlan and Fino fell to their knees, murmuring, "Fatewalker."

Umbel cackled, and Kofri swatted Yinlan on the back of the head. "Get up. It's just Kalish."

For now.

Wathi smiled. "I thought we might see you here, but I didn't want to get anyone's hopes up."

Tili's head whipped around. "How did you know Kalish would be here?"

This might take a while.

Kalish explained everything that she had discovered with Grandmother Ma and Tensa, described her and Norili's tumble off the cliff, and the task that was now before them, including the advisors' role in it.

Then Kalish asked about the battle.

"Caverna Clan arrived," Jenti said. "But by then we hardly needed them."

"At least half the Surefoots fought on our side, even before Norili died," Wathi explained.

"And when you went over the edge with her" — Kofri's tone said she'd seen it happen— "most of the remaining Surefoots laid down their weapons."

"We made them take the Fatekeeper oath, even though we knew" —Tili's voice broke— "even though we knew you were dead."

Kalish wanted to ask how they would prevent another power-seeking Norili from snatching control, how they would structure a new form of governance, who would make decisions. But those were not questions she needed to worry about. They were no longer her problems to bear. And she trusted her friends to do what needed to be done.

Her job now was to save the Fatewalker Realm. Save the world around her people so that whoever came into power next had a world to live in.

As she led her advisors to the nalati tree where they would perform the necessary ceremony, Kalish spoke to each of her friends, knowing her words were farewells. Whatever happened, however Kalish experienced the world after this, Kofri would never again swat Yinlan on the back of the head and say, "It's just Kalish."

Her stomach churned at the thought. This was the correct choice, right? If only Iskra were here to advise her. But if they were here, there would be no need to create a new god.

At the tree, the Fatecarvers among Kalish's advisors fawned over the legendary Tensa and verbally sparred with Norili. They hugged Dayo.

Kofri took Kalish's hands in her own. "Thank you. You've set our people on a better path. Saved us from ourselves."

Kalish blinked fiercely, fighting her tears. "No. Thank *you*. You believed in me when I didn't. I ... I couldn't have done any of this without you."

Kofri squeezed Kalish's hands and opened her mouth, as if to speak. She shut it again and swallowed. "I don't know what will happen to you when" —she shook her head and smiled weakly— "when you become a god. But we will always remember our Kalish. Don't be a stranger, okay?"

They fell silent, and Kalish knew it was time.

Her heart raced and her hands were clammy. She nodded to Dayo, Tensa, Grandmother Ma and Norili, and without a word, they gathered around the tree, offerings in hand.

Were there words to this ceremony? What if it didn't work? Fear lanced through Kalish and she darted a look at Dayo. He smiled and reached out to grasp her hand. Comfort flowed from his touch.

It would work. Kalish felt words rise in her throat. "Tensa, Dayo, Norili and Grandmother Ma. We step into the unknown today. Today we unite our spirits, our power, our hearts and minds in order to save our world and our people. Love, Life, Death, War, and the Unknown. The five Fates unite in Iskra, Nalatassa, the spark that inhabits everything. We offer tokens of the aspects of the god we become today, parts of a whole." Kalish held her rat in her cupped hand. Touching his mind with hers, she felt his excitement, his anticipation.

She let his uncomplicated thoughts soothe her own. "I offer Life in all its forms and exuberance." She squeezed Dayo's hand and he lifted his bead.

"I offer Love, the strongest of all bonds, and the power that transcends life and death." He turned to Kalish, smiling, but with tears streaking his face. He knew as well as she did that the love they had shared their whole lives was about to change irrevocably.

Grandmother Ma held her dead plant aloft. "I offer Death, the necessary respite for all who suffer life."

Norili brandished her knife. "I offer War, for love and life are inseparable from conflict." She said this looking directly at Kalish, and it felt like an apology. Kalish blinked, but the tears fell anyway.

Tensa shook her bag, heavy with something concealed. "And I offer the Unknown. The adventure to look forward to, the disaster to dread, that which every living thing steps into with each new moment."

All five stepped forward, offerings held out toward the tree. Kalish gripped Dayo's hand tighter as her other hand sank, along with the rat, into the tree's trunk. The sensation of warmth grew as she stepped closer, sinking her arm to the elbow, and then the shoulder. Now the heat burned, like the flickering of a flame. She squeezed Dayo's hand one last time, and then they all stepped into the tree.

I burn, I melt, I flow. Colours, sounds, sensations swirl in furious winds that sting my face. The hammer pounds, soft feathers brush my burning cheek, mud oozes between my toes.

I am stretched beyond the breaking point. I snap and shatter into glittering snowflakes, settling on the shoulders of giants in fur cloaks.

My feet, no hooves, no paws, no—

Roots, branches, leaves, clouds, rock.

Falcon, lantan, pebble. Golo beetle, mountain cat. Little puffer, warrior, lover. Mother, leader. Grandmother, rebel. Furred, whiskered thief. Fatecarver. Fatewalker.

Iskra.

I coalesce into being, resonating with the energy of rock and tree, earth and sky, life and death.

I feel their eyes, their breaths, their disbeliefgrieflovehatebeliefhope.

I hang the sun in the sky to warm their faces.

I soften the rocks along their way, hum in their dreams at night.

Did I know them once?

Were they not always me?

CHAPTER 34

Hana strolled among the saplings. They were only waist high, but nalati trees grew quickly. By next year, they would be above her head, and within five years, they would form a shady grove. It wasn't the deep green cathedral that had once graced Council Island, but someday it would become one.

Boluso stepped up behind her and wrapped his arms around her waist. "You're late."

Hana sighed. "I know. I was enjoying the peace here." Governing a people was hard work. Hana had no idea what she was getting into when she agreed to become the head of the new Treekeeper Council. The new council had been set up immediately after Hana's attacking force had taken back Council Island, which happened without any fighting once Norili's people knew their leader was dead.

Strolling through the nalati grove in the Fatewalker Realm was the only peace Hana got these days. Life in the real world was constantly busy.

But it was a good busyness. It was the busyness of rebuilding the strength of her people, building new ties with the Fatecarvers, celebrating many 'firsts'.

Today would be the first marriage between a

Fatecarver and a Treekeeper—Sendalee and Yinlan. As the Treekeepers' new spiritual leader—a role Hana still thought ironic—she was performing the ceremony.

That is, after she attended about five different meetings. There were committees for everything now—trade; dispute resolution; construction on Council Island; bladestone mining, manufacture and distribution—in theory, the committees made decisions separately from the council, which now only concerned itself with the general rules that governed society. In reality, the committee members wanted her input.

"Give me a few more moments. They can start without me—you know they don't really need me."

Boluso smiled. "You should tell them that one of these days," he teased. He knew she encouraged them to meet without her and rarely even spoke during meetings unless she felt someone was trying to take advantage of others. He kissed her on the cheek. "I'll let them know."

When she was alone again, Hana caressed a tree leaf. The ache of sadness throbbed in her chest.

She missed Kalish and Dayo. When they disappeared along with Tensa, Grandmother Ma and Norili into the nalati tree in the mountains, she'd held her breath. Surely they would step out again, transformed.

But they didn't. They were simply gone.

Iskra's hum didn't return until a few days later, and the intervening time was laden with grief.

Now she felt the god's hum in her fingertips as she stroked the glossy nalati leaf. She thought of Kalish. How she never wanted to be different, never wanted power. Only ever wanted a place to belong; a home. Yet she'd become a god in order to save all of them. Was there a part of her that still existed in Iskra?

"Kalish? Iskra?" The god had not spoken to her. She knew they were present, but she'd never heard their voice. "Iskra," she called again.

All the leaves in the nalati grove shivered, and Hana gripped the one between her fingers more tightly. "Iskra, are you there? Will you speak with me?"

The hum increased in volume. *Hmmm ... I know that voice ... Hana.*

Hana ... yes. A friend. Happy to be recognised. Yet she is sad.
For me, for us, for ... ah, for what we once were.
Hana, do not be sad. I am where I belong. I am home.

Just for you!

Subscribe to my newsletter and get an exclusive story!
Be the first to know about new releases.
Enjoy special deals and promotions exclusive to
newsletter subscribers.

Subscribe now at robinneweiss.com

ACKNOWLEDGEMENTS

Thanks to all my readers who begged for me to finish this series. I found this book particularly difficult to organise, and your encouragement kept me at it.

Special thanks, as always, goes to early readers: Ian, E.J., Liam, Loretta, and Maggie. Your feedback is invaluable!

And of course I'd be lost without my editor, Belinda O'Keefe, and cover designer Jenn Rackham. You ladies are amazing!

About the Author

Robinne is an entomologist and educator by training, but has never been able to control her writing habit. She has been publishing her writing since the 1970s, and has been known to answer entomology exam questions in verse. Unlike her exam answers, which were met with awkward silence by her Very Serious Professors, her  short stories have won multiple awards and her books get rave reviews.

Her books for children include the *Dragon Defence League* series and other books infested by unusual animals. For more mature audiences, she's written two cosy urban fantasy novels, and the YA epic fantasy series, *Fatecarver*. She also dabbles in non-fiction and poetry.

Robinne believes adventures are the key to writing. The list of her own adventures is long, and includes teaching with a live two-metre-long Burmese python, living in a mud house in rural Panama, and delivering a pair of goat kids in the middle of a dinner party. She writes from her office in rural New Zealand, where adventures can be found around every corner.

Visit her at robinneweiss.com.

OTHER BOOKS BY ROBINNE WEISS

Fantasy for adults
Demonic Summoning for the Modern Woman
Squelched

Fantasy for ages 13-18
Fatecarver
Fatewalker

Fantasy for ages 8-13
The Dragon Slayer's Son
The Dragon Slayer's Daughter
The Dragon Defence League
Dragon Homecoming
The Ipswich Witch
A Glint of Exoskeleton

Non-fiction
Insects in the Classroom
Backyard Bugwatcher

Poetry
Pandemic Poetry: Across the Fence